What was it that drew him back, time and time again to t

water evoked childhood memories of his long-dead father and nature provided a soundtrack of

rustling leaves moving in the occasional gust of wind and birdsong.

Jack Lunn took a moment whilst crossing the bridge, looking upstream to where a tributary spilled

over a small weir and joined the main body of the River Test. The river looked in good condition,

with the last couple of days of warm weather promising at least some fish rising and a hatch of

insects to encourage them. He flexed his right leg, trying to ease the stiffness in the damaged knee.

Peering down into the water through his polarised sunglasses, he could see a couple of trout

keeping station amongst the weed beds close to the bridge and a small shoal of grayling just to their

right. One of the trout rose swiftly to the surface, taking an insect caught in the waters grasp. He felt

a smile lifting the corner of his mouth.

Making for the bankside and the well-tended grass path alongside, he would take a while to get to

a favoured beat. The dew was heavy on the recently mown grass and the boots on his chest waders

made his footsteps easy to see.

His eye was drawn to a flash of blue, as a kingfisher dove into the water and returned to its perch

with a small fish. He took the birds prowess as a good omen.

After about a mile he passed the old stone bothy. Encouraged by the recent warm spell, the

trees had that sprinkling of fresh green from new leaf growth and the smell of the hawthorn's

distinctive perfume was a sure sign that Spring had arrived.

He put up a lone magpie, which chattered back at him as it flew away. A single bird had long been

considered an ill omen, so the mantra 'Good Morning, Mister Magpie. How's your wife and

children?' was muttered under his breath. A friend down in Kent trapped them during the nesting

season, otherwise they raided the songbird nests and slaughtered the chicks. The friend called

them 'the serial killer of the hedgerows'.

Keeping away from the river's edge, he crouched down as much as his now aching knee would allow. There was a bench a little further on and he set up there, retrieving Ibuprofen from his tackle bag and swilling it down with some water, before returning his attention to the matter in hand. What fly to choose? He selected an Olive Dun, tied it on to his leader, applied a little floatant and headed for a nearby clump of reeds that would cover his approach. There were a couple of fish rising and he elected to cover the closest first. With enough room behind him to make several practice casts, he stripped line off his reel and made his cast. It landed a little offline from where the fish had last surfaced, so he waited until it had drifted past before retrieving and recasting to better effect. The fish rose to his fly, but he snatched at the take and missed it. Having spooked the fish, he moved upstream to another clump of foliage and tried for the other fish he'd see rising.

 He could see a large tangle of weed heading his way but reckoned that a couple of casts were on. Trying to get the fly close to the bank at the head of the pool, where he'd seen the other fish rise, he cast out. The take surprised him, as it came almost immediately.

 Trying to keep tight to the fish, Jack struggled to stay in contact as it shot down the pool towards him. Turning and kiting to the right, the fish surged back towards the top of the pool, stripping line from the reel. Noticing the floating mass of vegetation was now a lot closer than anticipated put a frown on his face and holding the rod high, in an effort to keep the hard-fighting trout away from the obstruction. For a moment he seemed to be winning the battle, then it lunged to the left and buried itself in the accumulated weed.

 There was little point trying to haul it out and the best chance was to wait until the raft came to him, hoping that the fish hadn't thrown the hook.

 He noticed something entangled in the weeds. An old tarpaulin, or sack? Making the decision to climb into the river to haul it out, he unclipped and extended the net from the back of his fishing vest. Using it to steady himself into the river, which was only a couple of feet deep, he waited for the floating mass to arrive.

 As it came towards him, what as trapped in the weeds became more apparent and a knot grew in his stomach.

 The corpse lay face down in the raft of weed, a concave wound in the back of its head. He recognized the old waxed jacket on the body and was engulfed by sadness and disbelief.

Chapter 1

He'd known Elizabeth Lamont for over 20 years, often seeing her in the mornings and evenings as he cast a line on the clear chalk stream waters, and she walked alongside the river. A formidable character, with a reputation for not suffering fools gladly. Jack was glad he hadn't been amongst the villagers, neighbours, and tradesmen who'd felt the sharp edge of her tongue, or the acid prose of her lawyers.  But, over the years, they'd forged a good relationship and even a friendship, particularly after her husband had passed away. Enquiring after one another's family, talking business, local news and gossip, he'd got the impression of a somewhat lonely, but resolute woman and had valued their frequent bankside chats on her morning and evening walks.

His jaw ached, as he'd been standing with his teeth clenched looking at the body. What he saw caused the sadness to change to anger. Taking a sharp breath, he unclenched his teeth and moved his jaw around, then rolled his head and neck, as he could feel tension building across his shoulders. Looking at the fragile and broken body of the woman brought back memories of his own dead mother killed in a home invasion the previous year.

His hands were shaking as he returned the sunglasses to the peak of his baseball cap. Waving a damselfly from the tangle of weed, he patted his fishing vest to locate his mobile phone. The old woman's dead fingers moved slightly in the flow of the river. Lunn attempted a deep calming breath and made the call.


'Mick, you busy?' Lunn asked.

'This a social call, Jack?' DI Mick Sparkes replied.

'I've got a body here.'

'Thought it was a bit early for a chat. What do you mean, you've got a body?'

'Elizabeth Lamont is floating in the river with the back of her head smashed in,' he replied.

There was a moment's silence at the other end of the phone.

'Jesus, Jack. Where are you?' Sparkes asked.

'The Trophy Pool on the River Test, about a mile downstream from her house. Look, there's a car park by the river, downstream and on the opposite bank from the house. Use that and don't cross the bridge,' Lunn said and gave some further directions.

'Don't move, I'm on my way.'

'I can't go anywhere, Mick. She's resting against my waders.'

A skein of cloud blotted out the sun as he returned his attention to the lifeless body, the rivers flow animating it with a gentle movement.

He tried to think of something else but couldn't. He respected the Police of course and knew that they would do their best. But, standing there in the river, with the dead woman resting against him, he was helpless to the shock, anger and a deep sense of loss that almost overwhelmed him. There was no doubt in his mind that some responsibility fell on him to ensure that whoever was responsible for this crime was found.

Now he could hear the sirens. The first uniformed officers appeared about ten minutes later, closely followed by his friend and another tall, plain-clothes detective of mixed race.

'What bait were you using?' Mick Sparkes asked with his soft Hampshire burr.

Jack forced a smile. 'I don't suppose I can get out of the water anytime soon?'

The closeness to the body was becoming unsettling. A mixture of helplessness and a need to distance himself, allowing some perspective. He wanted to take a pace back, but fought that compulsion off.

'Not yet, I'm sorry to say,' Sparkes answered, then called to the uniformed officers. 'Cordon off the area. We're going to need both sides of the river searched and make sure that a unit is on its way to the deceased's home. Sorry, where are my manners? This is DC Marcus Taylor,' Sparkes pointed to the other detective.

'Good to meet you, Mr Lunn,' Taylor said. 'I hear you used to be DI Sparkes' boss?'

'A long time ago,' Lunn replied.

'Not what you normally see as part of the Independent Advisory Group,' Sparkes remarked.

'It's certainly a change from fly-tipping, petty theft and poaching with the I.A.G.'

'What can you tell me about her?' the DI asked. 'Any enemies?'

Lunn knew that Sparkes need something to work with and dipped back into his former job as best he could.

'She was a widow of about 80,' he said. 'Not the most popular figure in the area. She lived by herself, but had a gardener and cleaner in a couple of times a week. She upset a lot of people over the years, but enemies might be too strong a word. Her husband may have had some in his past.'

'Who did he upset?'

'There was some talk of London gangland connections, but nothing concrete that I'd heard.'

'When was this?'

'Back in the late sixties,' Lunn answered. 'He was a very clever accountant, so the story goes. Good at hiding money. The rumour was that he was involved with some less than scrupulous types from South of the river.'

'You're not suggesting that some old gangster from her husband's past has done this?'

Lunn gave him a wintery smile. 'Not, likely.'

Sparkes eyes narrowed and he looked over at Lunn thoughtfully. 'Could she have struck her head and fallen in?'

Lunn sighed. 'If you're asking my opinion, then judging from the position of the wound, it's more likely she was hit from behind and she either fell or was pushed into the river. The wound's clean, no blood. She was probably killed last night but may have been caught up somewhere. The river's flow increased about an hour ago, so the keeper upstream must have opened a couple of hatches and that could have released the body.'

'You haven't lost it then?' DC Taylor remarked.

*'How far that little candle throws his beams! So shines a good deed in a naughty world,'* Lunn replied, bowing slightly to the young detective and receiving a smile and the same in return.

'Not bad for a civvy. We'll have to wait for the C.S.I.'s assigned by FRMU to recover the body,' Sparkes informed him.

'FRMU?'

'Forensic Resource Management Unit.'

'Got to love the Police and their acronym's.' Jack replied. 'Then you'll get the dubious pleasure of watching me stripping off and getting fingerprinted?'

Sparkes smiled at his old boss. 'Tempting, but the only way you've touched the body is contact with your waders and net. Am I right?'

'I might have been out of the force for a few good years, but I remember enough not to bugger up a crime scene.'

'The victim's been in the water for some time, so the chances of getting forensic evidence are slim to zero and we'll take your DNA and some samples. Otherwise, a statement should suffice,' Sparkes said. 'Shame, most coppers would be happy to give a month's wages to see their old DI stripped down to his particulars.'

Lunn shook his head. 'What sort of person kills an old lady like this, Mick?'

'We'll find out,' the DI paused. 'Bringing back memories, is it?'

'They both deserved a better end. Lunn replied. *'Death lies on her, like an untimely frost upon the sweetest flower of all the field.'*

The three of them stood for a moment in silence with just the sounds of the running water from the river.

'Any family?' Taylor asked. Taking out his notebook.

'A son, daughter-in-law and two grandchildren in their twenties.'

'So, they'll be the beneficiaries?'

'I would think so,' Lunn said.

The uniforms were busy stringing up tape as four more figures approached. The first pair swathed in white coveralls and the other two were in scuba diving dry suits.

'Why the underwater recovery team?' Lunn asked. 'You could just pass me a pair of gloves and tell me what to do.'

'We have to follow protocols and Health and Safety,' came the reply from one of the coveralled men.

Photographs and video were taken before Sparkes offered a hand and Jack hauled himself awkwardly out of the river, wincing as he flexed his right knee.

'The old war wound playing up is it?' the DI asked.

'No worse than normal. Standing still doesn't help, particularly in a cold river.'

'Fishing probably not the wisest hobby then?

'I hadn't planned on standing in cold water with a body for half an hour,' Lunn replied. 'Do you mind if I take another look at the body?'

'Was it something in particular?' Mick Sparkes queried.

'I'm not sure.'

The C.S.I.'s were about to bag the hands and he saw what had troubled him.

'There!'

'What?' Sparkes asked.

'Her rings are missing.' Lunn said. 'You can see from the faint tan lines where they used to be.'

'Theft?'

'If they're not in her house, then that's certainly a strong motive. There was a wedding and an engagement ring for certain and maybe an eternity ring. Check the photos at the house and I'll bet you'll see what she had been wearing.'

'We should get you back to the station,' Sparkes said.

'Great, I get to go back to my old nick, drink your lousy tea and spell any words over two syllables for you.'

'I had to spell some long words to pass my Inspectors exam, I'll have you know.'

'Get your guys to look for footprints in the grass,' Lunn said. 'There was heavy dew last night and This weak sunshine hasn't burnt it off yet, so if they start from the house they should be able to follow the old lady's footprints straight to the crime scene.'

'Sure thing and why don't I tell them how to tie their shoe laces while I'm at it.'

'Never overestimate the modern police force.'

'You don't change, Jack.'

'Come on, Mick. I'll give you a lift back to the office.'


Back at the car park Jack returned to his car to start taking his waders off.

'It must cost a few bob to fish here?' Sparkes asked.

'It's not cheap.'

'Nice if you can afford it.'

'I don't pay,' Lunn replied. 'Got a day's fishing a week from the Lamont's about eight years ago, just before Mister passed away. I'd sold a couple of properties for them and rather than charge fees, I negotiated a rod on the beat. Best deal I ever made.'

Jack rolled up his right trouser leg, revealing a brace and a patchwork of scars around his knee. A reminder of why he was no longer a copper. Taking the support off, he massaged the area. After retrieving his shoes from the car boot and stowing his fishing gear, he clambered into the driver's seat. Mick slid in alongside.

'By the way, we won't be going back to Lyndhurst nick,' Sparkes said. 'You get to visit the new one in Southampton. You know where that is?'

'That glass and concrete thing? You can hardly miss it. I take it your boss is on his way down here?'

'The DCI is and the new Superintendent's waiting at the office.

'Geoff Cooke's the new Superintendent, isn't he?' Lunn asked.

'And he wants to talk to you, Jack. So, don't be a smartarse. I know you two have never got on, but I'll be the one getting grief if you clash with him,' Sparkes replied. 'He got confirmed on Monday. I'm surprised Marianne didn't tell you?'

'You know my ex-wife and I don't talk very often, particularly now that she's married to him.'

'That could have been you, Jack.'

'Would have, could have, should have. I'm more than happy to share what information and ideas I have, Mick. I just don't want her to end up as another crime statistic. I was her friend and I'll help in any way I can.'

'His first murder as a Superintendent, you know he'll want to wrap this up quickly.'

'I know you guys are stretched with all the cutbacks you've had, but it needs to be done right. Quickly is when mistakes get made.'

'Point taken,' Sparkes nodded. Still, you and Geoff Cooke working together again, now there's something I'd never thought I'd see,' Sparkes replied.

'Be careful what you wish for, Mick.'

## Chapter 2

'We'll get you logged in, take you upstairs, do the statement and get you out as quick as a flash,' Sparkes said.

'Suits me,' Jack replied. 'Sarah would have a fit if she knew I was here.'

'Rather you than me,' the DI replied.

They took the lift up to the Major Investigation Team's floor, Jack swept the baseball cap off his head, ran fingers through his greying hair and stepped out into a very modern open plan office.

He could see that every desk now had a monitor and keyboard. It was quite at odds with what he'd been used to, back when mobile phones were the size of half a house brick and computers relatively rare.

Sparkes knocked on a door and a disembodied voice from inside told them to enter.

Superintendent Cooke was sat behind the desk and barely glanced up at the new arrivals. His thinning hair was in full retreat towards his shirt collar and it was obvious that he rarely missed a meal.

'So, you discovered the body?' he said.

'Yes, Superintendent,' Lunn replied. 'Congratulations on the promotion, by the way.'

Cooke turned to Sparkes and a flicker of annoyance crossed his face. 'Get his statement and then get him out of here.'

Lunn cleared his throat and the Superintendent looked back at him wearily.

'What?'

'I know a fair bit about Mrs Lamont's life in the village and have a few ideas.'

'Of course you have some ideas. But I'm sure you don't have to be reminded that you're not in the job anymore,' the Superintendent said dismissively.

Lunn took a step back towards the door, 'Always such a pleasure to see you, Geoff.'

Sparkes closed the door behind them as they left.

'A one-track mind in a surround sound world,' Lunn muttered.

'Well, that went well,' Sparkes said.

'Any chance of that cuppa, then we can crack on with the paperwork?'

In just under an hour later Jack was signing his statement.

'I can give you a lift back to the river?' he offered hopefully.

'I'll call my boss and see where we are with the crime scene.'

'Who's the DCI?'

'Dave Richardson, he came down from Basingstoke. You might remember him?' Sparkes replied.

'He was a DS at Winchester back in the day, if I remember' Lunn said. 'Don't blame him for wanting to escape Basingstoke. The family has always said that the town's motto should be, "Basingstoke: better in the dark".'

Sparkes grinned. 'I forgot to ask why you weren't at work. Day off for a bit of fishing was it?'

'Something like that.'

As Mick spoke to his DCI, they made their way back to the car.

'You okay to drop me at the Lamont house?' Sparkes asked.

'No problem. How are they getting on there?'

'The search of the house and outbuildings is almost finished and the gardens are underway. They followed the footprints from the house to the crime scene,' Sparkes said, then caught Jack smiling. 'Yes alright, just like you said.'

Turning off the road on to a gravel driveway, they drove through an archway of trees down to an Arts and Crafts house. The pale sunlight threw wan shadows across the immaculately kept lawns and flower beds.

Jack had always admired the house, which the Lamont's had bought in the late 60's. On his occasional visits, he had seen a few of the downstairs rooms. The study, kitchen and drawing room were all impeccably decorated and furnished. Perfectly in keeping with the property, and with any trace of modernity only discreetly, almost apologetically, in evidence.

He brought the car to a halt and got out with Mick, recognising DCI Richardson as he emerged from the property.

'Mick, I need you to get coveralls on and liaise with forensics at the crime scene down by the river. Let me know if they need more uniforms for a fingertip search,' the DCI said. 'We're just finishing off the search of the house, but it doesn't look like anything has been stolen from here. Good shout on her rings though. If they're the same ones as in a couple of photos in the house, then they're worth a few quid.'

Lunn stuck out his hand, which Richardson took.

'Jack Lunn, Detective Chief Inspector. I found the body. Or more accurately, it found me and Mick has taken my statement and I've had the pleasure of meeting your Superintendent.'

'Good, good,' Richardson said. 'Well, if we've finished with Mr Lunn can we get him off the crime scene please, Mick?'

'Jack was my old DI, guv. He knew Mrs Lamont pretty well and might be able to give us some insight into what happened.'

Richardson studied Lunn for a moment.

'Jack Lunn? I remember you. I was a DS in Winchester when you got invalided out, must be getting on for 20 years ago,' he said. 'Now I've twigged how you know the Superintendent too. Bugger me, it must have been a shock when that body floated down the river?'

'Especially when you know the victim,' Lunn agreed. 'Mick, you've got my number. Good to meet you again DCI Richardson.'

He retreated to his car, grabbed his mobile phone and punched in a text to Sparkes.

'Call me later or meet me at The Blue Lamp. About eight-ish?'

Putting his sunglasses on, he slipped the car into gear and pulled away up the drive. Jack had friends were coming to dinner the following night and whilst preparing for that, he could give the mornings events some thought.

The dogs set up a plaintive chorus of barks as he parked on his empty driveway and once Jack came into the house they just started to bicker amongst themselves.

Taking a well-thumbed cookbook from the bookshelf in the kitchen, Jack propped it on the bookstand.

After inspecting the haricot beans that had been soaking in a pan overnight, he added an onion, along with some herbs from the garden and cubed pork rind. Setting the heat under the pan, he took a bowl of confit duck legs out of the fridge, along with a jar of duck fat.

Jack struggled to push the image of Elizabeth Lamont's lifeless body to one side but failed. In his time as a detective he'd dealt with enough killings to know that what he recognised was that gut feeling that this was murder.

As the family were the ones who had the most obvious gain, he assumed that investigations would start with them. If that didn't come up with anything, then the police would widen their enquiries.

Easing the flesh off the duck legs into a fresh bowl, Jack spooned a little of the duck fat into a heavy frying pan. He cubed the pork fillet, checked the recipe and transferred the pork into the frying pan, followed by the Toulouse sausage and lastly the duck. Once it had a little colour it went into the casserole pot. Into the frying pan went some crushed garlic, diced onion and celery to gently fry until they softened. He transferred all of this into the casserole with some tomatoes, tomato puree and a little more water. Setting the pot on the hob, it was allowed to simmer gently, whilst the beans continued to cook.

His thoughts couldn't help but return to the body resting against his waders and how he would tell Sarah.


'The shed' as it was usually known, occupied much of the far end of the garden, but shed undersold it. The oak framed and wood clad building's roofline extended to provide a veranda to the front and a pair of glazed doors led through to what was Jacks' refuge from the world. One section stored all the garden tools, lawnmower, etc. and in the other was his fishing rods, reels, tackle, fly-tying paraphernalia and any number of books. Under the big window that overlooked the garden, there was a desk and swivel chair with a bench for fly-tying alongside. As well as power and water, there was even Wi-Fi up there, so he could take his laptop up there to work. Tucked almost out of sight was a small barrel of ale, made by a brewery in nearby Ringwood. Jack rationalised that, if you had guests it would be rude not to offer them something stronger than tea.

Jack spun back to his desk and opened some of the many drawers to check he had sufficient fly tying materials, then taking out the laptop out, he plugged it in and waited for it to boot up. Jack went to his supplier's website and placed a small order for items he needed.

On the news websites; there were a couple of lines that a body had been discovered in the river, but no names yet. The police would want to speak to the family and get a formal identification from one of them before they released any details to the press, so it might be a few hours before the full details were on the local radio and TV channels.

Lunn hung up his tackle vest, putting the tackle bag away with the net next to it. The fly rods were in their rod cases and got hung up according to line weight. His sock drawer might not have a matched pair in it, but the shed was all in order.

It would be about 30 minutes before Sarah would be home, so Jack eased himself out of the chair, closed the door to his shed and returned to the house.

There was a text waiting on his phone from her, to say she was picking up her eldest daughter, Gemma, from Southampton.

Gem had been an Army Officer but, after leaving, she had been working for an NGO in Central America. Very bright, she had a ready wit, was well-read, spoke several languages and shared a love of film with Jack. They'd always been close.

Another text, this time from Mick Sparkes asking for a meet at Jack's local pub that evening.

He dug the chilli out of the freezer and stuck it on defrost in the microwave.

He rubbed his knee absentmindedly, realising that it was now aching and stiff. A couple of pain killers would sort that out.

He trusted that Mick would give him some idea of how the investigation was going. Having Elizabeth's body float down to him gave Jack all the justification for involvement he needed. He just needed to make sure that Sarah didn't get a whiff of what he was doing. But with time on his hands and his discovery of the body, Jack knew her antenna would be twitching like mad.

Chapter 3

Although Elizabeth Lamont had been a creature of habit, only a few people would have known the exact routes and times that her morning and evening walks took. Over the years she would stop and chat with Jack when he was fishing the beat and the more he thought about it, those in the know would have been a small number. The family, some of the fishing syndicate members, her cleaner and gardener at best.

Jack continued to mull over possibilities as he went upstairs to the bedroom, dumping what he'd had on in the clothes basket, dragging on a pair of jeans and a polo shirt. He inspected himself in the mirror. At a little over six feet tall, the greying hair complimented his blue eyes and whilst he might be carrying a few extra pounds, he wasn't in bad nick, all things considered.

On returning to the kitchen, the beans in the cassoulet had begun thickening the liquid nicely. He took the bouquet garni and onion out, then transferred the rest of the contents to the casserole pot, making sure that the meat was well-covered. Putting the lid on the pot, he stuck it in the oven on a low heat, where it would sit for another hour, so the flavours deepened.

Jack shut his eyes for a moment, trying to break his train of thought which kept returning to the eventful morning. Retreating to the shed for a while, he thought that tying a few flies would be a diversion. Instead he found himself on his laptop, scanning the local papers and news sites.

An hour or so had passed when he heard the dogs starting to bark, announcing an arrival and so he made his way back to the house.

The front door was flung open and the new arrival was welcomed by a barbershop quartet of dogs all clamouring for her attention.

'Good to have you home, Gem. Do you fancy a beer?' Lunn asked the new arrival, already knowing the answer.

The tall young woman extricated herself from the tangle of dogs and gave Lunn a hug and kiss on the cheek.

She swept her shoulder length dark hair back from her face and gave him a huge grin.

'It's so good to see you, Jack and a beer would be lovely.'

Sarah passed Lunn her coat took him in.

'You're home early. You normally stay for the evening rise?' she asked.

'I'll tell you later. I want to hear what your day has been like and catch up with Gem first.'

'You're up to something,' she accused him. 'What's happened?'

'I'll tell you later. Come on, Gem, it's beer o'clock and we need to have a catch up.'

Ten minutes later Sarah joined them and after giving Gem a hug took the mug of tea that Jack passed her.

'Mum told me about your job,' Gem said. 'She didn't tell me the whole story, said you'd fill me in. What happened?'

As a 30-year-old DI, Jack Lunn had been considered a highflier, until a drugs raid had gone wrong and a baseball bat shattered his knee and his career. After several operations, he'd been left with compensation and all the time in the world to contemplate on how to support a young family.

A meeting with his older brother, one lunchtime settled that. Dan had a successful estate agency in the village and was sat in the pub garden nursing a pint and cigarette.

Jack was struck by the pallor and tiredness in his brothers face and how his suit hung off him.

Dan told him that he had terminal cancer and wanted Jack to take over his business.

Four months later his brother was dead, leaving him the business and a cottage in his will.

Jack worked hard to build the business up, expanding to a second office and longer hours. Then Jack discovered his wife's affair and it was swiftly followed by divorce.

The bitterest blow was not seeing his two daughters every day.

Jack had opened the third office a couple of years after moving in with Sarah and then, just over three years ago, he'd sold his business to a corporate agency.

Jack had arrived at the usual monthly meeting with his Area Director knowing that the nine offices he oversaw were doing well.

His Area Director was a corporate man to the bone and not one for small talk. After going over the figures, ideas for new business and marketing, he'd got a sense that there was an elephant in the room. The meeting eased towards its usual finish, the Area Director sat back in his leather executive chair, cleared his throat and announced that Jack was being made redundant. The economic climate, rationalisation… blah, blah!

There hadn't been an elephant in the room but a dinosaur, him. Out of date, a relic and now on the scrapheap as far as the corporate machine was concerned.

He was told 'gardening leave' would begin immediately and that as the end of the meeting. He let the insincere 'Good luck' bounce off his back, as he walked out of the door.

Returning to his office in the village, Jack noticed that the manager, who he usually thought of and referred to as 'Corporate Boy', had the faintest glimmer of triumph on his face as Jack walked past him and up to the first-floor office. Alison, the office secretary, appeared at the door, wanting to know if he was alright. Jack assured her he would be fine and that apparently the future was downstairs. She had made a face, then asked what to do with his brother's old cottage. It had come up for re-let, so Jack asked her to put it on hold for the time being.

'The place could probably do with some re-decoration and updating. I'm going to have a bit of time on my hands now, so I'll get it done and let you know.'

Jack thanked her for all the hard work over the years, telling her to keep in touch.

He'd taken the files and mobile downstairs and put them on the manager's desk. Jack glanced up at Corporate Boy's Ego Wall. Pictures of him with minor 'celebrities', a signed Arsenal football shirt, various technical awards and in-house training certificates. The manager barely acknowledged him and refused to sign the required form until the company laptop was returned. Jack told the manager that he would drop the laptop off sometime later and left.

Chapter 5

'Backstabbing bastards!' Gem interjected.

'It's fine. I've done okay out of it with the redundancy package and they'll have to continue paying me rent for the two offices I own.'

'Mum seems quite sanguine about it. What will you do?'

'I haven't given finding anything else a real thought yet.'

'Sounds like we're both in the same boat.' Gem replied.

Sarah pointed a fork at her partner. 'You still haven't told me why you were home so early.'

'Ah,' said Lunn, 'Thereby hangs a tale.'

Jack had come to the conclusion that trying to keep his involvement from Sarah would be pointless, so told them of the fish diving into the raft of weeds that held Elizabeth Lamont's body, of the Police arriving and having to make a statement.

'Well, that's certainly put yesterday's redundancy in the shade,' Gem said.

'You're going to keep your nose out of this,' Sarah demanded. 'I know you and Mrs Lamont were quite friendly, but you poking around wouldn't be fair on Mick and frankly you have better things to do. Like getting another job.'

'I offered to help in any way I could, background, that sort of thing. But I won't get involved,' Lunn replied.

His partner looked far from convinced and decamped to the family room.

'She'll find out eventually you know. But I don't blame you for being curious about how it happened,' Gem offered. 'Are you're not going to do some snooping of your own?'

'The trouble is that you're far too clever for your own good, young lady. I liked Elizabeth Lamont and we got on. She'd been kind to me in the past and that meant a lot to me. I want to know who killed her and why. Is that too much to ask?'

'Of course not, but I doubt Mum will see it that way. Speaking of which, we'd better go and join her, or she'll suspect that we're plotting something.'

'As if.'

It was nearly eight when Jack announced he was going to take a stroll to the pub.

The Blue Lamp was right by the police station, hence the name and about a ten-minute walk from the house. The streetlights illuminated the thatched roof and as Jack opened the door, the hubbub from the chattering drinkers dipped slightly and then resumed its former volume. The beamed ceiling and flagstone floor gave the place a rustic authenticity and as it was a little off the tourist trail, it was favoured by the locals.

He'd just taken the top off his pint when Mick Sparkes walked in from the other entrance.

'Thanks for meeting up, Mick. I bet you could murder a beer.'

'Very funny. I'm bloody starving too,' Sparkes said.

'Let order you some food then.'

Jack came back to the table a few minutes later with a pint and a pack of pork scratchings and gave Mick an expectant look.

'Jack, this is a courtesy. I know you found her and are on the I.A.G., otherwise my lips would be sealed. The forensic team have the area tented and it was getting on, so we called it a day. Forensics will carry on working overnight and hopefully have a report to us tomorrow. Here's to a quick result.'

'What makes you say that?'

'Come on, Jack. You know I can't tell you everything.'

'Did you find her rings?' Lunn persisted.

'No sign of them.'

'Anything else stolen from the house?'

'Doesn't look like it,' Sparkes replied. 'We've spoken to the gardener and cleaner and nothing seems to be missing.'

'So, you have a possible motive then?'

'There was enough at the murder scene to give us a strong lead and I can't say any more.'

'Really? Geoff must be pleased,' he said, taking a mouthful of beer.

'He is.'

'Is it family?'

'You know I can't say. But suffice to say that as the daughter-in-law and grandchildren have some sort of alibi from your favourite curry house at about the time the old lady was killed.'

'What about her son?'

'Working late. We're checking mobile traffic, CCTV, etc.'

'Who's verified the family at the restaurant?'

'The owner says they ordered a takeaway and the son picked it up. Apparently, there was a bit of an argument about the bill and that's how he remembered it clearly.'

'I'm sorry, I didn't mean to press you.'

'You're in DI mode, Jack.' Sparkes said with a smile. 'This is strictly between us though.'

*'Sometimes the silence can be like thunder.'*

Sparkes thought for a moment. 'Is that Shakespeare?' he asked.

Lunn smiled. 'Bob Dylan. Eat your meal.'

'Why were you on the river, Jack?'

They were down to the last inch of beer by the time Lunn had told his former colleague of his redundancy. Sparkes cleared his plate and looked at the time.

'I had better get going; Emma will be on my back if I don't get home soon.'

'Will you keep me in the loop if you're able?'

'If it's going public, I'll let you know. I owe you that.'

'Thanks, Mick.'

As Jack walked away from the pub, his thoughts went back to his days as a copper and what a 'strong lead' would have meant to him. It all seemed to point to some sort of forensic or physical evidence and not knowing what just made him more determined to find out, one way or another.

Chapter 6

'Nothing on the main news,' Gem announced to Jack, as he arrived home a little after nine.

It was the second story on the local news.

'Sounds like they'll have it wrapped up soon,' Lunn said confidently.

Sarah looked over at him from the sofa. 'You didn't tell me Geoff Cooke was the senior officer?

There's another reason for you to keep your nose out of it, Jack.'

'Nothing to put my nose in to,' he responded, rather too quickly, noticing his partners daughter

was making sure that her expression of disbelief was safely hidden behind the screen of her laptop.


Getting into bed, Jack put his glasses on and picked up his book, as the dogs rearranged

themselves on the bed.

'Have you heard from Eden?' Lunn asked.

'Well, you know she's home in a few days,' Sarah replied, thinking about her youngest daughter.

'And there's apparently a new boyfriend on the scene.'

'From Uni?'

'No. He's apparently local, from what little I could wheedle out of her and that's the odd thing.

You know she's usually so open with me, but not this time. Won't tell me who he is and reading

between the lines, he's been up to Glasgow a few times.'

'I'm sure it's nothing sinister, she's just growing up and probably wants a bit of privacy.'

'You know what happened last time she was secretive over a boyfriend. Maybe I'm just being over

sensitive. It's a Mother thing,' Sarah conceded.

'I've an idea to try selling some of my tied flies,' he said, changing the subject.

'Do you think you'll make any money from it?' she asked, as she peered over her spectacles.

'No idea. But I've had enough of ten-hour days, so if I can make some cash and be at home

most of the time, then it seems to be worthwhile giving it a go.'

He read on for a while, finally switching his light off. Sarah followed suit and they snuggled

Down. It had been a long day and within minutes he was asleep.

Chapter 7

The few beers the night before hadn't given him a restful sleep, waking up twice during the night and struggling to get back off to sleep each time. The alarm roused him this time and slipping on his dressing gown, Jack made his way downstairs. After letting the dogs out into the garden and checking the chickens, he made tea and retreated upstairs. Putting the TV on, as Sarah was showering, the killing was being covered as part of the local news. He feigned disinterest when Sarah came back into the bedroom, but noticed that there was nothing new added from the reports of the previous night.

Her dressing complete, Sarah turned to Lunn.

'Will I do?' she asked.

''A thing of beauty is a joy forever'.'

'Thank you, kind sir. Flattery will get you anywhere. Tackle shops today?'

'Indeed, and don't forget we have guests tonight.'

'What time will they be here?'

'Between seven and half past.'

'I'm off then,' Sarah announced.

'I'll come down with you.'

He kissed her on the cheek and then watched as she drove away.

It was still a bit early to go around the various tackle shops in the area, but not too early for a stroll up to the village and a coffee.

There were a few cafés to choose from, but he made his way to his favourite. After getting a drink and a Danish pastry, Jack found a table and listened to the chatter as he ate. He eavesdropped on to a couple of garrulous local ladies on the next-door table.

'You could throw a stick down the High Street and hit half a dozen people she'd crossed over the

Years,' one of the women said.

'There won't be too many mourning her passing,' the other replied.

'I'd heard that even the supermarket had stopped delivering to her, as she was so rude to the drivers.'

There was no good reason to disagree with them. Plenty of tradespeople and local businesses had got on her wrong side over the years. Elizabeth Lamont was not gifted with a particularly forgiving nature and she'd had the memory an elephant would have been proud of.

Jack had always been good with names and quickly recalled who the women were. What was said next made his ears prick up though.

'Your Liam had a run in with her, didn't he?' One woman asked the other.

'There was no reason for her to threaten him with a loaded shotgun,' the other replied tartly.

'He was trying to rob her house.'

Jack leaned over towards them. 'I found her body,' he said conspiratorially.

The pair of them appeared taken aback by his interruption. The expression that passed across Mrs Galletly's face wasn't at all welcoming and her crossed arms seemed in concert with the look she gave Jack.

He caught the attention of the waitress, ordering tea and some cake for the ladies.

'Now then, you're Jack Lunn,' Mrs Cowan stated.

'You were a copper, weren't you?' Mrs Galletly asked, as he took him in and unfolded her arms.

'That was a long time ago, Mrs Galletly.'

'You were very kind to me when I had trouble with my ex-husband.'

Jack recalled her husband as a particularly nasty piece of work with a habit of hard drinking and beating up his wife. Jack had nicked him more than once. Unfortunately, the rumour was that the son was a chip off the old block and had a record of violence and theft to prove it.

'Just doing my duty.' he replied.

'So, you found the old girl?' Mrs Cowan chimed in.

'I was just out for a day's fishing when she floated down the river.' Lunn explained as the tea and cakes arrived. 'Now, what was that you were saying about there being plenty of suspects?'

'Well, it was common knowledge that she wasn't popular in the village,' Mrs Cowan said, taking a bite of cake. 'There was hardly anyone left she hadn't upset over the years,' she continued. Lightly peppering Jack with crumbs as she spoke.

'She was always very kind to me,' Lunn replied, turning to the other woman. 'What about you, Mrs Galletly? How did you find her?'

'She won't have a good word to say about the old girl,' Mrs Cowan interrupted. 'Mrs Lamont had her Liam arrested for breaking into her house.'

'Holding my Liam at shotgun point until the Police arrived. How do you think that made me feel? The other woman said crossly. 'It wasn't right, Mr Lunn. It was all a misunderstanding.'

'But your friend here said that Liam had been trying to burgle her house?'

'Well, I meant it was a mistake by Liam. He'd been drinking and was looking for somewhere to have a lie down. He was a bit disorientated. You know, with the drink.'

The other woman scoffed. 'So disorientated that he took a torch, jemmy and a couple of screwdrivers with him.'

'Just some of his tools from work. Like I said, it was all just a misunderstanding.'

'Is that what he told the magistrates when he was convicted of those other burglaries?' Mrs Cowan asked.

'And where is Liam now, Mrs Galletly?' Lunn asked.

'Oh, you'll like this, Mr Lunn. Liam came out of prison just a couple of weeks back,' the other woman interrupted again.

Jack watched as Mrs Galletly pursed her mouth and re-folded her arms, aware that the rest of the café was now listening to the exchange.

'I've had enough of this,' she said, abruptly getting to her feet. 'I'm not going to have my Liam slandered by the likes of you, Sandra Cowan. He had nothing to do with old Mrs Lamont's death and I'll thank you both to remember that.'

With that, she picked up her handbag and stalked from the café.

'So, the Police will be calling on Liam then?' Mrs Cowan asked Jack.

'I'm sure they'll be thorough in their investigations,' Lunn replied. 'I remember that Mrs Lamont had some trouble with a neighbour too.'

'Nasty boundary dispute, something to do with an illegally planted hedge and then there was that builder that she put out of business.'

'Both of which wound up in Court.'

'I cleaned for the neighbours. He had some sort of attack, dreadful business and ended up in a wheelchair with nurses having to come in. They moved soon after.'

'I sold them the house, a Mr and Mrs Brownlow. I don't suppose you remember where they moved to?

A smile lifted the corners of the woman's mouth. 'The wife and I exchange cards. Christmas and Birthdays, that sort of thing. I'll have their address at home.'

'Would you let me have it?'

'Why would you need it?'

'I'll bet the Police will be knocking on the door and asking for it. If you let me have it, you won't have the trouble of them visiting.'

She took a moment to think. 'I can drop it into your office if you like?'

'You know where I live, don't you?'

'I do.'

'Just drop by when you've a minute, please. You've been very helpful, Mrs Cowan.'

'I just keep my ears open,' she said. 'Thank you for the tea and cake.'

'A pleasure.'

With that, she left.


Finishing the last of his pastry and coffee, Jack thoughts turned back to what Mick Sparkes had last said to him. He doubted that Mick would have been so positive if they didn't have something concrete.

Making his way up the High Street, he saw Mrs Lamont's son coming towards him. Seemingly in a world of his own, Max had his head down and shoulders slumped.

'Max, how are you?' Lunn asked.

The man stopped and it took a moment or two before a flicker of recognition passed across his face.

'Jack, Jack Lunn,' he said. 'You found my mother.'

'I'm so sorry for your loss,' Jack replied. 'Are you and the family all okay?'

'I'm fine, just a bit distracted,' Max replied. 'I can't get it into my head that she's gone.'

'It's dreadful.'

'It must have been a shock for you too. But, I'm glad you're the one that found her. She liked you, Jack. I'm sorry, but with having to identify her and the Police, it's all a bit much at the moment,' Max replied. 'I'm sure you understand.'

'Of course and if I can help, just let me know.'

'I'll be fine,' Max replied.

Lunn asked. 'I understand the family was having a meal at home?'

'Still got your connections in the Police, I see?'

'It was mentioned when I was giving my statement. You were working late?'

'Tax returns, so our busiest time.'

'Straight home to the family and cold takeaway, was it?'

'I went for a drive in the Forest for a while,' Max responded. 'Just trying to blow the cobwebs away.'

Jack smiled reassuringly at him and put his hand on Max's arm. 'I used to do the same after a tough day. You can't beat a bit of peace and quiet and being surrounded by nature to help you unwind.'

'Have they a good chance of catching who did this?'

'They'll do their best and the Detective Chief Superintendent in charge of Major Crimes was my old boss. So, you're in good hands.'

'I hope so.'

'Look,' Lunn said. 'If there is anything I can do. If you just want to talk. I've been where you are today.'

'I appreciate that, Jack.'

'Let me know when the funeral is. I'd like to come and pay my respects.'

'Thank you,' The two men shook hands. 'I have to get on, but I'll be in touch.'

Chapter 8

There was no sign of Gem when Jack got home, so he packed some flies into boxes, picked up his car keys and mobile phone; it was time to try a new career path.

He'd decided to try three tackle shops where he was well known. At the first the owner wasn't in, so Lunn said he'd call back. The second tackle shop said no. He'd saved the final shop until last, as was one of his favourites.

The staff had always courteous and impeccably well-informed, but he also knew their stocking of flies was patchy at times. The owner welcomed him in, knowing that Jack was not averse to putting his hand in his pocket for an item of tackle he coveted.

He was a little taken aback when Jack wanted to talk business with him, but invited Jack into his office.

'It's been a trying day,' the owner explained. 'The police were here first thing about the death of Mrs Lamont. You've heard about that, I assume? We deal with the syndicate members for the river beats on her land and they wanted a list of names and addresses. Dreadful business. You fish there too, don't you?'

Jack nodded. 'They've already interviewed me.'

'Anyway, enough of that and down to business. How can we help each other?'

Jack showed him his flies, talking through what he proposed.

'You're right about our less than efficient stocking. That's my fault in some ways, but also partly due to the foibles of our supplier, who isn't local,' Wiseman conceded. 'I'm very impressed with the quality of your product. It explains why, in all the many years you've frequented my shop, you've never bought a single fly.'

'I'm glad I've been able to clear up that little mystery for you.'

'I think we can do some business, as I've been considering changing supplier for some time. But, whilst I can find plenty of mass-produced flies, many of my clientele demand a more bespoke item and are more than happy to pay a premium for a quality product.'

'I'm happy to help and you wouldn't have any worries about stock levels. I'm only a phone call and thirty minutes away,' Jack said, handing over his contact details.

Climbing back into his car, it occurred to Jack that he'd heard nothing from Mick Sparkes. Not a call or text and that was a little unusual. Jack sent him a message and almost immediately got a text back that he was tied up but would get in touch.

Chapter 9

Jack hadn't been long home when Gem came downstairs and joined him in the kitchen.

'What time do you call this?' he asked.

'Jetlag's a killer,' she replied. 'How did it go with the tackle shop owners?'

'I've got definitely one onboard and a foot in the door with another.'

'I've got a mate of mine who's a real computer geek, we could set up a website for you,' Gem offered.

Jack passed her a mug of tea. 'That would be incredibly helpful.'

'I'll call Henry and get him to come over.'

'Your mother mentioned something about Eden and a new boyfriend. Have you heard anything?'

Gem shook her head. 'Why do you want to know?'

'She's usually all too happy to discuss her relationships with your mother, but not this time. And you know what that could mean,' Lunn confided. 'I've tried her Facebook page, but no clues.'

'Let me dig around the rest of her social media and see what I can find.'

'Your mother is particularly protective when it comes to Eden. But I suppose any mum wants to know what's going on in their children's lives?

'Baby sister has not always made the wisest of choices in the boyfriend department. Message received and understood.'

'I saw Max Lamont in the High Street.'

'How was he?' she asked.

'In a daze.'

Their conversation was interrupted by Jack's phone buzzing.

'It's a text from Mick,' Lunn said. 'Says they have a prime suspect.'

'That's quick.'

Lunn nodded. 'I'm a bit surprised myself, but maybe they've got some good forensics. He must feel that they're close to an arrest.'

'Disappointed?'

'Mick said they had some decent leads,' Jack replied. 'Anytime a killer is off the street, I'm not disappointed. But this is a swift turnaround. I wonder who it is?'

'Do you miss being a policeman?' Gem asked, out of the blue.

Jack was caught out by the conversations sudden change of direction.

'I think what grates is that it was taken away, rather than me deciding that I'd had enough. You understand, unfinished business,' Lunn replied. 'Before you ask, I don't miss being an estate agent. I'd stopped being that person a few years ago, probably when I sold the business.'

'No more the corporate puppet.'

'Nope, just your mother's little helper. Which reminds me, she'll be home soon.'


They took Sarah's bags as she came through door and after changing out of her work clothes, she claimed a glass of wine.

'So, how did your meetings go?' she asked.

'One was a no, one was a maybe and then finally I got a yes,' Lunn replied.

'That's a start.'

'We're going to set up a website too, Mum,' Gem chipped in.

'Who's the 'we'? she asked.

'Henry Best and I.'

'Is he some sort of tech genius then? Because my recollection is of an average at best English scholar.'

'He has me for the spelling and he builds websites for fun.'

Sarah gave Gem a somewhat doubtful look and then turned her attention back to Jack.

'How long do you get redundancy pay?' she asked.

'Three months, why?'

'That's how long you have to turn a profit. If it's not a goer by then, you'll have to find a proper job. There's a decent nest egg tucked away, but I'm not sacrificing that. We agreed that that money was there to help the kids if they need it and for when we retire,' Sarah stated.

Jack capitulated. 'You're right, you're right. Gem, we'll need to get the pictures set up asap. Can you work on it over the weekend, please?'

'Yeah, sure. With the pictures you gave me and video of some flies being tied, I can make a start. With some help from Mark, we'll have you up and running before you know it.'

'And for that, you can help yourself to another beer from the fridge. But we have guests tonight, so leave the wine alone,' he pleaded.

'You've certainly got Gem on your side and if you're going to be working from home, who am I to complain if there is a nice meal ready and waiting when I walk through the door.' Sarah said, then gave Jack a peck on the cheek. 'What time is everyone arriving tonight?'

'David and Kimi should be here about seven and the others about half past.'

'I'm going to have a shower and get changed then,' Sarah replied.


'I notice you didn't say anything to Mum about Mick and an imminent arrest.' Gem observed with a smile.

'The less the case is discussed in front of her, the better.'

Chapter 10

The scent of cooking permeated the kitchen. Jack checked the oven, adding a little water to keep the cassoulet moist. He took the bread he'd left out earlier, cut it up and tossed it into the food processor, pulsing the machine to make breadcrumbs.

He was just tidying a few things away when Gem made a return to the kitchen.

'I'm going out soon, but I'll stay to say hello to everyone. Can I get a beer in the meantime?'

'Help yourself. I'm going upstairs to get ready.'

Sarah was in front of the bedroom mirror, putting a little make-up on.

'I'm just going to grab a quick shower and shave. David and Kimi should be here in about half an Hour,' he said.

'What's Gem up to?'

'Having a beer and then going out with some friends, from what I can gather.'

When he returned to the bedroom, Sarah was dressed and executed a quick twirl.

'You'll do,' he confirmed.

She smiled. 'I'm going to put the last touches to the table.'

'Okay, I'll be down in a few minutes.'

As she left the room Lunn's phone buzzed.

'We've made an arrest,' Mick's text stated.

Gem was watching TV and savouring a beer when Jack poked his head round the door of the family room to update her on the latest.

'No playing detective for you then. Never mind, you can have a nice weekend with your old friends.'

Jack left her and went through to the kitchen.

'The food smells delicious,' Sarah said, looking up from sorting out fruit for the Eton Mess. 'I've whipped the cream and the fruit is just about ready too. I think it's time for a glass of wine.'

He took a chilled bottle of Sancerre from the fridge. She wasn't a great drinker, but a glass of cold white wine always went down well. He poured himself a glass of red.

'Any news from Mick?' she asked.

Jack tried to look surprised but guessed that he was still under suspicion.

'I'll hear what's going on from the news, like everyone else.'

Sarah gave a snort of derision. 'Do you really think I'm going to believe that? In Mick's mind, you're still his boss. He'll let you know what's going on.'

There was a rush of barking dogs towards the front of the house, indicating that their guests had arrived. As they both made their way downstairs, he counted his blessings that Sarah hadn't joined the police. With the instinct she displayed for tracking down deception, plagiarism and just plain bullshit from her students, she'd have been Chief Constable by now.

They greeted their first guests, helping with the bags and hustling them into the house, where the dogs demanded some attention from the new arrivals.

David Anderson was a senior editor for a London based news bureau and had worked all over the world. Reporting from trouble spots in the Middle East, South and Central America, though this didn't explain how he'd managed to snag his attractive Japanese wife, Kimi. Jack and David had met at boarding school and had now been friends for the best part of 40 years.

Sarah and Kimi went through to the kitchen, as the men trucked the assorted luggage upstairs to one of the guest rooms.

Returning to the ground floor, they found their partners already nursing a glass of wine and discussing the children.

Gem emerged to say hello and help herself to another beer.

'How's was Central America?' David asked her.

'You should know. You've reported from practically every war there over the past twenty odd years,' Gem replied. 'I read your pieces from when you were in Lebanon, by the way. Great context and background to what's happening in the area.'

'And how's your Spanish now?'

'No como un nativo, pero bastante bueno,' Gem replied, with a shrug of her shoulders.

David laughed. 'It's better than mine now.'

As they talked, Lunn took a few moments to drag the cassoulet out, spoon the breadcrumbs on top and dribble some duck fat over them, before returning it to the oven.

Shortly after that, their second set of guests arrived bearing flowers and wine. Paul and Connie Clousden lived not far away, in Winchester. Connie taught Law at Southampton University and Paul, another old school friend, was a Q.C..

After the usual pleasantries, Gem said her goodbyes and left for the evening.

David proposed a toast to all of them and their respective children. Turning back to Jack, he asked, 'What all this about a murder down here?'

'Ever the reporter, mate, ' Lunn replied. 'A local landowner bashed over the head, nothing for a big city reporter like you to bother about.'

'Who was it?' Paul asked.

'Elizabeth Lamont,' Lunn said.

'Nicholas Lamont's widow?' the lawyer queried.

'Yes. I bought and sold a few properties for them over the years, so got to know her quite well.'

'Anything shady in the lady's past?' David chipped in.

'Not as far as I know,' Lunn replied. 'There was a bit of talk about her husband, but nothing concrete.'

'Jack discovered the body, or rather the body found him,' Sarah volunteered.

They all turned to Lunn.

'More drinks anyone?' he asked.

'You're not getting off the hook that easy,' Paul said in his best lawyer voice.

'Let me top everyone up, my learned friend, and I'll spill the beans,' Lunn replied.

Jack retold the events of the previous day, as he pottered around the kitchen, putting a pan of new potatoes on to simmer with some mint from the garden and offering the opinion that the killer was most likely a man, as it looked like the old woman had died from a single blow.

'So what's the latest on the case?' asked Connie.

'His old DC is the DI on the case, so will no doubt be keeping him informed,' Sarah chipped in.

'Really? Jack, you have to let me know what's happening,' David pleaded.

'David, enough. Let Jack feed us and stop being a reporter for a few hours,' Kimi ordered.

'We can talk later, mate,' David conceded. 'Kimi's right. Let's eat, drink and make merry."

Paul and Connie both raised their glasses. 'We'll drink to that.'

He hustled them out of the kitchen towards the dining table. 'Well, sit yourselves down and I'll see what poor fare I can rustle up.'

The other five drifted to the adjacent dining area, as Jack mixed a green salad in a large bowl. He turned the potatoes out, with a generous knob of butter slowly melting on the top. Jack removed the cassoulet from the oven, now with a crust of golden-brown breadcrumbs on top, placed it on the table, warning everyone that the pot was hot, but urging them to help themselves. Finally, he placed a couple of bottles of Crozes-Hermitage, which had been breathing for a while, in the centre of the table and did a quick round of everyone's glasses.

The cassoulet was deemed to be a triumph and the men adjourned to the shed, where Jack gave them a guided tour, a quick explanation of his redundancy and new business proposition.

Paul picked up a box of the flies. 'You made all of these?'

Jack nodded.

'They're all so intricate and so small.'

Jack picked up another box, this time with saltwater patterns in.

'What you've got there are freshwater dry flies, now these here are saltwater patterns,' he said and passed Paul the now open box. 'These are huge, by comparison.'

David looked at the flies with interest. 'I never really paid much attention to what you did in your man cave, on the few occasions I came up here. But, it appears to the layman's eyes that you have some talent.'

'Thank you, kind sir,' Lunn replied with a smile. 'Gem's been helping too and she has a real knack for it.'

He picked up three small boxes and ushered the men out, turning the lights off and locking the shed.

As they strolled down towards the house. Sarah appeared at the French doors to tell them that dessert was going to be served shortly.

The secret to Sarah's Eton Mess was the scoop of vanilla ice cream she placed in the bottom of the sundae glass. She'd already crumbled meringue into the whipped double cream and was now folding in the soft fruits, which she'd mushed up, to give a ripple through the cream. As she brought the finished articles to the table, Jack produced the three small boxes and placed one in front of each the ladies.

'A little keepsake and another of my brilliant business ideas for all those fishing widows out there.'

The boxes were opened to reveal rather exotic flies, tied on hooks with the bend removed and made into earrings.

'Jack, these are gorgeous,' Connie said. 'Very different.'

'Another innovation?' Sarah asked.

'Always a good idea to have a few strings to your bow,' Jack replied. 'I'm glad you like them.'

Coffees and brandies were poured and dark chocolate's circulated, as Paul and Connie engaged in a legally based full and frank exchange of opposing views on local planning laws, umpired by Kimi and Sarah. Jack slipped out to put the chickens away and David joined him.

'You know more about this killing than you're letting on, Jack.'

'We can't really talk about it tonight. But, I do feel some responsibility and there might be more information tomorrow.'

'Your old DC keeping you in the loop is he?'

'You might like to think that, I couldn't possibly comment,' Lunn replied with a smile, knowing that they were on the same wavelength.

'Come on, we'd better go and save Paul from the Oestrogen Gang, who'll now have banded together to verbally castrate him.'

Sure enough, the ladies had Paul cornered and he was using all his courtroom skills to try and parry their attacks.

'I appeal to my friends for support.'

David gave a derisive snort. 'I'd surrender with some grace if I were you.'

'The jury has spoken,' Kimi announced.

Paul waved his napkin in surrender.

Chapter 11

As he walked down to the newspaper shop that Sunday morning, his slight hangover dissipating behind the Ibuprofen he'd taken, Jack fished the phone out of his pocket and called Sparkes.

'I expected your call last night.' Mick said.

'I had guests.'

'Ah, that and a few drinks too many?'

'I'm wasn't driving anywhere. But yes, a glass or two was taken.'

'Anyone I know?

'Paul Clousden and his wife.'

'Old school friend and QC … and let me guess David Anderson? Those two always arrive as a pair.'

'At least you learned to put clues together when you were with me.'

'Ha, bloody ha, Jack,' Sparkes replied. 'The last thing I need is some Fleet Street hack poking his nose into this killing.'

'He already knows about it. But as you have a suspect, I'm sure that I can disabuse him of that line of inquiry,' Lunn replied. 'Who have you got for it?'

'Seth Walker.'

'Seth Walker the poacher? You're having a laugh, Mick!' he blurted out.

'It was well known that he poached on the Lamont land and that Mrs Lamont had pressed charges against him twice over the years. There was a net found close to the crime scene, he's got no alibi for the night and revenge is a pretty powerful motive.'

'I know that he's been caught poaching on her land, Mick. I bloody well caught him about 25 years ago,' Lunn said testily. 'He's denying it, I assume?'

'We're hopeful of getting DNA from the net and you'd expect him to deny it. Heat of the moment, lost his rag, thought he was going to get caught again,' Sparkes replied.

'That doesn't sound like Seth at all. Have you got a murder weapon?' Lunn asked.

'Not yet.'

'He's denying it because he didn't do it, Mick,' Lunn said. 'Seth might be a poacher, but he's never been violent. He's a runner or used to be when he was younger. Look at his file, he's never been any trouble when he's been caught.'

'Geoff is happy we have a primary suspect.'

'The trouble with your boss, DI Sparkes, is that he's got bugger all imagination and is just looking for a quick clearance. *Foolishness is the sister of wickedness*,' Lunn said angrily.

'More bloody Shakespeare?'

'Sophocles, actually.'

'The Superintendent is convinced he's the killer, Jack. Unless someone else more likely pokes their head over the parapet, or Walker can get someone to corroborate his story, he's in the frame. I'll let you know when the DNA comes in. Call me if anything comes to mind and keep the bloody reporter away from this.'

'I'll do my best, but I would be looking for another suspect if I were you, Mick,' Lunn said. 'Seth, just doesn't have the form for this.


The house was stirring when he got back and before long his guests and partner drifted down to be rewarded with the tea, coffee and croissants.

'Shall we take the dogs for a walk, ladies? It'll blow the cobwebs away.' Sarah suggested a little later. 'You men can meet us at the pub.'

'That suits me,' Paul replied, as the other two men nodded their agreement.

It only took a couple of minutes and the two parties headed out and then separated at the top of the road.

'What's the latest then,' David asked, once their partners were out of earshot.

'They nicked a local poacher, but I really don't think it's him.' Lunn replied, then relayed the information he'd been given.

'There's not much real evidence there, it has to be said,' Paul said.

'But you think it must have been someone local with a grudge?' David speculated.

'That's my best guess,' Jack replied. 'But Seth just doesn't feel right for it. Yes, he has a history with the victim, but I've known Seth for years and he hasn't got a nasty bone in his body. It's the net that really puzzles me, there's something not right about that and where's the murder weapon?'

They reached the pub, Jack and Paul went to the bar. David found them a table where they Reassembled, clinked glasses together and changed the subject to where David was off to next and Paul's latest cases.

They'd only been chatting for a few minutes when Jack became aware that someone was now hovering by his shoulder. He turned, taking in the dark-haired woman in her thirties dressed in black with very red nails and an equally red slash of a mouth.

'Can we help you?' he asked.

'I'm hoping you can, Mr Lunn,' the woman replied. 'I'm wondering if you'd care to comment on finding the body of Elizabeth Lamont for the local press?'

'You need to speak to the police, Miss?'

'Miss Adele Porter, Jack. A disgraced former employee of a now-defunct red top,' David said. 'You have fallen down the food chain, Adele. Not that a fall from the gutter was ever going to kill you.'

'David, what a pleasure. Still writing for that lefty news organisation, I note,' the woman said with a stiff smile. 'How about helping a fellow journalist out?'

David laughed. 'I'm always ready to help a fellow professional, Adele. But you hardly qualify, so jog on and find a phone to hack.'

She looked at Jack and raised a questioning eyebrow.

'I think my spokesperson has covered it for me,' Lunn answered and with that the woman left.

It wasn't long before the Sarah and his friends two wives joined them, insisting that, after just one more drink, it was time to get back to the house.


A rib of beef, aged and marbled with yellow fat, had been left on the side. Well out of reach of the dogs. Jack put the oven on to full heat and told everyone to get out of the kitchen whilst he was cooking, unless it was to get a drink or to watch the football.

Timing the meal, so it would be ready after the game was over was no problem. Once the meat was done, out of the oven and resting, he rearranged the roast potatoes and put the Yorkshire Puddings in. That left him time to get the table set and shoo the other men out, as he got ready to dish up.

After they waved their guests off later that day, Jack's thoughts returned to the news of the arrest. There wasn't any way he could reconcile his belief that they'd got it wrong. It wasn't about just joining the dots and then making what evidence you had, however circumstantial, fit what you needed to make the case. A case always made him think of a jigsaw with some pieces missing. Unfortunately, a newly promoted Geoff Cooke wasn't going to look a gift horse in the mouth. If he felt that it would help his clear up rates, he'd pursue the poacher like a hound on a scent trail.

It didn't take too long to get the dining room straight, clearing the dishes and glasses into the dishwasher. Gem arrived home and her eyes lit upon the remains of the beef joint and this was soon joined on a plate by the last few roast potatoes, veg and a generous ladle of gravy. Jack marvelled at how she could eat and drink whatever she wanted, but still stayed whippet thin.

As Sarah had settled down to some marking, Jack strolled down to the shed and slumped in his chair. Fishing his mobile phone out of his pocket he sent a message to Mick Sparkes.

'I know Seth and it would be totally out of character for him. Meet up soon?'

He looked in on Sarah, but it was apparent that she was only halfway through a mountain of essays, so he trooped upstairs and knocked on Gem's door.

'Fancy taking the dogs for a walk?' Lunn asked.

'Where were you thinking of going?'

'Down by the river, past Andy Fairford's place.'

'I see, stop off and have a chat with the River Keeper,' she replied. 'I hear they've made an arrest and you're not happy about who they've arrested, are you?'

Lunn shook his head, 'I'm not and maybe Andy can shed some light on my doubts.'

'Who have they nicked for it?'

'Seth Walker.'

'Seth? Now I can understand why you're not happy.'

Chapter 13

It only took a couple of minutes for them to gather the dogs and herd them into the back of Sarah's Volvo. Though they were only a few minutes walk from the open New Forest, it was worth the drive for the walk along the river, particularly when they could park at a rather decent pub, with a drink being purchased after the walk as a sort of parking charge. At least that's how Jack justified sometimes having a pint there.

Once their leads were clipped on, the dogs bickered for a moment amongst themselves, before some semblance of order returned and they made their way from the pub car park to the footpath alongside the river.

'How much further up were you fishing?' Gem asked.

'A couple of miles from here, above where Andy lives.'

'What are you looking for?'

'I'm not really sure. They've arrested Seth Walker, but I just can't see it,' Lunn replied. 'He's never been nicked for anything other than poaching and in the past when he's been caught, he accepted it as part of his lifestyle. He never resisted arrest and whilst he's been caught on the Lamont land in the past, why would he wait so long to take revenge? It just doesn't ring true.'

'He was really helpful when I was contemplating of joining up and you think that having a chat with the riverkeeper might throw up something?'

'It's worth a shot. I wonder if the Police have even spoken to him in the rush to put Seth in the frame. Whilst Andy and Seth aren't best mates, for obvious reasons, he's got to be worth having a word with.'

'How's he going to feel about possibly helping a convicted poacher?'

'Not great. But he's a fair bloke and maybe I can wheedle some information out of him without him catching on,' Lunn said.

'What do you think is behind Mrs Lamont being killed?' Gem asked.

'Not sure yet. But I always look for one thing, to begin with.'

'Is there some kind of secret method that they teach you at Bramshill?'

'God no. When it comes down to it, what motivates crime is usually one of the seven deadly sins,' Lunn explained.

Soon the river keeper's home came into view. The red brick Victorian house was tucked away behind high hedges right by the river and before long the dogs were replying to the barks of Fairford's Labrador.

A figure appeared at the gate to see what all the commotion was.

'Hello, Jack. I thought it was you when I heard all the yapping from your lot,' he said.

'Hi, Andy. How're things?' Lunn asked.

'Well, apart from all the excitement along the river in the last couple of days, we're all fine. Heard on the grapevine that you found the body?'

'And I lost the brownie I had on at the time.'

'That must have been the least of your worries,' The river keeper replied with a grimace. 'Dreadful business, poor woman.'

He turned his attention to Lunn's companion. 'How's you, Gem?'

'Good thanks, Mr Fairford.'

'Last time I saw you was just after you'd left the Army. So, what have you been up to?'

'I was working abroad, but that's finished now,' Gem said. 'Not sure what to do next.'

'I might be able to help there, if you're up for a bit of hard work?'

'Sure, what have you got?' Gem asked.

'Weed cutting in about six weeks' time.'

'I've nothing else in the diary, so I'm all yours.'

'The least you can do is help improve Jack's fishing.'

'Let's go down by the river, Andy,' Lunn suggested.

'Good idea. I can enjoy a smoke by the water.'

Lunn sat with the riverkeeper as he rolled himself a cigarette. Gem took the four dogs off the lead and they immediately decided that tormenting the resident Labrador would keep them amused for a while, whilst Gem followed them off up the bankside.

The two men sat for a couple of minutes, whilst the riverkeeper smoked, and they listened to the river tumbling past. Eventually, Fairford broke the moment.

'I haven't heard bugger all from the Old Bill, apart from them parking here, there and everywhere and trampling up and down my bankside with their bloody great big boots.'

'They haven't spoken to you?' Lunn enquired, somewhat surprised.

'Other than asking me where I was between whenever and whatever, not a word.'

'Had you seen anyone, or seen anything out of place?'

'I hadn't seen anyone odd if that's what you mean. The last time I saw old Mrs Lamont was the morning before she was found, when I was out walking the dog.'

'You didn't see anyone else?'

'Told the police that Frank Grayshott from the syndicate was tackling up, but he was the only one I saw.'

'What time did you do your rounds in the evening?' Lunn asked.

'I was early. We had family round for supper, so it was late afternoon and the Police were all over the shop next morning, when I started my rounds.'

'She was killed on her evening walk, most likely.'

'I told the Police I'd not seen any suspicious characters around, so the coppers upped sticks and left. Didn't stop them eating every biscuit in the house and drinking a gallon of tea.'

'You definitely didn't see anything out of the ordinary?'

'Not until after they'd gone,' said Fairford, before taking another slurp of tea and pull on his cigarette.

There was a moment's silence before Lunn broke it. 'When you're ready, Andy. In your own time.'

'I'd stowed a net in the store at the back of the bothy, came across it at the tail end of the salmon run last year.'

'And?'

'Well, the padlock on the store was broken and when I opened it up the net had gone.'

'What sort of net?'

'Typical salmon poachers net.'

'And it's been there for months?'

'Since the end of last season. I didn't see the broken lock until I walked the bank later in the afternoon and that was after the Old Bill had seen me,' he explained. 'Buggers made me late for my rounds. I always do this side of the river in the morning and the other side in the late afternoon or evening.'

'You've told the police this?'

'They'd been and gone and what's a net to do with the killing?'

'Pretty much everything. It's just occurred to me that it's not the start of the salmon run yet, is it?' Lunn asked.

'We always get a few early fish, but the main push is usually early May, when the season starts. Why do you ask?'

'Well if you were a poacher, you'd know that netting the river this time of year for salmon was bit of a waste of time?'

'Any poacher worth his salt would know that.'

Gem and Mrs Fairford rounded the corner of the house just then, accompanied by the dogs and it was like a cartoon light blinked on in his head.

'Dog!'

The River Keeper looked at him like he'd completely lost it.

'Dog?'

'Andy, did you ever see Seth Walker without his dog?'

'Seth without that lurcher of his, more likely to see him without his legs. But what's this got to do with who killed Mrs Lamont?'

'I'll call you later and let you know, but I've got to go. Gem, we've got to go, let's get back to the car,' Lunn said. 'Thanks for the chat, Andy. You've been a great help and I promise I'll call you soon.'

As soon as they were out of earshot, Gem wanted to know what all the hurry was.

'What Andy told me casts some serious doubt on this net that the Police have. He says it was from last year and someone had broken into a store and taken it on the night Mrs Lamont was killed.'

'And what else?'

'An alibi for Seth.'

'You have a plan?'

'Call Mick Sparkes, drop the dogs off and head into Southampton,' Lunn said. 'You fancy coming?'

'It could be fun.'

Mick Sparkes answered on the third ring.

'I'm busy, Jack. This had better be important.'

'It is. I'll be at the nick in about an hour and make sure Geoff Cooke is around, please.'

'He's here. Just don't wind him up, please.'

'He's going to thank me,' Lunn replied. 'I'm going to stop him making a twat of himself.'

'This I've got to see; he's going love you pointing out his shortcomings.'

'Better me than the media.'

'I wouldn't bet on it. See you soon.'

Chapter 12

They made quick work of getting back home and ushered the dogs in.

'We've got to go into town,' he explained to Sarah.

'What on earth for and why are you in such a hurry?'

'The Police arrested Seth Walker for murder and I'm certain he didn't do it,' he replied.

'When did you hear about Seth?' she enquired.

'Earlier today. Mick called me to let me know, just as a courtesy.'

'I wasn't born yesterday,' his partner said. 'And you just thought you'd drop in on the Fairfords?'

'How was I to know he had some good info?' Lunn protested.

'But you just thought you'd go and give that tree a good shake and see what fell out? You told me you weren't getting involved, Jack,' she said angrily.

'I wasn't,' Lunn protested. 'Until the police screwed everything up by nicking Seth. I told Mick they'd got the wrong man.'

'Come on, Mum,' Gem said, 'We've done a good thing and an innocent man won't get locked up.'

'What do you mean 'we'? You were in on this too, Gem?' she said. 'You're both as bad as each other. Get into Southampton and don't think you've heard the last of this either.'

Back in the hallway, Jack grabbed his work laptop on the way out and they jumped into Jack's car.

Making their way out of Lyndhurst, they headed through the village and past the fire station and Off through the Forest towards Ashurst and Southampton.


Mick Sparkes met them, arranged passes and escorted Jack and Gem upstairs.

'What's this all about?' the DI asked.

'Wait and see. You wouldn't want me to go off half-cocked, would you?' Lunn replied.

'I'm more worried that you'll be exchanging broadsides with the Superintendent.'

'All in good time, old mate.'

'You can't come into the meeting,' Mick said to Gem.

'That's fine by me; fireworks are always best viewed from a distance,' Gem said with a grin.

'I'm trying to help, Mick,' Lunn said.

'You might think that, but Cookie doesn't take advice very well.'

They walked briskly through the main office and were summoned into the inner sanctum, leaving Gem sat outside.

'To what do I owe the pleasure of another visit from you, Mister Lunn?'

'Some information for you, Superintendent,' Jack replied.

'We have a suspect downstairs in the cells, so what information could you possibly bring that we don't already have?' the Superintendent barked back, with a face like a bulldog chewing a wasp.

'The man you have downstairs?' he asked.

'Who says it's a man?' retorted Cooke.

'Okay, if you want to play that game, Superintendent. Seth Walker is sat downstairs, and you have him in the frame for this.'

'Who bloody told you?' Cooke looked at Sparkes accusingly.

'Not him. The New Forest jungle drums don't take long to get going when they see a bunch of policemen raiding a house in the area and carting someone off,' Lunn lied.

'Well, he doesn't have an alibi. The deceased had prosecuted him twice for poaching and we've recovered something that we believe will link him to the area that she was killed in,' Cooke said. 'Quite obviously he was poaching, she came across him, he attacked her and then dumped her body in the river.'

'Let's look at it another way shall we? Seth doesn't have a violent bone in his body. Not one of the times he's been arrested, and there's been a few, has he ever displayed aggression. You've got a net found at the scene of the crime, but that net has been in a store since the tail end of last year's salmon run. How do I know that? Well, if your team had kept in touch with the riverkeeper, they'd have found out that the store cupboard at the bothy had been broken into and the net was taken from there. Also, no poacher worth his salt would be netting the river this time of year, as the main salmon run is a month away.'

'Yes, all very imaginative. But he doesn't have an alibi and he does have a motive,' Cooke countered dismissively.

'Would you agree that if he has an alibi then he's free to go?'

'If he has an alibi, then he couldn't have been at the crime scene. But he says he was alone,' Cooke replied.

'Technically he was alone, but he had a companion.'

'Stop talking in riddles, Lunn?'

'Seth has a companion that never leaves his side. Your officers would have met that companion when they arrested him,' Lunn explained.

'I'm going to put a stop to this bollocks.' Cooke turned to Sparkes, 'Where's DCI Richardson?'

'In his office, sir. I'll go and get him.'

A flustered Dave Richardson arrived within a minute and looked at Lunn in surprise.

'Was there anyone else present when you arrested Walker?' Cooke asked.

'No one, sir.'

'There. No mysterious companion,' Cooke said angrily. 'No one to give him an alibi.'

Jack held a hand up.

'DCI Richardson, who was with Seth when you nicked him?'

'He lives alone, just him and his dog.'

'So, he wasn't alone then?'

'Well, I suppose if you put it that way, no,' Richardson replied.

Cooke got up from his chair in exasperation. 'I suppose the bloody dog is going to give us a signed statement that his master was in all night.'

'In a way, yes,' Lunn said. 'Have you got the pictures or video from the crime scene?'

'If it will stop you sticking your nose in where it's not needed,' Cooke barked. 'Sparkes, get the film footage.'

Mick returned to the Superintendent's office with a DVD, handed it to Geoff Cooke who stuck it in the machine, snatched up the controls and punched the start button.

'I assume there is footage of the grass showing how the victim and assailant got to the crime scene?'

Sparkes looked at a printed sheet of pages that gave a timeline for the video.

'From about four minutes fifteen seconds in, sir.'

The senior man fast forwarded to the time given to him and then started the film.

'Mick, is this the victim's or the attacker's path to the crime scene we're looking at?' Lunn asked.

'Victim's, why?'

'You can clearly see the path she took across the grass; it's disturbed, trodden down … agreed?' Lunn asked. 'Quite clear as just one person?'

'Yes, yes. What's your point?' Cooke queried.

'Let's look at the attacker's path, shall we?'

They watched the footage as the attacker's clear pathway could be traced both to and from the scene of the murder.

'Right,' Jack said. 'Three coppers in the room and I'll buy a pint for the first one to notice what's missing, if Seth Walker is the killer.'

It only took a few seconds before the penny dropped.

'It's just one person,' Mick Sparkes volunteered.

'Of course it's just one person, DI Sparkes. It's the bloody poacher, you idiot!' thundered Cooke.

'No sir, you don't get it. If it was Walker there would be two sets of tracks, him and his dog,' countered Sparkes

'He could have left it at home, maybe,' offered Richardson, trying to lend support to his senior officer.

'That dog goes everywhere with him,' Lunn said. 'He's never seen without it. I'll bet you another pint that in every report you have on his arrests it will have either that dog or, if you go back a good few years, that dog's sire with him.'

'You're saying that the poacher's alibi is the dog, who wasn't at the crime scene. And if the dog wasn't there, then the poacher couldn't have been either,' responded Richardson.

'Exactly. But don't stand on my word, check out his arrests, speak to his neighbours. The river keeper will confirm what I said about the net,' Lunn said looking over at the Superintendent. 'And where are her missing rings?'

Geoff Cooke was slumped back in his chair looking disconsolate, his nicely wrapped up parcel of a case unravelled in front of him. 'I suppose you have a prime suspect?' he asked.

'Can't help you there, Geoff. But keep your options open,' Lunn advised.

'Great. You swan in here, tell me my investigation and suspect are all a waste of time and then sod off without so much as a hint about who the real criminal is,' Cooke complained. You need to back right off and leave this to the professionals.'

'Look, I know that she'd had a run in with a builder a few years back,' Lunn said. 'Something to do with them not using the materials they'd originally quoted for and it ended in court. There was also a boundary dispute with a neighbour that got rather out of hand. The builder ended up going bust and the farmer, who had some sort of breakdown, lost some land to her.  You should also have a long hard look at Liam Galletly, a recently released from prison local, with a history of violence and house breaking. He tried to rob Mrs Lamont's house and she caught him red-handed. Held him at gunpoint until the cavalry turned up. That should give you some decent suspects to investigate'

Geoff Cooke looked up wearily from behind his desk.

'Mick, get over and interview the riverkeeper and I want CSI's at that store pronto. Dave, you'll need to get some detail about these other possible suspects from Mr Lunn and let's start fact checking. I want everyone in early tomorrow, understand?'

Both officers nodded their agreement.

 Cooked cast a look over to Jack. 'If you're waiting for thanks, you'll have a long wait. Bugger off out of my office, leave my investigation alone and don't let the door hit your arse on the way out.'

Jack took his leave, collecting Gem on the way.

'He didn't sound best pleased with you,' his partners eldest ventured.

'*How ill white hairs become a fool and jester,*' Lunn replied.

'I didn't see too much jesting from him and the hairs are disappearing rather than going white,' Gem said.

As Sparkes escorted them back to the lift, he gloomily observed to Lunn that his presence wouldn't be welcome anywhere close to the investigation.

'I'm sorry if I've dropped you in it, Mick. But I wasn't going to sit by and see an innocent man get put through the wringer,' he said. 'If I hadn't stepped in then somewhere along the line, you would all have looked like a bunch of numpties.'

'I know, I know. He's going to be like a bear with a sore head for days now, or at least until he has another suspect locked up.'

'Well, this was a woman of not inconsiderable means and greed is a great motivator. Look at who's going to gain from her death and where are those rings?'

'Good advice I'm sure, but I'm not the captain of the good ship investigation. Beyond my pay grade.'

'*Lions led by donkeys*,' Jack muttered.

'Not more Shakespeare, please,' Sparkes replied. 'I'm going to need that beer you owe me.'

'Just call anytime and if you happen to find out what the pathologist says killed the old girl, I'd be grateful to hear. Former professional interest I promise, nothing more.'

'Jack, you're an I.A.G member, so we can do some things officially,' Sparkes replied. 'But, try not to drop me in the shit.'

'Mick, we both have ladies in our lives, so we're used to always being in the shit. It's just the level that varies.'


Surrendering their visitor badges, they made their way out of the police station.

'What next?' Gem asked. 'Who is the fickle finger of fate poised over in your opinion?'

'It's not the old janitor who would have got away with it if it hadn't been for a bunch of pesky kids, that's for sure. We need to have a chat with some of these other suspects if we can.'

'Back to the Mystery Machine then?'

'If you're lucky there might be some Scooby Snacks at home.'

They both smiled and headed over towards Jack's car.


DI Sparkes was just picking up his jacket from by his desk, when Geoff Cooke summoned him to his office.

'If I find out that you had anything to do with supplying him with information from inside this investigation, you'll be finding yourself posted to the quietest station I can find in the arse end of nowhere. Have I made myself clear, DI Sparkes?'

'Sir, with respect, I've had nothing to do with what Jack found out.'

'Well, you would say that,' Cooke replied. 'Now get over to that river keepers house and get a statement from him.'

Once the DI had left the office, Cooke turned to DCI Richardson.

'Don't give him anything important to do.'

'You know that's going to be difficult, considering how thinly we're spread, Boss.'

'Just do as I say. I don't want Jack Lunn anywhere near this case,' Cooke demanded. 'Do you understand?'

'But he knows a lot of people and as a member of the New Forest I.A G., we should be using him.'

'You don't know Jack Lunn like I do,' Cooke said. 'He has a knack for poking his nose where it's not wanted and claiming all the glory.'

'Surely Chief Superintendent Blacklock will want some input on this?' Richardson asked.

'Chief Superintendent Blacklock has a blind spot where Lunn is concerned. She was always behind him when he was in the job. Pushing him forwards, getting him onto cases, helping him get promotion.'

'But he's not in the job anymore,' Richardson replied.

'So, he's not to be included in anything to do with this murder and that's my last word on the matter. Now get someone onto the arrest files of the poacher and let's see what they say about dogs. If what Lunn said is right, then we need to have a chat with Max Lamont.'

'What about the list that Lunn's just given us?' Richardson asked.

'Put them with one of the DC's. But get the son in first, he's who we need to speak to next. Inheriting all that money, now there's a motive.'

Richardson nodded agreement and closed the Superintendent's door behind him.

Chapter 13

Jack had decided they would swing past Corporate Boy's home on the way, to drop the laptop off. Gem stayed by the car, whilst he knocked on the cottage door. The lights were on and he could hear music playing but had to knock a second time before the door was opened.

'Oh, it's you.'

'I've brought the laptop.'

'You'd better come in for a minute, I suppose.'

Jack followed him into the sitting room, which held no surprises with its black leather sofa, flat screen TV on the wall, alphabetical array of DVD's and another wall of photographs, signed Arsenal shirt, souvenirs from trips to South Africa, the Caribbean and other trips abroad.

'Do I need to sign anything?' Lunn asked.

'I've got the form, let me get a pen.'

As Jack looked around the room again, he was struck by how it had the feel of something from a lifestyle magazine. Everything had its place and it was all about the effect. As he was proffered the pen, he heard a noise from the floor above. The manager's eyes reacted to the sound and then he looked back at Jack, who was making himself study the form.

'You've never liked me have you?' he asked Jack.

'With you being an Arsenal fan, there was so little to like,' Lunn responded, handing over the now signed form and pen. 'You've no thought of looking after your clients.'

'The office is making more money now than when you had it and it'll do better still.'

'At what cost? Sharp practice and cutting corners will only get you so far and the village is already wising up to you. Your core business is starting to dry up, you're having to pull in business from further afield and people talk,' Lunn warned him.

'You were on my back from the start and you came up with nothing. Not much good for an ex-copper, were you?' he scoffed.

'I knew enough not to trust you,' Jack shot back. 'That you weren't the person I'd have chosen to manage any office of mine.'

'I've heard enough and I'm not going to be insulted in my own home. Just get out.'

'I'll wipe my feet as I leave,' and with that Jack marched out of the door, leaving it ajar behind him.

'Did I hear raised voices?' Gem enquired, as Jack returned to the car.

'That little weasel just gets under my skin. I know I shouldn't react to him, but he just pisses me off.'

'That's all in the past now, isn't it?'

'You're right. Let's get home to your mother,' Jack replied. 'Oh, interestingly he wasn't alone.'

'Who else was there?' Gem asked.

'No idea. But there was someone upstairs, which is why he took a while to answer the door.'

'No accounting for taste.'


'You did the right thing, Jack. Geoff Cooke is just a silly little man who should be thanking you, not kicking you out of the station,' Sarah said later that evening, as Lunn recounted the events at the police station.

'Seth should be released soon, if he hasn't already been.'

'He should be very grateful to you and now keep your nose out of it, as you have a business to get started.'

'He shouldn't be grateful to me,' Lunn replied, 'his dog saved him.'


Jack checked the shed was locked and the chickens secure and returned to the house ready for bed. Sarah had already gone upstairs, so he poked his head in on Gem who was watching some TV.

'I'm off to bed now. Don't forget that your sister is coming back and we have the girls over for lunch this weekend.'

'It'll be good to have everyone around,' she replied.

A few minutes later he slipped into bed and picked up his book. Sarah, who was warmly ensconced beneath the duvet, nudged him.

'No more sleuthing, Jack,' she warned. 'I mean it.'

'You've made that abundantly clear. Fly-tying for me, love. The police can take it from here.'

'Good, the clock is ticking on you having to get a real job, kitchen bitch.'

'Always such a joy to receive the support of those who love you,' Jack responded.

'Love? We barely tolerate you and it's only your talent in the kitchen that's your saving grace. Now read your book,' she instructed.

Chapter 14

As clouds scurried overhead, it looked like the dry spell they'd enjoyed for the last week or so was going to break. Jack returned to the bedroom, after letting the chickens out and seeing Gem off on her morning run.

'How long will you be?' He asked.

'About an hour. I need to get back in my routine and a long run will help me get my body clock back on track,' she replied, as she tied her hair back.

As his Sarah was in the shower, he turned on the TV in the corner and flicked through the channels to try and get a local news update, whilst the dogs settled down on the bed next to him.

Before long she returned, towel wrapped and ready to make a fuss of the terriers. They stopped talking when the local news came on, with a shot from outside Southampton Police Station.

'Enquiries are ongoing into the murder of Elizabeth Lamont. But, I can report that a man that had been helping Police with their inquiries has been released without charge,' the reporter said to camera.

'You leave it alone, now,' Sarah warned him.

As soon as she had left for work, Jack sent a quick text to Mick.

'I see that sense has prevailed and Seth's been released. How about a beer Tues/Wed?'

Once showered, he went down to the kitchen and fixed himself a bacon and egg sandwich, then headed off to the shed. He wolfed down the salty bacon and rich egg combination, as he sipped on a mug of tea.

Who would the Police look at next and what would be his next step?

His thoughts were interrupted by a call on his mobile.

'Jack Lunn speaking.'

'Hello, Mr Lunn. This is Mr Wiseman and I'm in need of your services,' the tackle shop owner said.

'How can I help?'

'Well, I need of some Adams, Pale Morning Duns and Cahills, if you'd be so good.'

'How many do you need and what sizes?' Lunn asked.

'A dozen of each, on hook sizes sixteen to twenty inclusive, please.'

'I can have them with you by early afternoon. I might need to tie up a few, but I have a small stock of most of them,' Lunn confirmed.

'Excellent, I'm out of Adams completely.'

'I'll bring what I have to you this later morning.'

'There's also something I need to talk to you about, but that can wait until I see you.'

'No problem, I'll be with you in an hour.'

Fortunately, as it was early in the season and Jack always tied plenty of these typical patterns, he managed to round up between half a dozen or more of each, noted which ones needed adding to, then transferred them to a fly box. Jack produced an invoice, collected his keys and called up to Gem that he was going out for an hour or so.

He closed the front door and turned to find Mrs Cowan waiting at the front gate.

'I said I'd drop that address off to you,' she said.

'I'm just on my way out.'

'You can buy me another cuppa and cake next time you see me,' she said, handing over a slip of paper. 'You don't suspect that they had anything to do with it, do you?'

'I'm sure the Police will have a chat with them, that's all.'

'They're nice enough people,' she continued. 'They were stubborn about that damn boundary and it cost them dear.'

'You say 'they'?'

'Well, her mainly, as she wears the trousers.'

'Thanks, Mrs Cowan. I'll do my best to make sure they're dealt with sensitively.'

As he drove, Jack mulled over what he currently knew about the killing and where he would be focusing if he was part of the investigation. The victim was relatively wealthy, and the family would be the expected beneficiaries. Where there was a will there was a motive, Lunn thought. He'd definitely be taking a very close look at the family. Whilst he was sure that the some of the family giving an alibi for each other would be under close scrutiny. That left Max, who couldn't or wouldn't account for his movements fully. But, in Jack's opinion, he just wasn't the type. A random lone assailant, was it really just as simple as that? What and where was the murder weapon? That always gave you an insight into who the murderer might be. Mulling all of this over engaged him all the way to the tackle shop.

Mr Wiseman was just finishing with a customer when Jack entered the shop and so he waited until the old man was free.

It only took a few minutes to deal with the flies and payment and then Mr Wiseman told his assistant he'd be upstairs in the flat if he was needed and beckoned Jack to follow him.

There's something I need to talk to you about in confidence,' the old man said, one they'd reached the upstairs office. 'I believe you're an honourable and discreet man.'

'That's kind of you to say so,' Lunn replied. 'How can I help?'

'Mrs Lamont's murder, there's a family connection.'

Jack was taken aback. 'To you?'

He nodded. 'My daughter.'

'Did you tell the police about this connection when they came here?'

'They didn't ask and I felt it was old coals, best not raked over,' Wiseman responded. 'However, I've been thinking and I feel I have to talk to the Police. I remember you as a young bobby, coming in straight off your day shift, uniform in the back of the car and keen to wet a line. You seemed to be the logical person to talk to first.'

A smile formed on Jack's face, as he recalled those days. 'You'd better tell me what this connection is and I'll do my best to help.'

'My wife, God rest her soul, and I only had the one child,' the old man continued. 'You know how fathers are with their daughters, with two of your own.'

Lunn nodded in agreement.

'Apple of our eye she was, but not a good judge of men.' Wiseman said. 'She made a poor choice of a husband and against our advice. All mouth and trousers, my wife would say about our son-in-law. Decided he was going to be a builder but was a bit of a cowboy. Cutting corners, using sub-standard materials and workmen who had no real skills.'

Jack could see where this was heading. 'He did work for the Lamont's and got caught out?'

'He did indeed,' he replied, sadly. 'They took him to Court and bankrupted him. My daughter and grandson were going to be made homeless and it broke my son-in-law. We tried to help, but he wouldn't listen. He murdered my daughter and then killed himself.'

Jack remembered the case. He'd been trying to rehab his knee and get back to Police work at the time.

'What happened to your grandson?' Lunn asked.

'That's what made this worse,' Wiseman replied. 'The lad was a handful to begin with, but the death of his parents sent him completely off the rails and then my wife fell ill with Motor Neurone

Disease. We couldn't look after him anymore and he went into care.'

'Went off the rails how?' Lunn asked.

'Stealing from us and local shops, then the neighbour's cat went missing. They found it a few days later, the body mutilated. The police found the cats collar in the boy's room, along with some of the things he'd stolen. Fortunately, no one pressed charges and we bought the neighbours a kitten.'

'No one would blame you,' Lunn said. 'It sounds like the lad was damaged goods and you had your hands full with your wife.'

'I can't help feeling that we failed him in some way, but maybe you're right. Maybe it was all down to him being his father's creature and bad genes.'

'Did you keep track of him after he went into care?' Lunn asked.

'We tried to, but they kept moving him and then one day, he was gone.'

'Gone?'

'He just up and left. Broke into the office, stole money and his file, then just vanished.'

'How old would he be now?'

'Twenty-seven, twenty-eight.'

'You must tell the Police, George,' Lunn said. 'They need to try and find the boy. Do you have any photos of him?'

'Only ones from when he was a child,' Wiseman replied. 'You can't think that he was the one who killed Mrs Lamont?'

'Until they're eliminated from the enquiry, everyone's a suspect.'

'Would you speak to the Police for me?' Wiseman asked.

'Of course,' Lunn replied. 'But it would be better coming from you. I can get my old Detective Constable to call you?'

'Of course.'

'His names Mick Sparkes, he's a Detective Inspector now and I'll give him your number and outline what you've told me.'

'That's kind of you, Jack.'

Chapter 17

Having called Mick Sparkes, Jack decided to take a detour on the way home. He waited for a small number of New Forest ponies and a couple of donkeys to cross the road and then pulled up at the gates of a large house wound down his window and pressed the intercom button.

'Yes?' a female voice asked.

'It's Jack Lunn, Mrs Hayes.'

There was a moment's silence.

'I suppose you'd better come in,' the voice said.

The gates swung apart and Lunn drove along the paved driveway, parking close to the front door.

The house was built in the 1930's and was surrounded by beautifully manicured lawns and well-stocked borders.

As he walked up to the door it was opened by a woman in her fifties, dressed for the gym.

'I'm off to my yoga class. He's in the study, second door on the left,' she said, as Jack stood to one side.

'Thanks.'

'You haven't spoken to him yet. So, it's a bit early to thank me, don't you think?' the woman said tartly. 'He's in the study.'

Jack walked inside and down the hall to the second door on the left.

'Don't keep me waiting, Mr Lunn,' a voice said from the other side of the door. 'I haven't got all day for the likes of you.'

Lunn pushed the door open.

'How are you, Neville?' he asked, taking in the man sat behind the desk.

'None the worse for having you in my house,' Neville Hayes replied as he got up from the chair.

It was only when the man stood that Lunn recalled how tall 'Big Nev' was. At close to seventy years old he stood a good six feet five inches in his stocking feet and was immaculately dressed in black to show off his tan and shock of white hair.

'I won't stay long, but I was hoping that you would help me with a couple of questions.'

'I won't ask you to sit down then. Now, why would an ex-estate agent would have any questions for me?' Hayes said. 'Would this have anything to do with former DI Lunn finding a dead body?'

'I see the Forest jungle drums are in full swing,' Jack replied. 'And yes, it does have something to do with the murder of Elizabeth Lamont.'

'Oh, I get it. Because I did time for murder you thought you'd come and have a chat?'

'Not at all, Neville,' Jack said, 'I just wanted to find out if you'd heard anything, that's all.'

'Why would I know anything?' Hayes asked.

Jack laughed. 'You're still as sharp as a Stanley knife, so don't try and kid a kidder.'

'I'm retired now; my boys look after the businesses,' Hayes protested. 'And they're all legitimate. But, occasionally an interesting snippet of information comes my way.'

'I wasn't casting any aspersions,' Jack said. 'But I know you keep an ear to the ground and just wondered if you'd heard anything about the Lamont's that might be of interest?'

'Not that I know about these things you understand,' Hayes replied, 'But if you twisted my arm, I'd say that the old lady hadn't made too many friends over the years and then there is the matter of her long-dead husband.'

'I heard some rumours about him.'

'I'm not one to talk behind someone's back, as you know. But let's say that old Mr Lamont wasn't as clean as he might have liked to make out.'

'You can't leave me hanging like that, Neville,' Lunn urged. 'They're both dead and what you say to me will go no further.'

'This isn't speaking ill of the dead and I'm no grass, you understand?'

'Agreed.'

Neville motioned Lunn to sit down.

'The whole County Set thing that the Lamont's put about, it was all bollocks. She was a Bluebell Girl in Paris and they met when he was on a business trip. He was the money man for certain elements in London, back in the day. Long Firm fraud crews mostly. The word was that he was a genius at hiding money and got paid very well for it.'

'Then he retired and moved down here, buying the house with the money he made?'

'I don't think he fully retired straight after the move. But as the paper trails became more difficult to hide, he did less and less. He'd bought a lot of property in rundown areas in the less salubrious areas of London and when the 'do'er uppers' moved into those areas and started to make them fashionable, he cashed in.'

'So, he washed the dirty money via property deals.'

'He bought the big house and his property round here, set up his business in Romsey and went legit.'

'What about Max?' Lunn asked.

'Straight as a die,' Hayes replied. 'The old girl must have known where the original money came from though.'

'Do you think it could have been someone from back then who killed her?'

'Normally, I'd say no. If Nicholas Lamont had crossed anyone, then they'd have come after him. Back then, wives were strictly off limits and it was an unwritten rule that they were left well alone.'

'But now? 'Lunn asked.

'Sadly, we live in a changing world and today's villains have no code. But, why would they have waited so long? If you want my opinion, it's more likely to be a local. The Old Bill should be looking for someone with a grudge. You know what these village feuds can be like,'

'Point taken and the old lady certainly had a number of them over the years.'

'Neighbours, shop owners, builders, the butcher, baker and candlestick maker, I shouldn't wonder.'

Nothing much got past the older man, Jack thought.

'I'll see you out,' Big Nev said. 'You can't be too careful who you let in these days. They prey on pensioners like me.'

'I pity the fool who tries to pull the wool over your eyes.'

'It's difficult to pull the wool over anyone's eyes if your fingers are missing,' Hayes mused. 'I understand that you might be looking for a car soon?

'Nothing wrong with your hearing is there?'

'I heard what happened to you and there's just no loyalty these days. Go and see my boys at the showrooms when you're ready and they'll sort you out. Just let me know what you're looking for, I'm sure we can put our hands on what you want.'

'I'll bear that in mind,' Lunn replied, uncertain how to take the offer.

Hayes paused by a table in the hallway. 'I've got something for you, wait there a second.'

Lunn waited by the door and shortly Hayes returned with a plastic bag.

'Last years' plum jam and green tomato chutney from the garden,' Neville said with a shrug. 'Now I'm retired I've time on my hands.'

'And we all know what happens to idle hands, don't we?

'They get cut off?'

'Thank you for the preserves,' Jack said. 'I'd better get off.'

'One other thing. My other half said to ask you what layers pellets you use for your chickens?'

Lunn was taken aback. 'I don't know. Sarah gets the feed, but I'll find out for you? How did you know we had chickens?'

'Apparently, chicken keeping is a tight circle and when she asked around your Sarah's name came up,' Neville said. 'Libby is looking to take on some ex-battery hens and would like some advice.'

'Working with ex-prisoners, how apt,' Lunn said, unable to resist making the connection.

'Very droll, Mr Lunn.'

'I'll put her in touch.'

'I'll expect to hear from you very soon,' Hayes said. 'Here's my number. Leave a message if I don't answer, as the reception out here isn't great and anyway, I'll probably be in the garden.'

Jack took that as his cue to leave.

Chapter 18

Gem was in the kitchen when Lunn got home.

'Where've you been, Jack?'

'I stopped off to have a chat with someone I thought might be able to answer a little question I had,' Jack replied.

'About the murder?'

'Just trying to get a local perspective and maybe a bit of background on old Mr Lamont,' Lunn replied. 'I just wanted an opinion on it, that's all.'

'And where pray, did you find this opinion?' his partners eldest asked.

'Neville Hayes,' Jack said.

'You're a brave man, Jack. Wasn't he done for murder?'

'A long time ago.'

'Who did he kill?'

'Neville was one of four kids. Three brothers and a younger sister,' Lunn explained. 'The sister was assaulted and it was alleged that the brothers killed the man who had attacked her.'

'I can't say I blame them,' Gem replied.

'Neville took the charge and did the time, but the talk was that all three of the brothers were involved.'

'No such thing as DNA back then?'

Lunn smiled. 'I expect the Met would have just been happy to get the conviction. London was a bit like the Wild West back then.'

'What did Neville have to say?'

'That Mrs Lamont had a few enemies in the village, and he'd heard a good deal about old Mr Lamont and his somewhat murky past.'

'Murky past?'

'Connections to London villains, fraud, money laundering.'

'So, what about Max?'

'Clean apparently, but he has no alibi for the time his mother was killed,' Lunn replied. 'Come on up to the shed and look at what I've been doing.'

Jack unlocked the shed and sat down.

'It's good to have you home. Take a seat for a minute and let me just tidy up a bit and then we can talk. There's beer in the barrel and a couple of glasses on the side,' he said.

Gem poured the beer and then watched as Lunn completed a fly.

'It looks great, Jack,' she said.

'Let's just hope the buyers feel the same. So, what are your plans?'

'I'm really not sure. I could do another contract with an NGO, but I don't want to spend the rest of my life hopping from contract to contract.'

'A bit of a crossroads then?'

'Like yourself,' Gem replied with a smile.

'Touché, but I do have something in mind,' Lunn replied. 'Look, why don't you help me out?'

'With the fly-tying, or your snooping on this murder investigation?'

'Your Mother would kill me if you got involved in the latter, but you have some skills that would help.'

'I know you caught a lot of grief from her when you supported me going into the Army.'

'She was just worried about you and not exactly enamoured of the idea of you getting shot at.'

'And it helped that I chose the Intelligence Corps.'

'Absolutely. She was happy thinking that you were out of danger and sat behind a desk somewhere.'

When Gem smiled, it lit up her face. 'And Counterintelligence and covert surveillance is always best done from behind a desk.'

'I just didn't tell her anything that disabused her of the original conclusion that she'd reached.'

Gem took the scrunchy out of her hair and shook her head to release her tresses, then looked back at Jack.

'Do you miss the Army life?' he asked.

She nodded. 'It had a lot of plusses. A clear mission, targets and I got a lot of responsibility. But, I needed something more and the job with the NGO was like a year out for me.'

'Why don't you help me with the fly-tying for a while, whilst you look around for something? I could do with the help, you could do with something to occupy your mind and someone to put a few bob in your pocket,' he offered.

'What do I know about tying flies?' she scoffed.

'You were never a typical girl as a child,' Jack recalled. 'Whilst most of your peers were doing ballet and riding horses, you wanted to do Judo and make action figures. I remember your Warhammer action figures and how beautifully they were finished. And what did I know about tying flies, before I tied my first?'

'I'll give it a go, but I'd like to help you do a bit of investigation too,' she wheedled. 'As you said, I have certain skills in that area that may help.'

'What skills could you have possibly learned from sitting behind a desk for five years?'

'I could tell you, but then I'd have to kill you,' she replied with a wink. 'Let me give the fly-tying a go and see what you think.'

Lunn set up a second bench for her and showed her how to do a couple of patters. Gem tied them with aplomb and he left her to it and went back to his own bench.


An hour past quickly before Gem broke the silence.
'I've cracked on with some replacements for the flies you took, but I think we're going to need some more supplies.'

They were putting a list together when Henry called Gem.

'He'll be round soon to help get the website sorted,' his partner's daughter informed him.


Jack had forgotten how tall Henry was, maybe 6'4" and gangly with it. The lad was all angles and awkwardness but made the effort to come into the kitchen to see Jack.

'How are you Mr L? Gem told me you need some help setting up a website,' the lad said, sticking out a hand.

'I really appreciate you giving me some time, Henry and Gem told me that you're the man for the job.'

'I'll take him up to the shed,' Gem interjected. 'I think it'll help you get some ideas. Are you coming back up?'

'I won't be long,' Jack informed them. 'I'm just going to knock a cottage pie together and I'll be with you.'

Once the meat was done Jack stirred in the veg, added the now thickened stock and grated nutmeg into the mixture, before leaving it on a very low light to simmer and wandering up the garden to check on progress.

Jack's return to the shed was barely noticed by the Gem and Marc, laptop screens glowing and fingers flying as they worked on the website.

'We've really got creative for you, Mr L. Give us a day or two more and we can unveil it for you. I'm going to write your landing pages in the next hour or two,' Henry said.

'You might as well be talking Greek. Gem will explain it to me later and just make it easy to use, as well as easy on the eye, please,' Lunn requested.

'My dad likes to fish,' Henry offered.

'Fly or coarse?' Lunn inquired.

'Sea.'

'I've done a bit of that too.'

'I've seen the pictures, Mr Lunn. You do like your fishing.'

'Some have hobbies that only last a few weeks or years. My love of fishing started when I was a kid of six or seven and we lived between Bournemouth and Christchurch about two hundred yards from the River Stour,' Jack said. 'Gem's come with me when we've gone sea fishing a couple of times.'

'But you fly fish mostly now?' Henry asked.

'It feels more intimate to me. More of a challenge, more connected to the fish,' Lunn replied. 'My aim is to make a living out of tying and selling my own flies, so please crack on and get my website up and running.'

'We can shift over if you want to do some work, Mr L.'

'That would be good. I can tie a few flies for my order, if that's not going to disturb you guys too much,' Lunn said.

'No problem. You won't disturb us and if we're especially quiet and good you might care to offer us a small glass of the beer you keep in here?' Gem wheedled.

'Pushy little sod aren't you. We'll see.'

'That's a yes,' Gem informed Henry.

'Some music is called for,' Jack announced, turning Spotify on and selecting a playlist.

Jack had tied a few flies when he checked his watch.

'The boss will be home soon,' he said. 'I'd better get back to sorting dinner out.'

'We've got about another half hour or so, but give me a shout when mum's home and I'll come and say hi,' Gem replied.

'You don't have to rush home, Henry. There's food here if you want to stay for dinner,' Lunn said.

'Great, don't mind if I do,' Mark said.

He was peeling sweet potatoes when Sarah came through the door, to the usual greeting from the dogs. Dumping her bags in the hallway, she walked through to the kitchen as he was drying his hands.

'How was your day?' he asked.

'Good. Where's Gem?'

'In the shed working on my website with Henry, why?'

'I just wondered, that's all. How are they doing?'

'I've not got a clue,' Jack replied and then changed the subject. 'I'm going to have to dip into the money, to get a car. Nothing too fancy, but the company car will have to go back in the not too distant future.'

'I know. I suppose you'd better start having a look around for something sooner rather than later,' Sarah said. 'Anyway, what's for dinner?'

'Cottage pie, I was just doing the spuds,' he replied.

'Well, you had better get back to your duties then.'

'Yes, ma'am,' Lunn replied, tugging his forelock.

After changing Sarah went up to shed to see what was going on and once the potatoes were boiling, Jack turned the heat down and made his way up the garden. His knee was sore and playing up a little. His partner watched him come up from the house and spotted the way he favoured his bad leg.

'Knee giving you gyp?' she enquired.

'Just a bit sore, I'll take some Ibuprofen later.'

'You don't wear your knee brace as often as you should,' she chastised him.

'You're right and I'll try to remember to stick it on first thing.'

'How long will food be?' Gem asked.

'Just under an hour.'

'How's the website coming along?' Sarah asked.

'We should have it up and running tomorrow, Mrs B,' replied Henry.

'I remember you telling me that your essays would be in the next day, Henry. So that doesn't seem like much of a guarantee,' Sarah quipped.

'*Tomorrow, and tomorrow, and tomorrow, creeps in this petty pace from day to day*,' murmured Lunn and Gem together.

Sarah shot Jack a glance.

'Time for me to get back to the kitchen, I think,' he said.

'There you are, Gem. A man who knows his place. I'll come with you,' said Sarah.


They walked back to the house together, the dogs trailing after them. Sarah went through to the family room to get some marking done, whilst Lunn turned the oven on and tested the potatoes with a knife to see if they were cooked. Another couple of minutes would do the job.

After spooning the meat and vegetable mix into an ovenproof dish, topping it with the mash Jack put the dish full of cottage pie into the oven.

'Is that the pie going in the oven?' a disembodied voice asked.

'Yep, should be just about half an hour.'

'Good, I'm starving,' Sarah said.

Jack ambled up to the shed to let the workers know when food would be ready, taking three beer glasses with him.

'Time for an aperitif,' he declared, pouring beer from the barrel into the three glasses, holding it up to the light. 'There you go, Henry. This is what proper beer drinkers have, not that carbonated, over-chilled and tasteless muck most of you youngster's drink.'

After the meal, Gem and Henry volunteered to clear up, so Jack and Sarah moved to the family room to watch some TV.

Gem poked her head around the door. 'We're just off to the pub for a drink.'


'What are the police going to do about the killing, Jack?' Sarah asked, now they were alone.

'They'll look for another suspect I guess, why?'

'Well, call me old fashioned, but having a murderer loose in the area isn't my idea of a great deal of fun.'

'I'll make sure I lock the doors up properly and we have dogs, so we're going to be okay, love.'

'Will Gem and Henry be okay?' she asked

'They'll be fine. I think the killer targeted Mrs Lamont specifically and it wasn't as if she hadn't made a few enemies over the years,' Lunn replied. 'I told the Police that they need have a word with her old next door neighbours over an old boundary dispute and there's the son of a builder she put out of business. And then there's Liam Galletly.'

'Liam Galletly, now there's a blast from the past. Why would the Police want to talk to that little waste of space?'

'Not so little these days and old Mrs Lamont caught him breaking into her house.'

'I'd forgotten about that. Holding him at gunpoint until the Police arrived, she should have given him both barrels.'

'Well, he'd be high on my list of suspects.'

'I taught him, or at least tried to. Not so much the shallow end of the gene pool, more like the footbath by the side of the shallow end,' Sarah said. 'And Mick will be keeping you up to date?'

'I haven't heard from him since Sunday.'

'Just so long as you understand that Mick is a useless liar and his wife is part of my department. I'll know if the two of you try and sneak around behind my back. You have a business to get going and I don't want you ending up being chased around by a murderer.'

'Wouldn't be much of a chase with my dodgy knee, love,' Lunn replied. 'You know I couldn't stand by when they arrested Seth Walker and I'm not going to turn my back on Mick, if he's looking for a bit of help.'

'Alright, alright. Just keep it at arm's length, please?'

'You know he and I will talk, but I'll try and keep it to that,' Lunn conceded.

'Good, just make sure you do. My spies are everywhere, Jack.'

'Bloody hell, woman. It's like living with MI5 in stilettos.'

'And don't you forget it. You can fetch me a glass of wine now.'

'Your humble servant obeys your every command.'

'That'll be the day. Now fetch me my booze.'

Chapter 19


After a shower and shave, Jack made his way down to the kitchen and out across the lawn. Gem had already left for her morning run, so he put some music on and worked through the list for the tackle shop, before breaking off at about nine o'clock.


He picked up his mobile and called his eldest daughter.

Abi picked up. 'Hey, Dad, what's up? Discovered any more dead bodies?'

'Not since the last one,' Lunn replied. 'How're things with you?'

'All good. How are you enjoying retirement?'

'It's called redundancy and I'm pretty busy trying to set up my business.'

'Oh yeah, Gem mentioned she was working on a website for you.'

'When did you talk to Gem?'

'Text, Dad, text.'

'Ah, the joys of social networking.'

'You should get Gem to set up a Facebook page for the business.'

'Why? So I can spend all my time 'friending' people I've never met, nor ever likely too.'

'No, Troutman, so you can interact with related businesses and see if you flog them some of your shoddy goods.'

'Shoddy! Shoddy! You mean handcrafted, artisan, piscatorial works of art, young lady.'

'Whatever. Are we still on for lunch on Saturday?' she asked.

'You bet, kiddo.'

'Pub first and lunch after?'

'Sounds like a plan,' Lunn agreed.

'I'll be there.'

'Will you pick up Grace on the way?'

'I'll talk to Eden and we'll sort something out.'

'Speaking of Eden,' Lunn said. 'Have you heard about this new boyfriend of hers?'

'Not a thing. She's being very mysterious about him. I'll let you know if I hear anything though.'

'See you Saturday and maybe speak to you before.'

His youngest daughter's phone went to voicemail, so Jack left a message for her to call back and went back up to the shed. He'd tied about half a dozen flies for the order when the phone went again.

'Hi, Mick. You looking to collect on that beer I owe you?'

'Seems like a good idea. I'd like a chat and I guess you might like to listen, Jack.'

'I've always been a good listener, mate. Where and when?'

'About half three at The Waterloo?'

'Good enough,' Lunn replied.

'See you later.'


It was about an hour later when Grace rang.

'Hey, Pops.'

'How are you?'

'Good thanks. How's the fly-tying going?' his daughter asked.

'It's what I was doing when you rang,' he replied. 'I spoke to Abi earlier and either she or Eden will pick you up on Saturday, assuming you're still coming?'

'Definitely. Wouldn't miss it. Particularly as Eden is down too and I'll see if she wants to go shopping.'

'You could stay Saturday night if you like?' Lunn offered.

'I'm out with friends Saturday night and my guess is Eden will be out with the new boyfriend anyway. Have you met him yet?'

'No. She's keeping him under wraps,' Lunn replied. 'Has she said anything to you about him?'

'No. Every time I try and get her to tell me about him, she changes the subject.'

'Same with us, which isn't usually like her at all. Do me a favour and see if she'll open up to you about him at the weekend?' He asked. 'There must be a reason why she's being so coy about this one and her mother is naturally very curious.'

'I'll see what I can do, but you know what Eden can be like. She'll only tell you what she wants you to know.'

'Well, it'll be great to have you all under one roof for a change.'

'Roast dinner and pub, perfect day.'

'See you then and call me later in the week.'

'You're so needy, Dad,' Grace said.

'It's my age and being on the employment scrapheap.'

'Get back to fly-tying. Love you.'

'Love you too and catch you later.'


Gem wandered up from the house at about half-past eleven, with Henry in tow.

'How's it going, Jack?' she asked.

'Well, I've tied about a third of the order for the end of the week. And good morning to you, or should I say nearly afternoon,' Lunn made a pantomime of checking his watch.

'I do my best work after eleven in the morning, Mr L,' Henry said.

'Just as well it's not a nine to five job then, young man. You guys get started and I'll rustle up some breakfast,' Lunn offered.

'A bacon sandwich or two wouldn't go amiss,' Gem ventured.

'I'll see what I can do.'

With the bacon under the grill, Jack stepped out of the kitchen. He hoped that Mick would bring some interesting news about the murder investigation; maybe some idea of what was used to kill Mrs Lamont and who the killer was. He walked the supplies up to the shed where the workers were hunched in front of their flickering screens.

'That's what I call breakfast, Mr Lunn,' Henry said, as Jack put plates in front of the two lads.

'It's what I call a very late breakfast then,' Lunn replied.

'That'll keep the brain fed, Jack,' Gem said.

'Well, I've got something I need to do and can you drag yourself away, Gem,' Lunn replied. 'We'll only be out for an hour or so, Mark.'

Chapter 20

They drove over to a house in Minstead, pulling up to the wrought iron security gates, wondering just why it was that some people seemed to think they had to construct battlements and a moat to keep the world out. Pressing the entry phone button, he identified himself and the gates eased slowly apart.

Leaving the car outside, they walked down the gravel drive, past the two, matching silver Mercedes sports cars and up to the front door.

Dressed in black, Imogen Lamont opened the door with a suitably sombre look on her face.

'This really isn't a good time.'

'We came to pay my respects, Imogen,' Lunn replied. 'I felt obliged, as I found her and you might remember my partner's daughter, Gemma as she was in the same year as Sebastian?'

'The police mentioned something about you finding her,' she muttered. 'I'm sorry, Gemma, but I can't really remember you.'

There were a few moments of awkward silence before she continued, 'I suppose you'd better come

in for a minute.'

Jack and Gem followed her along the oak-panelled hall and into a modern kitchen that was open plan with skylights to the dining area, with large bi-fold doors opening onto a paved patio and neatly manicured lawn.

'It must have been a shock finding her?' she asked.

'It's always dreadful when you know the dead person and I'd known your mother-in-law for about 25 years. She could be single-minded and challenging to deal with at times, but we got on,' Lunn replied. 'She reminded me of my own mother in some respects.'

'In what way?'

'Maybe it's that generation,' Lunn mused. 'They don't stand fools gladly, seldom forgive and never forget. But they can be incredibly kind and generous.'

'She was a force of nature,' she replied. 'And I'd definitely agree with the first part.'

'Your mother-in-law was very good to me when my marriage broke down, very understanding. Even made the effort to come into the office and speak to me.'

'I always thought that when Elizabeth gave you fishing rights on the river, it was just her way of getting another bailiff on the cheap. After all, wasn't it you who caught the salmon poacher for her?'

'They weren't really connected,' Lunn replied. 'I was just doing my job when I caught Seth poaching and my rod on the river was in lieu of me charging fees on the sale of a property.'

'And now the police have arrested that poacher for her murder.'

'Who are you?' a voice said from behind Jack.

He turned to see a younger version of Imogen Lamont looking sulkily at him.

'I'm Jack Lunn, Georgina. You were at school with my partner's youngest daughter, Eden Bryce and this is her sister, Gemma. I found your grandmother and we just stopped by to offer our sympathies.'

The young woman ignored Gemma, looked away from him and over to her mother. 'Where's Seb?'

'Busy and you need to get ready, as we're leaving soon,' her mother said.

'You must be upset by your grandmother's murder?' Gem enquired.

Georgina Lamont took a sideways look at her and then back at her mother. 'We're all devastated by Granny's death,' she said in almost a monotone.

'Death?' Gem scoffed. 'She didn't die, someone killed her.'

'Well, they have the murderer now, don't they?' the mother stated.

'You obviously haven't heard that the poacher was released without charge, Lunn replied. 'Turned out he had nothing to do with it.'

'What will they do next?' Georgina asked.

'I expect they'll start widening the search to everyone connected with your grandmother.'

'What if it's some random stranger?' the daughter queried.

'There's a good chance that the killer is known to your grandmother. So, as I said, they'll start by looking at everyone who touched her life.'

He had watched the surprise register on the daughter's face.

'The Police say that you were all having a takeaway together, but Max was absent?' Lunn asked, as he turned back to Imogen Lamont.

'He was working late,' she responded. 'Went for a drive to clear his head or something.'

'That's right, he mentioned it when I bumped into him. It must have slipped my mind,' Lunn replied.

'We've all spoken to the Police. Now thank you for coming over, but we have errands to run.'

'I didn't mean to pry, Imogen,' Lunn said apologetically. 'I was just hoping to see Max and find out when the funeral is going to be.'

'He's at the office,' the daughter replied.

'That's right,' Lunn said. 'End of the tax year isn't it.'

'I'll show you the door,' Imogen Lamont said.

'I'm sorry if you feel we were intruding. This must be a terrible time for all of you.'

'It is, but I'm sure you'll respect our privacy,' she replied, ushering him down the hallway. 'We're all trying to come to terms with Elizabeth's death.'

'Of course,' he replied. I just wanted to offer my condolences. You will let me know when the funeral is. She was a friend to me, Imogen and I found her. So, I want to make sure that her killer is found, whoever that might be.


Lunn waited until they were back in the car and out of the gates.

'What did you make of that?' He asked his companion.

'Hardly wracked with grief and I think we just got shown the door,' Gem replied. 'Not even the offer of a cuppa, that was downright rude. But, they have an alibi and I'd be having words with the husband.'

Chapter 21


On returning home, they walked up to the shed to look in on Henry.

'How's it going?' Jack asked.

'Few more hours and I'll have you up and running, Mr L,' Henry replied. 'I've added some more features, which have taken a bit longer than I'd originally planned.'

'You need to start your list of chores for Mum,' Gem reminded Jack. 'You don't want to get on the wrong side of the mistress of the house.'

'We could really do with some footage of you catching fish with one of your own flies, Mr L,' Henry said.

'Can it be uploaded later? I just want to get a website up and running and then you can add the frills later,' Lunn replied.

'No problem. We can upgrade as we go,' Henry confirmed.

'I need to get a bunch of flies tied now and then get some housework done. So please excuse me for sticking on some music and getting stuck in.'

The dogs settled down on the floor. Soon the only sounds were Bruce Springsteen, fingers tapping on keyboards and the odd sounds made by Jack tying flies.

Lunn stopped when two o'clock came around.

'Okay, what will this puppy you're building do?'

'Come and have a look,' Henry said.

Jack sat behind the two young people explained how the website would work. How it was linked to his eBay account and that they had uploaded some of the photos and film to animate the site.

'There's a fair bit more we'll go live on, but this will do to start with,' Gem said.

'It looks pretty impressive so far and I really appreciate it.'

'Good luck, Mr Lunn and we've got some upgrades that I can do over the next couple of weeks,' Henry said.

'Thanks, I think this will help a lot,' Lunn replied. 'God, look at the time! I have to go out for a while, so will you tidy the house up a bit, Gem?'

'Sure. Where are you off to?'

'Just out for a while. I'll be back before you know it,' Lunn replied.

'Quick assignation with the esteemed DI Mick Sparkes?' Gem enquired.

'If you ever think of becoming a copper, God help the criminal classes.'

'Ain't no big thing. It's not like you're letting the matter drop.'

'Mr Lunn, there's still a murderer out there then?' Henry asked.

'Well the Police don't have anyone for it, so yes. Chances are they are not passing through; they live in the area and are linked to the victim in some way,' Lunn explained. 'But, Elizabeth Lamont didn't have many friends, never mind close ones and she'd certainly made a habit of upsetting a few locals over the years.'

'You know a bit about this stuff then?' Henry asked.

'It's Murder 101. But I haven't been in the middle of an investigation for more years than I care to mention.'

'Do you think the police will be looking at the family?' Henry asked.

'It's where I'd start?' Gem interrupted.

'Alibis, you always start with alibis,' Lunn said. 'Get them to tell you why it wasn't them and then see if their story holds water.'

'What happens when someone can't give you an alibi, or they were at home watching telly by themselves?' Henry queried.

'They're a suspect, for sure. Ask what programme they watched, though with the ability to record stuff these days, that's not as cut and dried as it used to be,' Jack said. 'You're then looking for physical evidence to link a suspect to the crime and generally, you should have motive if they're family, or close to the family. Serial killers are a different kettle of fish of course and you have all this mobile phone and CCTV stuff these days. In this case, my first guess would be to follow the money. Who got what, who gained from her death and who didn't get anything. So, if someone's in line to get a ton of money that's great motivation to kill,' Jack said. 'The first is motivated by greed, the second by jealousy or anger. Remember, this was a lady who had legal run-ins with a few people too. Boundary disputes, clashes over works, that kind of thing and the Police will talk to the parties involved. There was even a local caught trying to break into her house.'

'Murder isn't always just a flash of temper,' Gem offered. 'Sometimes it's cold-blooded revenge over a real or imagined slight.'

Jack nodded in agreement.

'So, who have you got in the frame then, Mr L?' Henry asked.

'As Gem said, you can't dismiss the family, but there are three suspects I'd want to have a chat with as well. A builder who did some work on the house about 10 years ago. There was a disagreement about the work he'd done, she refused to pay the bill and it ended up in a protracted court case. The builder ended up losing and went bust. Unfortunately, he then killed his wife and then committed suicide, leaving a child behind. So, where is that child? He'll be grown up now and could certainly be harbouring a grudge against the Lamont family. The argument with the neighbour started out over a hedge and concluded with Mrs Lamont showing that he'd encroached on her land, cutting the hedge down and taking the land. But that wasn't the end of it, if I remember correctly, the dispute continued for months afterward, with the neighbours erecting spotlights shining on to Mrs Lamont's house, rubbish being fly-tipped on her land, that kind of thing. Eventually, the neighbours moved and things settled down. Embarrassingly, I'd sold them the house. And there's the burglar, of course.

'How do you know about the rest of this?' Gem asked.

'Fishing her stretch of the river,' Lunn replied. 'We sometimes talked and I think she was quite a lonely person after her husband died. Plus, as the village estate agent, you do hear all sorts of gossip.'

'I know the local who was caught trying to rob her house,' Henry added. 'Low life, Liam Galletly.'

'That drunken scumbag, really?' Gem asked.

'She covered him with a twelve bore until the Police rolled up.' Jack confirmed. 'He's just been released from prison too.'

'A jailbird too. He must be top of the list, surely?' She queried.

'Let the Police do their job, Gem.' Lunn replied.

Chapter 24

It took about ten minutes for Jack to walk down to the pub. He got a beer and as it was a warmish day, adjourned to the pub garden. He was deep in thought when DI Sparkes arrived, placing a file on the table.

'Mick, you're looking a little harassed.'

'Not something that can be said of you, Jack.'

'Well, Sarah is at school teaching with your good lady wife and I've got Gem doing most of my chores for the day.'

Mick pointed at Lunn's now nearly empty glass.

'Another?'

'Why not.'

'I'll get them in, you do some reading,' Sparkes said, pointedly leaving the file on the table. 'Oh, And we'll have someone joining us soon.'

Lunn raised an eyebrow.

'It'll be a nice surprise for you,' Sparkes remarked.

The report included the breakdown of the autopsy. Fragments of wood and varnish had been found in the head wound and sent for analysis, with the estimated time of death at between nine and ten at night. Considering the body had been in the river for a few hours, they were lucky to recover much in the way of forensics at all. The wound size and shape interested him, it was unusual and the coroner hadn't seen anything similar in his experience but was still looking to try and pin down a murder weapon. The large depressed wound suggested a round or hemispherical weapon, like an oversized wooden ballpein hammer, according to the report. But it would take a while to analyse the type of varnish and wood. That was the unique part to the case that Jack always looked for, find this weapon and you usually had your killer.

Mick arrived back with another beer for Lunn and a soft drink for himself.

'How's the investigation going?' Lunn asked.

'As you predicted, we've been looking at the family.'

'What's the score there?'

'The wife and kids are alibiing each other for the night, but the old girl's son doesn't have any alibi.'

'Let me guess. As he gets the cash, he's the name in the frame?' Lunn asked.

'There's a logic to it, you have to agree?'

'You wouldn't be here if you didn't have a few reservations.'

'He just doesn't seem the type,' Sparkes replied.

'*Ah, is evil something you are? Or is it something you do?*'

'Another quote from The Bard?'

'A little more recent than that, mate. Returning to the family, the wife and kids are alibiing each other?'

Sparkes raised his hand and waved to someone behind Lunn. Jack turned to see a smartly dressed brunette walking towards them, accompanied by a familiar figure.

'This is Scarlett Ribbans, Jack. She's the Deputy Scientific Services Manager for Hampshire Police,' Sparkes said.

'Scarlett, a pleasure to meet you,' Lunn stood to shake hands with the first new arrival. 'Unusual first name?'

'Scarlett's a nickname I seem to have picked up,' she said as they shook hands. 'Blood is my specialty and policemen do like to have their little jokes.'

'It's a schoolboy humour thing,' he replied. 'Mick was just telling me about the family's alibi. But that can wait whilst I get you a drink.'

'Lime and soda, please,' she said.

Lunn turned to the familiar figure accompanying the scientific officer. 'Hello, Rhona. I didn't think it would be long before I saw you. Are you well?'

'All the better for seeing you,' Detective Chief Superintendent Rhona Blacklock replied. 'Are you going to offer your old boss a drink too?'

'Glass of Pinot Grigio?'

'No bloody chance, I'm afraid. I have a meeting with the ACC later, so it'll have to be an orange juice.'

Jack returned a few minutes later to find the three of them going over the file, the papers spread over the table. Lunn placed the drinks on the table and then turned his attention back to Sparkes.

'About the wife and kids?' he asked.

'They were having a meal together.'

'At home together isn't much of an alibi.'

'They were having a takeaway from your favourite Indian,' Sparkes said.

'It's still not much of an alibi, Mick,' Lunn said. 'What's the story on Max Lamont?'

'He says he was just driving around, no one with him and he didn't stop anywhere.'

'What does the wife say in support of hubby?' Lunn asked.

'Not a lot really, just that it's the end of the tax year and a very busy time.'

'So, have you had the husband in yet?'

'He's being picked up in about an hour for a nice chat,' Sparkes said.

'Hence your soft drink. Looks like you'll have a long night ahead of you, Mick. I agree he doesn't seem the type, but he'd be who I'd have been speaking to next,' Jack said. 'He'd definitely be top of my 'to do' list. But, having said all that, I don't think he did it. You guys need to be looking for the people I gave to Geoff.'

'What makes you so sure about Max?' Blacklock asked.

'I bumped into him in the village a couple of days ago and he looked like a man who had lost his mother, not killed her,' Lunn replied. 'I know you have to look at him, but I just don't fancy him for it.'

'Well, you've always had good instincts,' Blacklock said. 'I've asked Geoff and his team to track down the people you gave him. But trying to find the builder's kid is going to take time. He went through a series of homes and then did a vanishing act.'

'I thought you'd come to tell me to keep my nose out?' Lunn asked.

'Quite the opposite,' Blacklock replied. 'I come with an offer.'

'Is this a bit like, *'beware Greeks bearing gifts'*?' Lunn asked.

'On the contrary. I spoke to the Assistant Chief Constable about your contribution in respect to the poacher.'

'I'll bet that went down well.'

'I got to him before Superintendent Cooke, so he got the unvarnished story,' Blacklock replied. 'I told him that you were arguably the best detective I'd ever worked with. You're a member of the Independent Advisory Group for the New Forest, so you already work with us and you know the area and the people well.'

'I see,' Lunn said. 'You want to keep me inside the tent pissing out?'

'Strangely enough, that's exactly how the ACC put it. I understand from Mick that you're not exactly overwhelmed with work currently.'

'You know I'll help,' Lunn replied. 'Not a word to your missus though, Mick. Sarah will kill me if it gets back to her.'

'Now, where were we?' asked Blacklock.

'Talking about the old woman's son, guv,' Sparkes replied.

'Is he where you'd start, Jack?' Scarlet asked.

'I'm assuming he's going to be the main beneficiary in her will, so that seems like a good place to focus. The autopsy report is a bit vague on what exactly killed her though,' Lunn replied. 'My other favourite would be Liam Galletly, our local thug and thief. He had a run in with the old lady a while back,

whilst trying to burgle her house and ended up getting nicked for it.'

'I remember,' Sparkes said with a smile. 'Uniform tuned up to find him lying on the floor and the old lady stood over him with a loaded shotgun.'

'Oh, I dropped in on Max Lamont's house earlier, by way of offering my condolences.'

'You're pushing it,' Blacklock warned him. 'What did he have to say?'

'He wasn't there, just the wife and daughter.'

'How did they seem?' Sparkes asked.

'A little surprised that the poacher had been released.'

'That just slipped out did it?' Blacklock said with wry smile.

Jack put his hands up. 'I must be getting careless in my old age.'

Rhona Blacklock raised an eyebrow at that remark.

'Any more information on what killed her, Scarlet?'

'Other than it being varnished wood we can't pin it down and we're still working on what type of wood,' the CSI replied. 'It reminds the pathologist of the Yorkshire Ripper injuries, he mentions a ballpein hammer.'

'Well, Sutcliffe's safely tucked away in Broadmoor and I guess we not looking for a copycat,' Blacklock replied

'No chance. A copycat is going to use the real thing, not something wooden,' Ribbans said. 'And the victim was hardly frequenting an area favoured by sex workers.'

'Did I hear sex workers being mentioned?' a voice enquired.

Jack recognised the voice and turned in his seat. 'Ladies and gentlemen, this is Adele Porter. A reporter for the local paper.'

'I know exactly who Ms Porter is,' Blacklock replied. 'This is a private meeting, Ms Porter, and the Press are not invited.'

'I'm just looking for a quick quote, Superintendent Blacklock. And you're meeting with members of the public in a public place.'

'Mr Lunn is an Independent Advisory Group member and found the body, and it's Detective Chief Superintendent. There's nothing for you here.'

'If you change your mind, I'll be at the bar,' the reporter replied, turning on her high heels. 'I'll see you around.'

'Not if I see you first,' Blacklock said, sotto voce. 'That one would sell her own kidney for a story.'

'So that brings us back to the son and his lack of alibi,' Sparkes said, after making sure the reporter was out of earshot.

'Indeed it does,' Lunn said. 'Without some corroborating physical evidence, you'll need to keep an open mind.'

'I'll do my level best,' Sparkes replied.

'Now, changing the subject, how's the fly tying going?' Blacklock asked with a smile.

'Well, I've knocked off for the day and if this is the shape of things to come, I would say it's a winner.'

'You like the humdrum of self-employment then?'

'I've left the lads putting the finishing touches to the website and it'll go live later tonight or tomorrow. I've made a couple of hundred quid this week from the one contact and I've got another to chase up that'll give me a chunk of orders two or three times a year. So it's all good, thanks,' Lunn replied.

Sparkes finished off the last of his drink and gathered up the file.

'It goes to say that you haven't seen this file.'

*'Silence is a true friend who never betrays.'*

'Does Shakespeare have a quote for everything?' Mick asked.

'It's Confucius, DI Sparkes,' Scarlett corrected him.

'I assume you'll be having a fun evening questioning the son?' Lunn asked.

'I'm off back to the nick, as Dave Richardson is bringing him in,' Sparkes said.

'Under arrest, or just helping you with your inquiries?'

'The latter. No doubt we'll get an extended interview time to give us a good opportunity to see if he'll cough to it,' Blacklock said.

'Well, it's not about getting a quick result; it's about getting the right one,' Lunn replied. 'As for a judge giving you extra time, I wouldn't bet on it without physical evidence and you've now got a few more suspects to take a serious look at as well.'

'It'll keep us busy. We'll catch up in a few days if that's okay?' Blacklock asked.

'I'm at the end of the phone. Just give me a call,' Lunn replied. 'It was nice to meet you, Scarlett. I'll let you know if I hear anything of interest, Mick.'

'Cheers, Jack,' they chorused.

Lunn took another mouthful of ale. Max Lamont would be top of his suspect list now, but there was a nagging doubt. Sarah's children had gone to the same school as the Lamont's, with Dom a year below the son and Eden the year below the daughter, so they had been no more than nodding acquaintances.

It was obvious to anyone with a pair of eyes and half a brain that Max didn't wear the trousers. The wife was the driving force without a doubt. So, what would have compelled the son to kill his own mother? It wasn't as if he wanted for anything. There was a reasonably well-thought of accountancy business set up by his father when he'd been alive. The cars were replaced at regular intervals, the family holidays at the same place, at the same time of year.

Max was a man who appeared to live his life to a pattern, then he makes an excuse of having a drive in the Forest at about the same time his own mother was being murdered.

That's what puzzled Jack it wasn't what he'd had observed when they'd come across each other on the High Street. What he'd seen was the face of a grieving son trying to come to terms with his mother's death, either that or he was a very good actor. Murder seemed such a departure from Max's usual box of life choices. Jack would have had a team tracking down some of the other villagers who'd crossed words with Elizabeth Lamont.

He finished the last of his beer and got to his feet. The damn knee was playing up again and he'd need a couple of Ibuprofen soon. Sarah would be back in about half an hour, so he could get home, check on the boys before she got back. She'd be expecting him to be preparing something for the evening meal, but Jack had other plans. He got up, made his way out of the pub and started heading towards home.

'Hello again, Mr Lunn.'

'Ms Porter,' Lunn said. 'You're staying closer to me than my own shadow.'

'Just trying to do my job,' the reporter replied. 'I understand that you had your doubts about the arrest of the poacher, then made rather a fool of Superintendent Cooke by proving that he didn't do it. That Superintendent Cooke just happens to now be married to your ex-wife, must have been a happy biproduct for you?'

'Who Superintendent Cooke is married to is neither here, not there.'

'I hear that you and he didn't get on when you were in the force either. That he headed the investigation that failed to find your mother's killer, isn't that right?' she asked.

'It's still an open case, Ms Porter,' Lunn confirmed.

Jack watched as a look of realisation formed on the reporter's face.

'Ah, so this is about redemption then, Mr Lunn?' the reporter queried.

'I really don't know what you mean,' Lunn replied.

'Come on, you used to be a copper.'

'I'd like both of their killers to be brought to justice,' Lunn retorted.

'Your story makes interesting reading,' the reporter continued. 'Losing your father at an early age. A stepfather you didn't get on with and who alienated you from your mother. You got a scholarship to a boarding school for seven years, played county rugby and went to university, getting a degree in geography and then the police. How am I doing?'

'You've obviously done your homework.'

'You were on the fast track for high rank. Well-thought of, good results, a senior officer who mentored and supported you and then it all goes wrong.'

'Best laid plans,' Lunn said with a wintery smile.

'You got injured and it stopped your career in its tracks, even after a number of operations and months of rehab.'

'I was never going to be anything other than a desk pilot and that didn't appeal to me.'

'Then your brother gets cancer, dies and leaves you his business,' she continued. 'That must have hit you hard?'

Lunn said nothing.

'So, you throw yourself into building up that business and it costs you your marriage.'

'I made sure that my kids were looked after and I think I was a good dad,' Lunn replied. 'We're close.'

'And how do you get on with your ex-wife?'

'We don't always see eye to eye, but what divorced parents do?'

'It can't have helped when she married Superintendent Cooke?' she asked.

'Being a stepfather is a minefield.'

'Your children don't like him?'

'I didn't say that,' Lunn replied. 'My girls live their own lives and I'm sure that he does his best to support their mother.'

'Is that what you do with your partner and her children?'

'What's that got to do with all of this?'

'How did your partner take it when you lost your job?'

'I didn't get sacked; I was made redundant.'

'And so here we are.'

'Of course, the facts don't always tell the full story.'

'I'm a good listener if you want to flesh out the bare bones.'

'I'll pass on that,' Lunn replied. 'What I don't understand is your interest in me?'

'You're a determined man, Jack Lunn. You were focused when you were in the police and in your business. Now you're focused on finding Elizabeth Lamont's killer, or killers.'

'And you feel we have that in common?' Lunn asked.

'Determination, yes. Mine may have led me astray in the past.'

'That's an understatement,' he said sarcastically. 'You were a good lawyer away from bed and board courtesy of Her Majesty.'

'I've learned my lesson,' she replied. 'I won't make that same mistake again. I want to be a good reporter and if you think that the police have been barking up the wrong tree, then I believe that you're right.'

'A little flattery goes a long way.'

'I'm not blowing smoke up your arse.'

'Really?' he asked. 'Why should I trust you? You've broken laws and betrayed trust in the past.'

'Because you believe that people should have second chances. Because my current employers gave me a second chance and because I think you aren't motivated by a clear up rate, but by wanting to make sure that whoever killed Elizabeth Lamont is found.'

'Look, I just feel some responsibility to her,' Lunn responded. 'Everyone thought that she was this hard-faced old woman, but I got to see a different side to her. She didn't deserve to end her life face down in the water with the back of her head caved in. No one had the right to do that to her.'

'And that brings us back to your mother.'

'You're very close to crossing a line,' Lunn snapped back.

'I'm sorry,' the reporter replied. 'I don't want to upset you.'

'Then stay out of my way. Get your information from the police, as whatever I have they will have.'

'We have the same aim.'

'You'd need to prove that and stop following me.'

'How was your trip to the Lamont's house, by the way?' the reporter asked. 'And who was that with you?'

'My partner's daughter, Gem. She was at school with both the Lamont children. We were just paying our respects, that's all.

'The husband wasn't at home on the night his mother was murdered, was he?'

'And?' Lunn asked.

'He's going to be the next suspect for the police, isn't he?'

'You might like to think that,' Lunn replied. 'But, I couldn't possibly comment. You really should be speaking to the Police media people.'

'They aren't going to give me anything more than the usual 'dog and pony show'.'

'And you'll get the same from me. I'm not going to compromise the investigation.'

'I'll see you around then,' the reporter said, then turned on her heel and started to walk towards the car park. Lunn watched the retreating figure, then called out to her.

'Ms Porter.'

She turned back towards him.

'Tread carefully.'

She smiled, and half waved to him.

'I will and thanks.'

Chapter 23

Jack returned home and went straight to the shed.

'How's it going?' he asked.

'Pretty much ready to go live. We were just waiting for you to home, so we could walk you through the site,' Gem replied.

'Take my seat, Mr L,' Henry offered. 'I'll do the honours.'

They took a few minutes to show Lunn over the website and they were just demonstrating how it connected to his eBay account when Sarah arrived.

'Oh! I see this is how your days are spent, is it? Computer games and beer drinking, whilst I go out, bring home the only wage in this house,' she said.

'Hey, I've had a payday this week. These guys have finished the website and we're about to go live, if you don't mind,' Lunn replied.

'In that case you are temporarily forgiven, so long as I get to watch the official start of the website.'

'Why don't you take it live, Sarah,' Lunn said.

'What do I press to get it going then?' Sarah asked.

Henry showed her what to do and the site went live. Gem explained that they would start to put product on to eBay now and that should start to generate some orders.

'Well, I thought we'd have a takeaway to celebrate,' Lunn announced.

'Chinese or Indian?'

'I thought Indian. You love the Tandoori fish from The Darjeeling Limited.'

'And you can talk about football to Mr Khan whilst you wait,' Sarah said.

'That thought hadn't crossed my mind, but now you mention it,' Lunn replied with a smile.

'Incorrigible,' as she kissed Lunn on the cheek. 'I'm off to get changed.'

'I'd better go,' Henry said.

'Sure you won't stay for a curry?' Lunn asked.

'Better get back, thanks.'

They strolled back down the garden and Jack thanked Henry again for all his hard work.

'When are you going to order?' Gem asked.

'I'll phone at six and then wander up. Should be back here within half an hour, if you want to come? It'll give your mum time enough to put her feet up for a while.'

Sarah reappeared in jeans and a jumper.

'Are you having your usual from the Indian?' Jack asked.

'Mmm, yes please. That fish with a bit of rice, an onion bhaji, a poppadum or two and some salad will do for me. I'll set the table.'

'I'm going up with Jack to fetch the food,' Gem said, slipping on her coat.

'And no doubt also have a cold beer, whilst there is discussion of the dubious merits of Tottenham Hotspur.'

'It'll be my cross to bear, Mother dear.'


Jack closed the front door and snuggled a little deeper into his coat, the late April evening was turning chilly and a recent shower had turned the streets to patent leather under the streetlights.

'This takeaway isn't just a whim then?' Gem asked.

'I may have a question or two for Mr Khan.'

'Was it something Mick said at the pub?'

'He may have given me a titbit of info that needs clarifying, that's all,' Lunn said, as they turned the corner and crossed the Romsey Road. 'And they've picked up Max Lamont for questioning.'

'I guess that's not too much of a surprise,' Gem replied. 'You know, I can be your bag man.'

'You have been watching too many old cop shows.'

'Was Mick your bag man?'

'I guess he was, though I never thought of him that way. 'Bag man' always seemed demeaning to me,' Lunn replied. 'I'd like to think I was his mentor.'

'He still trusts you though, even after all these years?'

'I hope I've never let him down and he has been a pretty good friend to me over the years.'

'I'll bet he talks to you about cases?' Dom asked.

'Mostly in an abstract sense. Never anything like this, but then I haven't made a habit of discovering bodies on a regular basis.'

Lunn nudged his companion.

'Thirsty work this walking malarkey. What say you to a cold lager?'

Gem grinned. 'Hello, cold lager.'

'Good answer,' Lunn shot back, as they reached the door and walked into The Darjeeling Limited.

'Mr Lunn, what a pleasure to see you. The food should be about twenty minutes,' said Mr Khan the owner as he shook hands with Jack. He then turned to Gem.

'And how are you, Gem?' the restaurant owner asked. 'Last I heard you were working abroad.'

'I was and I'm very well, Mr Khan. How's the family?' Gem replied.

'All good, thank you for asking. You'll have a drink whilst you're waiting?'

'It would be rude not to. Let me settle the bill and we can enjoy a cold beer,' Lunn said.

'I understand you found that poor woman's body?' Khan asked.

'A dubious distinction,' Lunn conceded. 'I understand that the family had ordered a takeaway that night?'

'Indeed they had. The boy made a bit of a scene when he picked it up.'

'Really, what happened?' Gem asked.

'A small misunderstanding over the bill. He claimed there was a dish missing.'

'Awkward?' Lunn said.

'Yes, but a storm in a teacup, there was no mistake.'

'Of course not.'

They finished their drinks and were escorted to the door with appropriate handshakes.

'He confirmed that Seb Lamont picked up a takeaway from there.' Gem pointed out.

'What else?'

'Not much, other than young Master Lamont has poor manners and doesn't care who knows it. He was always an arrogant little shit at school, with so little to be arrogant about.'

'Come on, let's get a move on. Your Mum will be starving, and the food will get cold.'


'You look pensive, Jack,' Sarah stated, as she dished up the food.

'It's just that I'm due a day's fishing this week and I've been thinking about going in the next few days. Also, I'd like to see if I can get some casting instruction organised on one of the nearby fisheries. If you fancy the idea, Dom?'

Gem looked up from her food for a moment, nodding vigorously. 'I'm up for that. Would it be on the river where you found the body?'

'Let me sort out something out for a stillwater. It's the best place to have your first proper lessons,' he explained.


As Sarah and Gem cleared the table and Jack took the time to shut the chickens away for the night. He watched the bats flit overhead chasing insects, dodging around the shrubs and trees of the garden. Sarah joined him from the kitchen.

'We have a good life, Jack. I hope this fly-tying thing takes off for you. I'd hate to think of you having

to get a proper job.'

'Cheeky beggar. Gem and Henry have done a great job on the website and I'm not going into competition against the mass producers. I'm going to send some flies to a couple of the magazines, see if I can get a positive review. Now that really would help sales a bit.'

'Well keep having the ideas, as we need the cash,' Sarah said.

'I thought I'd start looking for a car,' Lunn said. 'I'll have a look online and have a wander

up to have a chat with the garage in the village and see what they have on offer,' Lunn replied.

'Just don't spend too much.'

'I'll make sure I get a good deal.'

'I know you will, but a good deal isn't something for twenty-five thousand,' Sarah reminded him.

'Be sensible about the price and get something practical. I get it.' Lunn replied.

'Back in the house with you, enough fresh air.'

Chapter 24

Jack stood on the doorstep the next morning in his dressing gown with Sarah's laptop slung over his shoulder, as she put her other bags in the old Volvo.

'Looking sexy, Jack.'

'Luckily, I don't venture into the village like this. The elegant, effortless style and finely tuned, athletic body,' Lunn mused.

'Deluded mind, dodgy knee, greying hair.'

'Always so supportive. Have a good day,' Lunn smiled and hugged his partner.

'You too.'

Jack went back into the house, making his way upstairs to knock on Gem's bedroom door.

'Why such an early call?' Gem asked sleepily.

'Early? This is what morning looks like for most people and I need some help today,' Lunn said. 'So, I'm going to teach you how to tie a couple of different fly patterns.'

When Gem arrived in the shed, Jack had already set up a second bench for her to work at.

'I'm going to show you how to tie, the Adams and Parachute Adams. Every dry fly fisherman has these two patterns in their fly box,' Lunn explained.

'Is it an English pattern?' she asked, whilst watching Jack tie the two types of fly.

'American actually. They have a great dry fly tradition too.'

Then Gem tied a couple of each pattern, with Jack marvelling at her dexterity and speed. The flies were tied precisely and with flair. She had game.

'You're a natural and they look great,' he said. 'I'll show you a few more patterns in the next few days and you can tie a few for our trip.'

'I see what you're doing, Jack. I catch a fish on a fly I've tied myself and I'm the one hooked.'

'Thoreau once said 'that many men go fishing all of their lives without knowing that it is not fish they are after'.'

'Fishing as philosophy?'

'I love being able to appreciate an early morning or evening sunset, the wonder of nature and just living here in the New Forest, close to some of the best chalk stream fly fishing in the world,' Lunn replied.

'What shall we do now then?'

'Let's get the dogs together and take them for a walk?'

Locking the front door behind them and taking two dogs each. They walked down the High Street and past the Lyndhurst Park Hotel and on to the Forest, continuing up the hill to Bolton's Bench with its the old yew tree. Letting the dogs off their leads they carried on walking past the cricket pitch and followed one of the paths that wound over the heath.

Their walk was interrupted by Jack's mobile, the screen showing it was Paul Clousden.

'Hello, Paul,' Lunn answered. 'An unexpected pleasure.'

'Just wanted to call and thank you for the hospitality the other night and to pass on something I heard about your murdered lady.'

'It's always a pleasure to have you guys round, but what's this about Mrs Lamont.'

'I was at a working breakfast with some of the solicitors and the subject of her murder came up,' Clousden replied. 'One of them acted for her and mentioned something about a recent change to her will.'

'I don't suppose you got any idea what those changes might have been?' Lunn asked.

'I didn't push for details, but I gathered there was a change to the beneficiaries.'

'Any idea who the winners and losers were?'

'Something to do with the son's family, that's all I got.'

'Thanks for calling and let me know if you hear anything else?'

'I'll keep my ear to the ground and thanks again for dinner the other night.'

'Your turn next time,' Lunn replied.

'Better start getting the recipe books out then.'

Lunn laughed. 'It's not a competition.'

'You try telling Connie that,' Clousden responded. 'Talk to you soon.'

'Well?' Gem asked.

'A titbit of information from Paul,' Lunn replied. 'The solicitor who acted for Mrs Lamont told him that the old lady had made some changes to the beneficiaries in her will.'

'And?'

'It was to do with Max's family and the will, but he had no details.'

'Worth passing on to Mick Sparkes?'

'I'll make sure he knows.'

Before long they were back at Boulton's Bench by the yew tree, gathering up the dogs to clip their leads back on, as they started back towards home. Crossing back over the road by the garage, they headed towards the cut through to Wellands Road, when Jack saw something that caught his attention. Pausing to go into the showroom, he beckoned over one of the salesmen.

'Is the XC90 in for a service or going to be sold?'

'We're going to be selling it, sir.'

'Any idea on price?' Lunn asked.

'I'll get the manager.'

They wandered over to the car, dark metallic grey, full leather seats. He handed the other two dogs over to Gem and took a lap around the vehicle before the manager emerged from the showroom.

'We've only just taken the car in, sir. Are you looking for something like this?' enquired the manager, as he approached.

'I might be in the market, Simon,' Lunn replied, turning towards him.

'Hello, Jack,' Simon Court said. 'I didn't recognise you in mufti. Giving up the company car are we?'

The two men shook hands.

'More like the company car is giving me up. What are you going to ask for it?' Lunn replied.

'I think we'll be putting it up for about eighteen thousand.'

'And what would you be taking for it?'

Court smiled. 'You interested?'

'I think we need to be closer to seventeen thousand than to eighteen, don't you?'

'Seventeen's too low,' Court said.

'Seventeen three hundred?'

'Would you consider seventeen four fifty?' the car salesman asked.

'Maybe, with the car fully valeted and a full tank of fuel. You get the car turned around nice and quickly and off your forecourt?'

'Point taken, seventeen four fifty it is.'

'Do you need a deposit?'

'Give me five hundred now and we'll get the valeting done later today. It'll be ready for pick up tomorrow or the day after at the latest, if that suits you?'

After sorting out the down payment, Jack left the showrooms and spotted Gem and the dogs.

'Let's get home for a cuppa,' he said.

'Did you buy it?' she asked.

Jack nodded. 'It's a decent deal'.

'That was quick work. What will Mum say when she finds out you've bought a car?'

'She knew I had to get one and told me not to go mad and spend twenty-five thousand. And I haven't,' Lunn said. 'Plus, when I get bored with it and her car finally gives up the ghost, she can inherit it.'

'Have you spoken Mick Sparkes yet?' Gem asked.

'Thanks for reminding me, I'll do it now,' Lunn replied, fishing his mobile out of his pocket.

'Mick, how's the interview going?' Lunn asked.

'He's not really saying much and his solicitor is telling him to keep his answers to the bare minimum, which isn't helping him look innocent.'

'You might want to ask if he was aware of any recent changes to his mother's will.'

'What have you heard?

'My information is that there was a change of beneficiaries and Max's family was directly affected.'

'Thanks. That'll give us something to work with.'

'Anything to help, mate.' Lunn replied, terminated the call. He turned to Gem. 'They'll have Max Lamont for thirty-six hours and apparently he's not being very cooperative. Hopefully, what I've just told Mick might give them some leverage to get him to be a bit more helpful.'

'Are you sure he could have done it?'

'I'm not convinced, as he looked bereft when I met him in the High Street. But a change to his mother's will would certainly give him motive,' Jack said. 'Maybe he wasn't going to inherit after all and he doesn't have an alibi. You can't blame the police for taking a good look at him.'

Lunn's mobile rang.

'Jack's phone.'

'Can I speak to Jack Lunn, please?'

'Jack speaking.'

The caller identified himself as, Ben Carpenter, the owner of the first tackle shop he'd visited.

'How are you?' Jack enquired.

'Good thanks. I said we would get a date sorted out so that we could get my Florida trip together and see if we could put some orders your way. Maybe get you to tie a couple of flies as a demonstration. I'd like to take a look at your freshwater flies again too and see if there's something we can do together, as you're local.'

'Happy to help if I can. Let me check my diary and I'll come back to you soon,' Lunn signed off.

'Another bit of business?' Gem asked.

'Hopefully. Let's see what happens. No counting of chickens before hatching,' Lunn advised.

'Any thoughts on food for tonight?'

'Well, speaking of chickens, we have eggs. What about frittata? You could cook if you feel like it?'

'Actually, I rather do feel like cooking tonight.'

'Plans for tomorrow?'

'Show you a few more patterns, get those flies posted from the order on eBay, deliver the order to the tackle shop and then get on the river for the evening rise.'

'Full diary then?'

After the evening meal, Jack spent an hour back up at the shed tying some more flies and after watching a bit of TV, he followed Sarah up to bed.

'Things seem to be going okay with your fledgling business then?'

'I'm happy so far, we'll make a few quid this week and I've got a meeting with some guys who are off to Florida too.'

Lunn picked his glasses up from the bedside table, along with his current book. 'Oh, I bought a car and so I'll need to transfer some money from the account.'

Sarah looked at Jack over the top of her glasses.

'And you left it until now to let me know about it!'

'Yes, sorry about that. Just slipped my mind,' he said apologetically.

'I'll bet. What did it cost?'

Jack explained the haggling and the deal he got, which mollified his partner somewhat.

'Well, at least you didn't go too mad,' Sarah said. 'Just transfer the money online.'

'I'll do it tomorrow morning and I thought I'd catch the evening rise tomorrow. My last day didn't exactly end very well after all,' Lunn said.

'You should definitely go fishing,' Sarah agreed. 'A getting back on the horse kind of thing.'

'Well, I wouldn't have put it quite like that. But it will be good to cast a line again.'

Chapter 25

Jack was up early again the next day. His partner's youngest daughter would be home in the evening and he wanted the house looking nice for her return, as well as getting all the other things on his list accomplished. With the house clean and his chores done, he'd worked it out that he could get an hour or two's fishing in and still be home in time to get Southampton Airport to pick her up at about nine o'clock.

Pouring himself some fruit juice, Jack looked in the medicine drawer for some painkillers. A couple would do, taking the edge off at least. His visit to the doctors after the last set of X-rays was revealing. The doctor told him there was good news and bad news, he'd responded predictably asking for the bad news first.

'The bad news is you're going to have to get the knee joint replaced.'

'And the good news?'

'It won't be for a few years yet, you've kept your weight at a reasonable level and whilst you can't run, or even break into more than a jog for more than a few steps without the knee buckling, you've a reasonable degree of flexibility. So long as you continue to manage your pain and wear a brace whenever you can, you'll stay off the operating table.'

He hated wearing the damn brace. But he was going to be walking and driving a fair bit that day and with the knee giving him some pain already, he'd have to wear it if he wanted to enjoy his fishing later.

Gem arrived back in the house from her morning run.

'Don't forget the other flies that need tying,' Lunn called out.

'I won't.'

'And remember your sister is home this evening and the house needs to be kept clean and tidy for when she gets here.'

Closing the front door, he turned to find a familiar figure with a lurcher at his side.

'Alright, Mr Lunn?' Seth Walker asked.

'Hello, Seth. What are you doing here?'

'Just wanted to say thank you for what you did.'

'I Just did the right thing,' he replied. 'I know you and I haven't got a lot in common, but I knew you couldn't possibly have done it.'

'You didn't have to stand up for me though and I appreciate it,' the poacher said. 'Just a little something to say thanks.'

The poacher handed a bag over and Jack looked inside to find a couple of rabbits.

'Should I ask where these came from?'

'If you don't ask, I can't tell no lies,' Walker said with a smile. 'If there's anything I can do for you in the future, you'll let me know?'

'Thanks for offering,' Lunn said. 'Just stay off the river, please.'

'You'll not see me, sir.'

He watched as the poacher walked back down the short path with his lurcher at heel and disappeared down the road. After putting the rabbits in the freezer, Jack walked up to the village, making his way over to the garage, where he was welcomed into the manager's office.

'It'll be tomorrow before we can hand the car over if that's okay with you?' Court asked. 'We can sort out the paperwork and then deliver it.'

'That's fine. I've transferred the money already, so let's get the paperwork done and I'll come down to pick it up.'

Gem was showered and in the kitchen when Jack got back.

'Did you pick up the new car?' she enquired.

'They offered to drop it off tomorrow, but I'm just going to walk down and collect it.'

'You back later?'

'Yes. I'll pop back and get my gear and go and wet a line. Mick Sparkes asked me to meet him this evening, but I said no and put him off until tomorrow.'

'Are you trying to keep this thing at arm's length?' Gem asked.

'A bit. Particularly whilst your sister is home and Emily and Grace are over. It'll be nice to have a family weekend without any drama.'

'Not likely with all the girls here,' Gem quipped.

'Bloody comedian.'

Jack went down to the shed and collected the flies to take to the tackle shop and made his way back down to the kitchen, where Gem was filling the dishwasher.

'Have you got everything?' the young woman asked.

Jack nodded.' I'll be back in a couple of hours to pick up my gear and then hopefully get some fishing in. I'll call Avington and book us in there early next week and get you some casting lessons. See if we can get a fish tugging your line.'

He called the fishery from his car and made the arrangements and then reversed off the drive and turned right on to Romsey Road, heading towards Cadnam and Junction 1 of the M27. Jack passed Broadlands Lakes and Rownhams Services, before bearing left and joining the M3. It wasn't a long drive and soon he was turning on to the forecourt parking of the tackle shop.

Chapter 26

Mr Wiseman was busy with a customer when Jack arrived. So, like most fishermen in a tackle shop he couldn't resist looking for things to spend money on. He was rummaging through the books, when there was a cough behind him, he turned to find the owner and the customer.

'Mr Lunn, can I introduce you to Steven Ingram, editor of *Game Fisherman*. He's been admiring the small selection of flies that you supplied earlier in the week.'

'I'm pleased you like them,' Lunn said as he shook hands with the man.

'Do call me Steve,' the man said. 'George always calls me Steven and he's the only one who does, other than my mother.'

'Well, Mr Wiseman is old school. From a time when a man's word was his bond and quality was always more important than quantity.'

'That's very kind of you, Mr Lunn,' the tackle dealer said. 'I rather think that Steven may have something of interest to say to you.'

'Really? Can we adjourn to your office upstairs and I'll happily trade being Jack if you allow me to call you by your first name?' Lunn enquired.

'I was about to suggest that myself, Jack,' the tackle shop owner said. 'Gentlemen, if you'd please follow me.'

The shop owner led the way upstairs to his office, offering the men a seat and the magazine editor asked if he could take a look at the new flies Jack had brought in, taking his time examining them closely.

'These flies are really quite special. The mass-produced flies are fine, but what you're making is way beyond fine,' he said. 'They're classic flies, with a twist. Not wacky, more like another stage on from the original and beautifully tied.'

'You can understand why I was keen to stock them,' Wiseman said.

'And you tie them all yourself?' Steve asked.

'The first batch was all my own work, but this batch is partly my partner's daughter's work.'

'Really, how long has she been tying?' asked the magazine man.

'About forty-eight hours,' replied Lunn, waiting for the reaction.

'You're joking! All of these flies are so well tied, and she's been tying just a couple of days. Which are hers?'

'She's a natural. If she sticks with it, she could be one of the greats,' George said, finding his tobacco pouch and starting to fill his pipe. 'I take it she fishes?'

'She has natural dexterity, a wonderful memory and eye for detail. She has always aimed high and she wants to tie the best flies. The Adams and Parachute Adams are hers, and she's going for her first casting lessons next week,' Lunn said.

'Where?' the editor asked.

'Avington. They have a good tutor and she can target fish in the clear water there.'

'You tell me what day you're going to be there and I'll meet you.'

'That's incredibly decent of you, Steve.'

'I'll be bringing a photographer with me and we're going to do an article about the flies you're tying. Put her at the centre of it. A young woman coming to the sport as a novice, that kind of thing. What's her name anyway?' Steve asked.

'Gemma. Everyone calls him Gem and I call her a few other choice names when she borrows things without asking, or drinks my beer,' Lunn joked.

'It'll be a nice article, Jack. We can fish the carrier stream for the Itchen as well as the lakes and catch a few fish on your flies. What do you say?' Ingram asked.

'I'm more than happy. Can I call you to confirm?' Lunn asked.

'No problem, here's my number. You're not in a hurry, are you?'

'So long as I get the evening rise, I'm happy to stay as long as you'll have me.'

Half an hour later Lunn walked back down the stairs with another order from George Wiseman. There was also the promise of a piece in one of the leading game fishing magazines from a renowned fisherman. In a slight daze, he sat in his car on the forecourt of the tackle shop and called up Mick Sparkes.

'Hi, Jack. Are you calling to meet up?'

'Sorry, No. I just thought I'd see if you guys had got anywhere with Max Lamont?'

'We had to release him last night, but he's still under investigation. He's not giving us anything. The same old story about working late and then going for a drive.'

'Seriously, he just played a straight bat at everything?' Lunn asked. 'He must have balls of steel and a heart of ice if he did kill her. You've got no physical evidence to link him to the crime scene at all and there's not much in the way of CCTV in the Forest. To be honest, you didn't have much choice other than to release him.'

'I heard from the uniforms that his family has decided he did it. The wife's had the locks changed and his stuff was in suitcases on the doorstep. He's moved into his mother's house and we're going to check in on him.'

'Well, his family have obviously made their minds up. Poor bloke. If he didn't do it, he must be feeling pretty down and if he did do it, he'll be feeling pretty exposed.'

'He knows he's got to talk to us again at some point. He's sticking with the 'driving around' alibi, but you know that isn't an alibi at all. Let's just say that he remains a person of interest.'

'I'm off home,' Lunn said. 'Picking up my fishing gear and trying to get the evening rise in, as my last outing was so unexpectedly interrupted.'

'Well good luck, or whatever fishermen wish each other.'

'That would be tight lines then, mate,' Lunn replied. 'Catch you soon.'

Chapter 27

Gem was still in the shed when Jack walked up the garden.

'You seem in a good mood. Do you have another order?' she asked.

'I do. In addition, you and I are going to be part of a feature in *Game Fisherman* and the editor is going to give you casting lessons.'

'You're bloody joking!'

'I'm bloody not,' Lunn said. 'This could give the business a massive boost and it'll do you no harm to get a few lessons from one of the top fly fishermen in the country.'

'But, this is your business.' Gem replied. 'I don't want to steal your thunder.'

'Steve Ingram, the magazine editor was blown away by the quality of your work. So long as you will tie flies for me when you're at home, I'll make sure you get a decent bit of spending money.'

'I want some credit for the flies on the website and in the article.'

'Of course,' Lunn laughed. 'I'll make sure you're mentioned in dispatches.'

Gem held out her hand and the two of them shook on the deal.


It was a glorious evening in the New Forest, with a weekend to follow. His daughters and Eden would be around, so there would be a full house. Jack couldn't help smiling, as he drove along the sun-dappled road.

Two fellow fishermen were finishing their preparations as he climbed out of the car. Jack recognised them as part of the syndicate and wandered over to exchange pleasantries. Slipping on his fishing waistcoat, Jack wedged his baseball hat on, took his polarised sunglasses out and walked up the road, through the gate on to the footpath down towards the river. Stopping on the wooden bridge, gave his sunglasses a final polish, put them back on and took a couple of minutes to enjoy the quiet and solitude.

Strolling over to the far bank, he started to walk up the beat to the first bench, settling down to rig up. On a lovely, warm late afternoon, he could enjoy the burst of green, as the trees started to get dressed in new growth.

The river was in good condition. The warm weather might encourage a hatch and hopefully an evening rise. He carried on walking along the bankside, past the bothy and the past where Elizabeth Lamont's body had interrupted his last day's fishing. A shiver went down his spine, as if someone had stepped on his grave, but took a few moments to stand on the bank opposite where the body had come to rest against him.

'I'll find out who did this, Elizabeth,' he whispered under his breath and touched his fingers to his cap.

There were fish rising in the Trophy Pool, but he felt uneasy casting to them after what had happened there. Carrying on towards the Lamont house, which as now looming up to his right, Jack dropped his tackle bag to study the water.

As a few flies were coming off, some fish were rising. He stripped line from the reel, made a couple of false casts and then covered the closest fish. The trout studiously ignored Jack's offering, remaining on station between the beds of ranunculi. He cast again to cover the same trout. This time the fly landed on the right line, Jack put a mend in the line, the fish moved slightly off station.

'Sir.'

Jack tried to keep his attention on the trout now moving towards his fly.

'Sir!' the voice called more insistently.

The fish moved towards his fly.

'Excuse me, sir.'

Distracted, he turned slightly towards the voice, trying to see who it was as the fish rose. He missed the take, striking too late by which time the fish had rejected the fly.

'Sir, you'll have to move,' the voice stated.

He turned around to see a uniformed police officer approaching. Jack didn't recognise him, so knew he wasn't local.

'You'll have to move, sir. This area is now sealed off.'

'I didn't see any tape up,' Lunn replied. 'And I know all about the body.'

'Do you now, sir?' the constable said. 'You'd better come with me then.'

'I'm trying to have a pleasant evening fishing, officer. You've just made me miss a take,' Lunn complained.

'This way, sir.'

Jack recovered the line on to his reel, picked up his bag and walked alongside the policeman.

'How do you think I can help?' he asked.

'The plainclothes officers will want to talk to you at the house,' the policeman said. 'What's your name?'

'I think you might find that some of them know my who I am and won't want to see my ugly mug.'

'You're known to us?'

'I was one of 'us',' Lunn confirmed.

'Oh, I thought you were just a member of the public,' the policeman said, as they reached the back of the house. 'The detectives are around the front, near the body.'

'Body?'

'Yes, the body,' the officer said. 'The body you said you knew all about.'

A small knot of detectives loitered just outside a taped off area with their backs to him. Past them and through the open front doors Jack could see the body of a man, the face towards him. Jack found himself open-mouthed with shock and disbelief. Max Lamont's neck was at an awkward angle and the tangle of limbs resembled a broken puppet.

'Sir, this man says he knows all about the body,' the uniformed officer called out.

'Officer, you might want to listen to me first,' Lunn stage whispered.

The detectives all turned towards Jack and the policeman.

'Says he knows about the body, does he?' said an instantly recognisable voice from within the group.

'Good evening, Superintendent. What an unexpected pleasure,' Lunn said as Geoff Cook emerged from the middle of the scrum. 'A misunderstanding with the officer, I'm afraid.'

'Really, and how did that come about?'

'No idea really. I was just fishing, the officer told me the area was being sealed off. I told him that I knew all about the body, not realizing he was talking about Max,' Jack replied.

'So, you don't know anything then?'

'Not this time, Superintendent. How did poor Max end up at the bottom of the stairs?' Lunn asked.

Mick Sparkes emerged in the hallway, clad head to foot in a crime scene coverall and pulling his mask down.

'Looks like we have a message from the deceased, guv,' he called out, a somewhat bewildered expression passing over his face as he caught sight of Jack.

'We might have an answer to your question, Mr Lunn,' Geoff Cooke said.

'Well, if it's an answer, the question is whether it's the right one,' Jack fired back.

Geoff Cooke bustled up to his former colleague, deliberately invading Jack's space, his reddening face inches from Lunn's.

'I want you out of here, away from this body, away from this house and above all away from my investigation. Do I make myself clear?'

'I was merely following the good officer's request to accompany him.'

Cooke turned on the young uniformed booby, who was still standing close by. 'And you thought it was a good idea to bring a civilian to a crime scene, did you?'

The young officer flushed red. 'I thought you'd want to speak to him as soon as possible, sir.'

'I'll bloody well tell you when to think. He could have been the killer, or contaminated the crime scene.'

'It's not his fault, Geoff,' Lunn intervened. 'Don't take it out on him. I've caught a glimpse of poor Max through the open front door and must have been at least thirty feet from the body. You haven't got a coverall on and you've probably been closer than I have.'

'You stay out of this,' Cooke said with a sneer and returned his attention to the young bobby. 'Get back to the river and get that tape up. I'll be speaking to your sergeant about this.'

'Don't drop him in it,' Lunn appealed. 'He's just a youngster who made a mistake, Geoff.'

Cooke's features flushed a deeper shade and he appeared to be on the point of apoplexy as he inched even closer to Lunn, a thin trail of spittle at the corner of his mouth.

'You were always a smartarse. Flying by the seat of your pants, leaving proper policing to the likes of me,' Cooke said. 'Perhaps, instead of poking your nose into everyone else's business, you should have spent more time beefing up the security at your mother's home. Now piss off!'

Jack felt his hands turn into fists and fought the urge to punch Cooke in his smug face.

'That was low. Even for you,' he replied, then turned on his heel and started back towards the corner of the house, where he had dropped his fishing gear.

'Jack Lunn, what are you doing here? The best detective I ever worked with.' Lunn turned to see Rhona Blacklock approaching.

Rhona noticed Geoff Cooke for the first time. 'No offence, Geoff.'

'There'll be some taken,' Lunn said under his breath, noticing a few smirking policemen.

'Detective Chief Superintendent Blacklock, always a pleasure to see you, ma'am.' Lunn stepped away from the group and shook his former boss's hand.

'You can drop the ma'am, Jack. What the bloody hell are you doing here? Finding the first body not enough for you?' Blacklock enquired.

'Well, this very nice uniformed officer invited me to accompany him when we had a bit of a misunderstanding,' Lunn replied. 'But, Superintendent Cooke feels that I've outstayed my welcome and I'm trying to keep my dead body discovering down to a minimum.'

'Stick around a minute,' she said, then turned to the coterie of detectives. 'Now then, did I hear that we have a note from the dead man?'

'Not so much a note as a message, ma'am,' Sparkes answered.

'What sort of message?' asked the DCS

'On a laptop. It says that he's sorry.'

'Is that it?' Rhona Blacklock asked. 'Does it explain how he ended up at the bottom of the stairs?'

'No, ma'am, but the half-empty bottle of scotch might,' said Sparkes.

'So, summing up, Superintendent?' Blacklock asked, turning to Geoff Cooke.

'Wife kicked him out, so he returns to the family home. Gets on the sauce and is overcome with guilt. Begins typing out some sort of confession but doesn't finish it. He starts up the stairs but, half-pissed, he loses his balance and takes a dive to the hall,' Cooke answered.

'No sign of a struggle?' Blacklock asked.

'No, ma'am, looks like he was by himself. The gardener arrived at the house and the front and back doors were unlocked. He'd seen Lamont's car outside, so came in, found the body and called us.'

'Right,' said Blacklock. 'What does the message say, Mick?

'Just two words,' Sparkes replied. ''I'm sorry.''

Blacklock turned back to Lunn.

'And what were you doing around here?'

'Fishing. I've a day a week on the beat here,' he explained. 'Last week's day got interrupted by Mrs Lamont arriving in my swim.'

'And you knew the Lamont's well?' Blacklock asked, for the benefit of the gallery.

'I'd dealt with Mr and Mrs Lamont over the years,' Lunn replied. 'It used to be mostly business, though Mrs Lamont and I always chatted when I was fishing. I knew Max and his wife, as the kids went to the same school as Sarah's.'

'And you told Superintendent Cooke this?'

'Not really. I indicated to the Superintendent that I might have some insights he'd find useful, but it was made abundantly clear that I was surplus to requirements.'

'Well, Jack is an I.A.G. member and a former police officer, Geoffrey. You should take advantage of his insights.'

'Well, it does seem that we can now close the murder off, ma'am,' Cooke said hopefully.

'Let's dot all the i's and cross all the t's this time, please. Make sure that forensics are fully completed. Jack, is there anything else you want to add?'

'No. I didn't think he was the type, but I know that he didn't appear to have an alibi.'

'You can't be right every time, Mister Lunn,' Geoff Cooke snarked. 'He's started to write a confession on the laptop.'

'He wrote that he was sorry, not what he was sorry for,' Lunn countered. 'Pretty open to interpretation, in my opinion. What about the other suspects I told you about?'

'We haven't spoken to them yet,' Geoff Cooke replied. 'Doesn't seem much need to now.'

'Max Lamont had no alibi for when his mother was killed,' Richardson chimed in.

'But, you've got no physical evidence connecting him to that killing,' Lunn said, then looked back at Blacklock. 'I'm sorry, just playing devil's advocate here.'

'You've made some good points, Jack. But this is best left to us now, don't you think?' Blacklock asked.

Lunn took the hint; his old boss had momentarily put a comforting hand on his shoulder for old time's sake and now the door was now being closed politely, but firmly, in his face.

'Absolutely, leave it to the professionals,' Jack said.

'Let's walk and talk, Jack.' Blacklock said and led Jack away from the group.

'I've got the hint,' Lunn said. 'Geoff seems to have this one wrapped up and you don't want an amateur ex-copper muddying the waters.'

'You were always quick to catch on and this matter hasn't been handled as adeptly as it might have been,' DCS Blacklock said. 'Geoff Cooke is a good solid copper, trying to do the best he can with fewer resources than he should have.'

'We're all victims of the recession in one way or another, but he would have had Seth Walker banged up given half a chance,' Lunn replied. 'And calling Geoff Cooke a good solid copper is just your way of saying that he's by the numbers, unimaginative and concerned about his clear up rate.'

'You two never did get on, did you?' Blacklock said. 'Why do you think Max Lamont didn't kill his mother?'

'I'm not saying he didn't,' Lunn explained. 'What evidence there is points to him. However, the evidence is pretty thin and circumstantial, don't you think?'

'What would you do next?'

'I passed on to Mick what I'd heard about a recent change to Mrs Lamont's will,' Lunn said. 'I think that's worth looking at. And I would want to know where Max was the night his mother was killed and those other suspects should be tracked down and interviewed, particularly Liam Galletly. Look, I sold the neighbours the next-door house and I've got an address for them. I don't know them very well, but do you mind if I have a chat with them, prior to Geoff marching in with his size 10's?

'We've spoken to the solicitor and the will had been changed a few months before the old lady was killed,' Blacklock replied. 'The other three need following up. But, if you have a bit of history with the neighbours, by all means have a chat with them. But, take Mick with you and you're just there to do the introductions. As for Mr Galletly, I agree he has both the form and a motive. So, let's see what Forensics come up with first, shall we?'

'Are you going to tell me how the will was changed?' Lunn asked.

'The old dear had named the two grandchildren as beneficiaries. Then she took them out a couple of months ago, leaving everything to Max. Gives him a pretty good reason for offing her don't you think?'

'And the grandkids and wife were having a nice takeaway curry at home from my local Indian when Elizabeth Lamont was getting bashed over the head,' Lunn said. 'Did the kids know granny had disinherited them?'

'The lack of alibi and that note left by the dead man means he's at the top of the list as far as we're concerned. I know the family having a meal together isn't much of an alibi and we'll speak to them again now Max is dead and we know about the will. I've told Geoffrey to leave no stone unturned. I don't want another screw up like the poacher.'

They'd reached the river.

'I guess the wife will get the money now?' Lunn said.

'That's up to the lawyers. But the good news is that your day of fishing is safe.'

'Really, how so?'

'The old woman had made a change to the deeds of the property so that you and your descendants have a day on the beat in perpetuity,' DCS Blacklock said.

'Max didn't say anything to me about that.'

'You haven't heard it from me of course, but it seems the old lady liked you.'

'Well, it wasn't expected. I was only told the other day that she just regarded me as an ad hoc bailiff.'

'With the prime suspect dead from booze and a fall, it does look like we can close the case,' Blacklock said, then caught the look that Lunn gave her. 'Yes, I'll remind Geoff to get the people on your list seen and interviewed too.'

'Thanks, Rhona,' Lunn replied. 'Mick hasn't told me anything, you know?'

'And I'm the Easter Bunny,' Blacklock scoffed. 'Everyone knows he keeps in touch and even asks you for advice. He hasn't got your intuition, but he's a good DI and better than most, to be honest.'

'Don't let Cooke give him a hard time. Geoffrey can be a bit of a twat when it comes to holding a grudge.'

'Will you ever forgive him for marrying your ex?'

'Geoff as stepfather to my kids doesn't exactly fill me with joy. It was just so out of the blue, I didn't know he'd held a candle for her for years.' Lunn said. 'I guess my intuition let me down well and truly then.'

'But you're happy now?'

'Meeting Sarah was good for me, I was drinking a fair bit and had been before the separation,' Jack replied. 'I'm happier, so I drink less. Don't get me wrong I still like a glass of wine or a decent beer. I just try to mostly save it for the weekends now, as it keeps the weight off and that helps the knee.'

'I've only met her a few times but you two seem to be a good fit,' the DCS said. 'I'd better get back to the house. Speaking of drinks, we should get together sometime?'

'I'd like that.'

'Well, if you do hear anything that you think might be useful, let Mick or me know and good luck with the new business.'

Lunn didn't miss the oblique invitation to keep his ear to the ground.

'Message received and understood.'

'Good, I've got your mobile number and we'll have that drink soon. Give my regards to Sarah.'

Blacklock strode purposefully back towards the house.

Jack made his way back down the bankside, past the bothy and on to the bridge. He paused and took a few minutes to watch the fish in the clear water and think over what he'd seen and heard in the house.

Max Lamont a murderer. Well, he certainly had the motive with his mother's will giving him all the money and property, and apparently had the opportunity. It grated against the meeting they'd had in the High Street and unless there was some strong physical evidence Jack couldn't help feeling that assumptions were being made.


Rhona Blacklock arrived back at the front of the house and called Geoff Cooke over.

'Let me make this as plain as I can, Geoff,' The DCS said. 'Jack Lunn has already got us out of a jam regarding the poacher and you will co-operate with him.'

'But-'

'But nothing, Superintendent. You'll make sure that this Galletly character and the grandson are all interviewed, and this investigation is watertight. Make sure you have an answer to every question, the forensics are all present and correct and that you don't screw this one up for the sake of a quick clear up.'

'He just gets under my skin.'

'You're not some bloody schoolkid,' Blacklock snapped back. 'You're a senior police officer, so start behaving like one. The ACC is very grateful for Jack's intervention and appreciates that he stopped us getting egg all over our faces. Do your job, Geoffrey, do I make myself clear?'

'As day,' Cooke replied.

'Have you got somebody going to see the wife?'

'I'll get one of the local bobbies to do it.'

'No,' Blacklock said. 'Send Mick Sparkes with Michelle Taylor. Tell them to treat it like a sudden death and no mention of what was on the laptop.'

'Will do.'

Lunn made tracks away from Elizabeth Lamont's house, he saw the figure watching him from under the branches of a bankside willow.

'I didn't see you at first, Ms Porter,' he said. 'Loitering somewhere shady?'

'You seemed somewhat distracted, Mr Lunn.'

'Just watching the fish.'

'And talking to DCS Blacklock.'

'So, you've been watching for a while?' Lunn asked.

'What's going on?'

'Try the police media relations people.'

'They're being very tight-lipped about all this activity,' she responded. 'I thought you could give me a helping hand.'

'Miss Porter, there isn't a chance I'll give you anything,' Jack said. 'I have too many friends involved to jeopardise that by giving information to you. Especially when you're, how can I put this, not without some previous.'

'I'd hoped that my past indiscretions would not be taken into consideration,' Porter replied. 'I thought that you and I might help each other.'

'Not much likelihood of that,' Lunn said. 'You should go and talk to the DCS and if she's willing to give you anything, then settle for that.'

'And how are you finding working with your old colleagues?'

'You have done your homework,' Lunn replied. 'But, I've no story for you.'

'Oh, I don't know. Our readers love a human-interest story and you're involved in all of this. You knew the old lady and her family, know the police officers involved and I'm sure you'd make wonderful copy. What's going on?'

Lunn smiled. 'Don't write a story yet, Ms Porter. I will say that I'm not certain that this is what it at first seems.'

'Okay,' she replied. 'I'll go and chat to the DCS.'

'Tread lightly. Keep Rhona onside and you might get a story to get you back to Fleet Street.'

'I just want to get a break on the old lady's killing.'

'Then you'd better hurry along and ask Rhona about the second death in the family,' Lunn replied. 'But you haven't heard that from me.'

'A second death?'

'Go and speak to the DCS,' Lunn said. 'And stop following me.'

'I knew you were an interesting man, Jack.' With that, she walked quickly towards the house.

Lunn crossed over the river, walking up the footpath, through the gate and onto the road leading back to where the car was parked. Two sessions and not a fish to the net, perhaps he'd stay away from the river for a while. Perhaps people would stop dying?

Jack shook his head at the ridiculous connection he just made.

Chapter 28

As he arrived home, Sarah was just climbing out of her car.

'I thought you were staying for the evening rise?' she queried.

'So did I, but I bumped into Rhona Blacklock, who sends her regards to you.'

'Your old boss? I haven't seen her for ages.'

'Well she remembers you,' Lunn replied. 'You seem to have made a good impression on her for some reason.'

'Possibly because I rescued you from a lonely existence. Where did you run into your old boss anyway?'

'At the Lamont house.'

'What was she doing there and more to the point, what were you doing there?'

'She was working, and I was fishing.'

'She's working on Mrs Lamont's murder?'

'In a way, yes,' Lunn said evasively.

'You're being obtuse, Jack, which means you're hiding something. You'd better come clean, my lad,' Sarah ordered, as she stood on the bottom step of the stairs.

'I like your interview technique; will you be taking down my particulars?' Lunn asked suggestively.

'In your dreams! Tell me what Rhona was doing.'

'They found Max Lamont's body at the foot of the stairs at the family home.'

'Oh my god! Poor man. Is it another murder?' Sarah asked.

'Looks like he'd been drinking. Apparently, the old woman had changed the will a couple of months ago and took the grandkids out. Max was due to get it all. The police think that he killed her for the inheritance, but they couldn't get anywhere when they interviewed him,' Jack explained. 'Imogen threw him out, so he went to the house, drank about half a bottle of scotch. On the face of it, he started typing a message saying he was sorry, went upstairs and took a dive to the hallway.'

'Come on, I thought you said that Max wasn't the murdering type,' she said.

'I don't see him as a killer, least of all of his mother. What they had on Max was circumstantial at best. They still have a few people to interview, but unless something else comes to light, I guess they'll close the investigation.'

'No more helping the police with their inquiries for you then?'

'I suppose.'

'Go and have a shower whilst I change. Have you thought about food for tonight?' Sarah asked.

'We could swing by the supermarket, get the makings for a nice risotto and maybe a bottle of wine?'

'That does sound good, now get in the shower.'


It didn't take long to scoop up a few provisions for the evening meal, after which they made it to Southampton airport with plenty of time to spare and grabbed a coffee.


Lunn's mobile phone buzzed. It was Mick Sparkes, so he left Sarah in the coffee shop as he took the call.

'Mick, sorry I didn't get a chance to have a chat with you earlier.'

'Thanks for winding Geoff Cooke up.'

'I always have time for that. Any news?'

'C.S.I.'s are still on site, but there was no sign of a struggle and it looks like he was by himself,' Sparkes said. 'I had to give the sudden death message to the wife. She looked suitably shocked and upset. Said it was a mistake making him leave the house, but that when the Police hauled him in for questioning it seemed the right thing to do.'

'That's it then, as far as you guys are concerned?' Lunn asked.

'Pretty much. We'll wait for the autopsy results and the forensics before making it official though.'

'Any luck tracking down Galletly and the builder?'

'Geoffrey says he has a couple of DC's working on your list and Liam Galletly has disappeared from his mother's home.' Sparkes replied. 'Now there doesn't seem to be much urgency about seeing them though.'

'He won't be far and Geoff needs to make sure everything is tied up tight. Did Rhona mention coming with me to see the old neighbours?

'Yeah, she said you'd be in touch to sort a date and time out.'

'Do you think Max did it, Mick?'

'Not my call, though the lack of physical evidence is a concern. It's Geoff's show, but I don't think Rhona is best pleased about how he's has been handling the case. You turning up and showing that the poacher wasn't the killer certainly hasn't helped his stock,' Sparkes replied.

*'How are the mighty fallen.'*

'Set myself up for that, didn't I?' Sparkes replied. 'I'd better go, Jack. We should have the autopsy results back soon and the forensic boys are finishing up at the house.'

'I'll speak to you soon. I'm going to have to go, Eden's plane is about to land and I'll be in real trouble if I'm not there to greet her.'

'Cheers, Jack. Catch you soon.'


Lunn returned inside the terminal and Sarah waved him over.

'Looking forward to seeing her?' he asked.

'Of course, she's my baby.'

The Arrivals board told them the plane had landed and about a quarter of an hour later Eden came through the doors, dragging her case behind her. After hugs and kisses all round, they made their way back to the car, loaded up the luggage and started back towards home.

Eden was such a contrast to her mother, all long blonde hair and cornflower blue eyes, which she got from her father. Her mother got a hug and then the young woman slipped her arm through Jack's.

'So, murder most foul. Do tell, Jack,' she said.

'The found Max Lamont dead in his mother's house today,' her mother interrupted.

'Two murder's, OMG, are we talking serial killer?'

'Serial killers are three murders or more,' Jack corrected her. The Police think Max wasn't a murder, that he was in the process confessing to killing his mother, got rather drunk and fell down the stairs.'

'And you don't buy into that?' Eden asked.

'That's completely contrary to the visibly upset man I saw in Lyndhurst High Street shortly after his mother was killed. Anyway, it's in the hands of the Police now.'

'So, who's got the case, Mick Sparkes?' she asked.

'No such luck, Superintendent Geoffrey Cooke,' Lunn replied.

'Geoffrey got promoted? Your ex must be pleased.'

'I'm sure she's ecstatic.'

'Can we change the subject, please,' Sarah asked.


Before long they were pulling on to the drive at the front of the house.

Gem was busy in the kitchen, as Sarah and Eden made their way through, but she stopped to hug his sister. Following up at the rear, Jack made himself a bet that it would be less than twenty-four hours before they were complaining about each other, but promised himself that he would enjoy the harmony in the meantime.

Gem poured a glass of wine for her mother, a cold cider for Eden.

'Do you want a beer, Jack?' she asked.

'I think I'll have a glass of wine whilst I'm cooking but help yourself to one. There's some cold Moretti in the fridge,' Lunn said, knowing that Gem had a weakness for the Italian beer.

'Don't mind if I do. Mum just told me about Max Lamont. Have you heard any more?' Gem replied.

'It's horrible. But it'll take them a couple of days to get all the forensics together, but I'm not expecting any surprises. They'll wrap it up and that'll be the last if it. The Imogen gets the money and will sell the house, I expect.'

Jack poured himself a glass of red and raised his glass.

'Here's to us, guys. Welcome back to Eden for a few days. Thanks to Gem for all her help with the fly tying and website,' Jack toasted them. 'I'll have the risotto on the table in about half an hour.'

'Can I get another beer in a minute?' Gem asked.

'Help yourself.'


With plates assembled, Gem spooned the now ready risotto on to them, before Jack topped each off with a sea bass fillet. He called Sarah and Eden to the table, where a salad was waiting, along with a chilled bottle of Sauvignon Blanc.

'Well, I'm as fat as a pig,' Sarah announced, as she finished her last mouthful.

'That was great, Jack. The perfect meal to come home to,' Eden said.

'Go and put the TV on and Gem and I will clear up.'

'Thanks for volunteering me there, Jack,' Gem said, making a face at him.

Eden's phone rang. It was Grace, Jack's daughter and she left the room to take the call. She was back in a couple of minutes.

'Grace isn't working tomorrow, so I'm going to pick her up for a coffee and a catch-up.'

'Seeing the new boyfriend tomorrow night?' Dom asked.

'Having a meal sometime in the next couple of days,' Eden confirmed.

'Don't forget, family lunch on Saturday, you promised,' said Lunn. 'What about inviting your boyfriend along?'

'Too early for that,' Eden answered, ending any debate.

Gem and Jack settled in the two chairs, whilst Sarah and Eden cuddled up on the sofa and the dogs settled down into whatever space remained.

'Do you think the Police will close the case now?' Eden asked.

'No reason for them not to. He was their prime suspect,' Jack replied. 'Wraps it all up nice and neat, with no loose ends.'

'So, we're safe in our beds then?'

'No one would dare to try and get in here with the well-known attack Yorkies on guard,' Lunn quipped.

'Has it been weird being so close to an investigation again?' she asked.

'Do you mean has it been weird butting heads professionally against my ex's new husband?' Jack replied. 'All I did was stop him publicly humiliating himself. He should be thanking me. But instead, I just got a bunch of hostility.'

'That, and he's not who you wanted to be a stepfather to your children?' Eden said.

'I'm sure your father feels the same way about me.'

'That would pre-suppose that Dad is any sort of father to us, Jack,' Gem chimed in.

'So long as you keep the place clean and do the cooking, you'll always have a place below stairs here,' Sarah contributed.

'Thanks, love. Luckily, I know my station.'


Later that night, as they got ready for bed, Sarah hugged Jack.

'My kids know they are lucky to have a good man in their lives.'

'If I find out who he is, I'll kick the crap out of him.'

'What, with your dodgy knee? You couldn't catch him and even if you did. You'd take one swing with your good leg and the bad one would give up the ghost and put you on your arse. Now brush your teeth and go and warm my bed up,' she said affectionately.


Chapter 29

When Jack arrived at the shed the next morning, Gem was already there, sat in her running kit. Her hair pulled back and she was tying some of the flies for the orders.

'You're keen,' he said.

'I like to keep busy, Jack and thought that a shower could wait. I'm not stinking the place out, am I?'

Jack shook his head. 'I'll fetch us some tea and we can crack on.'

They turned their full attention to working over the next few hours. Jack also checked the website noticing a couple of small orders had come in, which he gave to Gem to tie.

The barking dogs announced that Sarah was back from work.

She called up the garden. 'Trying to kill my daughter with hard work?'

'I've tried poison and it's had no effect. Work might take a little longer, but I'll get her in the end,' Lunn replied.

'When are you thinking of picking the car up?'

'I've got some things to finish, so we could walk down later to pick it up.'

'That sounds good. I'll leave you to it then,' Sarah said.

Jack's mobile rang again, and it was the Florida trip organiser wanting to come over on the Monday evening. Jack confirmed a time and was told there would be a party of six.

'That sounds encouraging,' Gem said.

'Let's not count our chickens,' Lunn counselled.


The manager of the garage was busy as Jack and Sarah slipped into the showroom later that afternoon.

'Is this the point where you tell me you've actually signed up for a Maserati?' Sarah teased.

'No surprises, I promise,' Lunn assured her.

Simon Court appeared from his office and he and Jack shook hands, who introduced Sarah and they were ushered over to the office. Jack started the paperwork required.

'We had the manager from your office here in yesterday,' Court said.

'Not my office anymore, but what was he after?' Lunn asked.

'Strangely enough probably a car, Jack,' Sarah said.

'He's got a company car, so not much reason for him to buy something else,' Jack replied.

'Nevertheless, it did appear he was more than window shopping.' Court replied.

'Well, he's not my responsibility anymore,' Lunn replied

With the paperwork out of the way, Jack and Sarah went out to the vehicle.

'Shall we go for a little drive?' Lunn asked.

Twenty-five minutes later they pulled up outside their home.

'Happy?' asked Sarah.

'I am,' Lunn said. 'I'm really looking forward to having the kids around on Saturday too. But, I really have to get some of the orders filled.'

Gem was in the kitchen having a snack when they got back. Sarah announced she was going to get on with her marking and lesson planning, so Jack took the chance to make a beeline for the shed.

Gem appeared a few minutes later.

'Mum seems pleased with the car.'

'You can't go wrong with a Volvo in your mother's eyes and thanks for your help with the order, mate. I'll just finish my bit and then we can take a swing at some of the flies for Florida. Come on I'll show you how to tie a Crazy Charlie.'


They'd been tying saltwater flies for about an hour when Jack's phone rang. It was Mick Sparkes, he was about five minutes away and was going to drop in. Lunn walked down to the house to meet him and collect another glass.

'Are you expecting somebody?' Sarah asked as she enjoyed a glass of wine, having finished her work. Jack got the glass down from the cupboard.

'Mick should be here in a couple of minutes.'

'Social call?'

'I'm assuming so. They should have had all the evidence bagged and tagged by now,' Lunn said.

'Well, don't go mad,' Sarah advised.

'A glass of beer hardly counts as a booze-up.'

'Make sure it stays at just a glass. He's got to drive home and you've still got to sort out food.'

'Bread, cold cuts, cheese, and pate doesn't take too much effort, love. But I'll try and make sure we don't turn Mick's visit into a bacchanalia.'


The doorbell rang and the dogs made a dash for the door, barking as they went. Jack and Sarah both scooped up a dog each on the way down the hall, opening the front door to find a tired looking Mick Sparkes, his shirt rumpled, and tie loosened.

'Hello, Mick.' Sarah gave him a kiss on the cheek. 'You look like crap?'

'Knackered, but on the way home,' Sparkes replied. 'You look good. Having Jack around the house full time obviously suits you.'

'Having someone do my cleaning and cooking certainly does. Though how his offering today of bread and cheese qualifies as cooking is beyond me,' Sarah said. 'I'll let him lure you up to that den of iniquity at the top of the garden and pour you a beer. I'll catch up with your lovely wife at school and we'll sort out a supper soon.'

'I'll let her know.'

Lunn handed him a glass and they walked back through the house and into the garden.

'I guess the investigation is complete?' asked Jack.

'Nothing out of the ordinary. The autopsy was pretty much what we expected.'

'Pretty much?' Lunn asked as they reached the shed.

'He hadn't drunk as much as we'd thought.'

'Enough to be drunk?' Lunn asked.

'Hello, Gem,' said Sparkes, as they made their way into the shed. 'Depends how much of a drinker he was and it was clear he hadn't eaten.'

'Is this the recently departed Max Lamont under discussion?' Gem asked.

Mick nodded.

'It doesn't take that much when you haven't eaten, Mick,' Lunn said, pouring a beer for the dishevelled policeman. 'How many times have you had a couple of beers on an empty stomach and felt like you'd had four pints.'

'You're right,' the DI said, taking the glass from Lunn and having a gulp of his beer. 'That does hit the spot and enough of work for today.'

'Take a pew. You look all in.' Gem advised, giving up her seat.

'Thanks, I am,' Sparkes said, as he slumped into the now vacant chair.

'Geoffrey must be happy?'

'I think he's just relieved the case is closed. That way he doesn't have you involved, or the Chief Super on his back.'

'He did seem a little hostile yesterday when I turned up at the house. Not sure why?'

Sparkes laughed wryly. 'Everything about you rubs him up the wrong way, Jack. He always envied the way you sifted through the evidence to solve a case. You also had a wife and kids and he wanted that life for himself.'

'He's got my ex, so that's punishment enough,' Lunn growled.

'Don't you think that grates on him. He also wanted the sort of relationship you have with Sarah's kids,' Sparkes took another mouthful of beer.

'All I have to do with Gem is give her a beer every so often and slip her the odd tenner.'

'A bit harsh, Jack. Accurate, but harsh,' Gem responded. 'He's a balding little man in a job that is beyond him and married to your ex-wife. That's a combination to screw up most people.'

'Poor bloke was always a bundle of neuroses, to begin with. No wonder he's so angry so often,' Lunn said.

'I had better get off,' Sparkes said, draining his glass and standing up.

'I'll walk you to the door,' Lunn replied. 'How did the wife take the news that her Max was dead, by the way?'

'Surprised, shocked, but calm.'

'Too calm?' Lunn asked.

'I think she was definitely shocked,' Sparkes said. 'I'm not sure what's going on with your list. Geoffrey has kept me out of the loop and it's not like I don't have other cases.'

'Loose ends, Mick. I hate loose ends.

'I'll try and find out what's going on.'

They left the shed and walked back to the kitchen, where Sarah was tidying up.

'Are you off, Mick? She asked. 'I'll buttonhole Rachel at work and we'll arrange that supper.'

'That would be great. Just so long as the two of you talk about something other than school,' the policeman replied.

'That's a deal,' Sarah said and then kissed him on the cheek.

Lunn watched Sparkes wearily climb into his car and drive off.

'Are we going to eat soon?' his partner asked.

'I thought we'd take the dogs for a walk and then sit down to eat.'

'That sounds good.'

'I'll give Gem a shout and see if she wants to come.'

Chapter 30

It was a bright Friday morning, as Jack limped up the stairs.

'Knee playing up?' Sarah asked as he returned to the bedroom.

'Yeah. I'll take some Ibuprofen later,' Lunn replied, looking down at the knee joint and the old scars.

'If you'd stop drinking red wine that would also help.'

'The slow erosion of the few small pleasures left to me continues.'

'It would stop you snoring too.'

'And now the lies begin. It was probably one of the dogs snoring,' Lunn answered, as he slipped back beneath the duvet.

Lunn picked up his book and glasses.

'Gem's coming with me this morning, but we'll be back by lunchtime and I want to get the rest of the flies tied for the guys going on the Florida trip.'

'Any plans for late afternoon and early evening?'

'Having had my last two fishing trips buggered up, I thought I'd take a walk on the beat and get a few casts in. It's going to be a lovely morning and I think we'll have a hatch this evening.'

Sarah was first into the shower, waking Eden up on the way, whilst Jack let the chickens out and sorted a few biscuits out for the dogs.

Fifteen minutes later Lunn was showered and shaved. Eden passed him coming out of the bathroom.

'Morning, love.'

'Bloody Gem's been using my towels,' his stepdaughter replied. She wasn't exactly a morning person.

'I'm sure she didn't mean to; it was probably just a simple mistake.'

'She's not a retard, Jack and does it deliberately to wind me up. She's being a dick.'

And with that she stomped off, slamming her bedroom door behind her. Lunn poked his head round Gem's door.

'You're up early,' he said to her. 'Leave your sister's towels alone.'

'What happened to my 'simple mistake' defence?' Gem asked, with a smile on her face.

'You blew it by being either a retard or a dick. Your sister's version of Hobson's Choice, smart arse,' he replied. 'I want to leave in half an hour, so get some breakfast.'

Sarah looked up as Jack came back into their bedroom.

'Has civil war been declared' she asked.

'We got a couple of days of peace you were being a little optimistic if you were banking on much more,' Lunn replied. 'What are your plans for the first day of half term?

'Well, Eden and I are off for a bit of Good Friday retail therapy and gem is staying with you, so A little peace and quiet may be possible.'


An hour and a half later Lunn drew up outside the tackle shop and rang the bell to the flat above. The owner opened the door a few seconds later,

'Good morning, George.'

'Morning, Jack,' the tackle shop owner said. 'Is this young lady, Gemma?'

'It is,' Lunn replied. 'Gem, this is Mr Wiseman, purveyor of fine angling products, a scholar and a gentleman.'

'Jack speaks highly of you, sir,' Gem said. 'It's a pleasure.'

'I've seen some of the flies you've tied, and the pleasure is mine. Now, can I see the order you brought with you, please.'

Gem handed the flies over.

The shop owner opened the boxes, balanced his spectacles on the end of his nose and examined the flies.

'I understand that you completed most of the order, Gemma?'

'Yes, sir,' she replied.

'Then you shall have a just reward.' The tackle shop owner reached into the corner behind his chair and picked up with a rod bag. 'This is for you.'

'Mr Wiseman, I don't know what to say,' Gem managed to squeeze out, as a huge grin spread across her face.

'You've rendered her almost speechless,' Lunn said. 'I'd have said that was nigh on impossible.'

'Gemma, this isn't a sale. This is a gift from Jack and I. We've included a reel and line, some leaders and empty fly boxes that we think will get filled up swiftly.'

'I'm truly grateful.'

'Get your stuff in the back of the car and I'll be out in a minute,' Lunn said, passing Gem the keys.

Once she had left the shop, Lunn turned back to George Wiseman. 'Have the Police been to see you yet?'

'I had a call from a detective, and they're going to come and see me at some point.' Wiseman replied. 'There didn't seem to be much urgency, to be honest.'

'They're pretty sure that they have their man. I'm guessing you're not a priority, just a box they have to tick.'

Jack said his goodbyes and went back to the car.

'Your mother's cooking her lasagne tonight?' Lunn asked.

'I'm still taking in the gift from you two. But, mum's lasagne as well, the day just gets better and better.'

'It's a very good rod, so listen to Steve Ingram when he coaches you. Learn good habits now and you won't have to have them coached out later.'


They got the usual boisterous welcome from the dogs when they returned to the house. Jack put some food out for them, whilst Gem made a sandwich for them both and before they went up to the shed accompanied by the dogs.

A couple of hours had passed before Sarah appeared in the doorway.

'I just thought I'd let you know we're back,' she said.

'How was town?' Lunn asked.

'Crowded, but we got what Eden was looking for. A minor miracle in itself.'

'Did you manage to wheedle any more information about the man of mystery boyfriend?'

'Not a single titbit. She's playing her cards very close to her chest.'

'I can't imagine where she gets that from.'

'Don't overstep the mark,' Sarah replied with a smile. 'I don't want my daughter making another mistake like last time.'

He stepped through the French doors into the kitchen as Eden appeared, hung about with a variety of bags.

'Looks like the shopping went well?' Lunn asked.

'I got exactly what I was looking for. Want to see?' Eden replied.

'Sure.'

Jack was given the full fashion show treatment.

'Looks like you've got some really nice stuff, love. I hope the new boyfriend appreciates it.'

'I'm going to see how Gem is getting on,' she announced. 'And I wish everyone would stop giving me the third degree about my love life.'

Chapter 31

It was about five o'clock evening when Jack pulled into the small car park, he'd come to twice in the last two weeks and each time previously coinciding with the discovery of a body.

He decided to change his routine, assembling his rod, mounting the reel and attaching the leader before setting off for the river. As it was warm and sunny, there was a real chance of a few fish rising to an evening hatch.

Taking out a couple of the dry fly boxes from the tackle bag, Jack stowed them in his fishing vest. He took out his sunglasses, gave them a polish and put them on, followed by his baseball cap. Lastly, Jack clipped his landing net on to the back of his fishing vest and locked the car.

After walking along the road, Jack turned right through the gate, making his way along the footpath and onto the bridge. He stopped for a minute or two and took in the river, before carrying on over the river to the far bank.

Deciding to return to the pool by the house, he walked past the Trophy Pool and bothy, before keeping low as he approached the spot at the bottom of the Lamont property. Edging up to a clump of balsam, he crouched down with his knee complaining at the discomfort.

There were one or two fish rising to a hatch of insects, so he stripped some line off the reel before making a couple of false casts to get the line out, then casting out towards where one of the fish had recently risen. The fly disappeared in a splash and Jack lifted into the fish, feeling the resistance as the fish bore away from him.

He could feel that the fish wasn't going to break any records, but after an empty net for the last fortnight he'd be happy with pretty much anything and concentrated on keeping contact with the trout. As it zigzagged its way upriver, Jack put some side strain on, and it darted back down the river to a spot below where he was standing, as he did his best to quickly recover line back on to his reel.

Before long the fish was tiring. Unclipping the net from the back of his vest, Jack extended it and placed it easily to hand, whilst manoeuvring the fish back up towards where he was. The net dipped and he smiled as the fish was his.

Placing it in the shade and wetting a hand to remove the barbless hook from the scissors of the trout's jaw, he returned the brown trout to the water. Holding it in the current gently, Jack helped the fish recovered some strength before it slipped off into the weed in the river. Jack washed his hands and stood up, looking around as a voice called out.

'You. Yes, you! What the bloody hell do you think you're doing?'

Lunn looked away from the man, who was now marching down towards the river from the gardens of the Lamont house and tried to see who he was shouting at. It dawned on him that he was the target of the question.

'I have a fishing rod in my hand, which might give you a clue,' Jack replied, recognising who it was for the first time and that the advancing figure was carrying a shotgun.

'Don't try and be bloody clever, you're trespassing. Now get off my land!'

Lunn took in the young man as he drew closer. Six feet tall, dark hair, well cut clothes from well-known labels, with a petulant look. A few years had passed, but he'd knew him straight away.

'Sebastian Lamont,' Lunn said, as he stuck out his hand.

Jack had often used the tactic to break any tension in awkward or threatening situations. Stick out a hand to most men and they'll automatically respond in kind. Sebastian Lamont was one of the exceptions however and he studiously ignoring the proffered hand.

'What if I am? Not that it's any of your business,' Lamont replied. 'Now get your stuff together and get off my fucking river, or I'll have you done for poaching and trespassing.'

'Please do call the police. I'm sure they'll be interested to find out if you have a licence for the shotgun and there are no signs up saying that trespassers will be prosecuted. That leaves the poaching,' said Lunn.

'I suppose you're a member of the syndicate then?' Lamont asked and then continued without waiting for a reply. 'I would have thought you'd have a little more consideration with our family's recent losses.'

'Your grandmother and father both knew me reasonably well,' Lunn replied. 'But I'm not a member of the syndicate.'

'So, you admit you're a bloody poacher then?' Lamont said taking a firmer grip on the gun. 'I'm sure the police will overlook my lack of a licence, when I explain to them that I had to use it to keep the poacher from running away.'

'My knee is in no condition to run anywhere, even if I wanted to,' Jack replied. 'And I've just released the fish I caught, so I'm no poacher. I've permission from your grandmother to fish here one day a week and I'm exercising my right by way of a tribute to her. It's interesting that you're referring to the house and gardens as your land, with your father not even cold in his grave and his will yet to be read. Don't you think you might be getting a little ahead of yourself?'

'Who the bloody hell are you anyway?' asked Sebastian Lamont.

'Jack Lunn. I acted for your grandparents when they bought and sold property for a good few years.'

'You're the one who came to our home.'

'That's me,' Lunn replied. 'You went to the same school as my step kids.'

'Who are?'

Lunn was pleased to see the gun being lowered. 'Gemma and Eden Bryce.'

'You're Gemma Bryce's stepfather?' Seb replied with a surprised note in his voice. 'I should just carry on and kick you off my land, poking your nose in where it's not wanted or needed.'

'Gem mentioned you came out on the wrong side of a run in with her. She's home for a few weeks, so you might bump into her some time,' Jack said. 'As for my visit here, I was just paying my respects.'

'Bit of a barrackroom lawyer are we, Mr Lunn? This is my family's land and we've had two people die here in the last week, so I really couldn't give a toss for your rights,' Sebastian Lamont replied. 'After what you've just said, I'd have thought you'd have enough respect for my grandmother to leave without creating a scene. Now be a good fellow and bugger off.'

'Barrackroom lawyer, not a bit of it,' Jack said. 'I'm ex-police and your grandmother was very kind to me over the years and I'm just respecting her wishes by fishing here.'

'You're being a pain in the arse. Now, sod off!' Sebastian said and then turned on his heel to walk back towards the house.'

'Not the first or last time that's been said to me. I'll be seeing you.'

The retreating figure didn't bother to acknowledge Jacks words, but continued back up the garden with the shotgun slung over his shoulder and mobile phone clamped to his ear.

Jack picked his net up, collapsing it and hooking it on the back of his fishing vest. The confrontation had left him a little unsettled. There was a thuggish, entitled streak to the young man. Sarah's kids had been spot on when they'd said that he was arrogant and felt he was a cut above everyone else. His carrying the shotgun was definitely a concern, but Jack had seen that it was broken and not loaded. But there was enough to inform him that Sebastian Lamont was a dangerous bully used to getting his own way. Jack looked back at the river, but the few minutes with Lamont Junior had robbed him of any enjoyment he'd have got from carrying on fishing, so he started to walk back along the river to pick up his car

A little under half an hour later Jack closed the gate from the footpath behind him and turned left along the road back towards the car park. A glimpse behind him caught a dark coloured car pulling out of a side turning and coming up the road towards him. He kept close to the ditch on his left, as he limped in the direction of his car.

The vehicle was almost upon him, before a change in its engine note made Jack take a hurried glance back over his shoulder, registering the dark shape speeding towards him in the evening gloom and Jack was dazzled by the lights on full beam.

He made a split-second judgement and dove to his left, the damaged knee barely holding up under the stress, as the car clipped his trailing tackle bag and spun him into the ditch.

Nettle stung and bramble scratched, Jack limped heavily back to the car park where a member of the syndicate was assembling his rod. Looking up as he approached, Lunn recognized him as Bob Stacey. A local developer who he'd worked with on and off over the years.

'Evening, Jack. What's happened to you?'

'I just took a tumble into a ditch.'

'You okay?' Bob asked. 'You look shaken.'

'Just getting old,' Lunn replied, still a little dazed and shocked by the near miss. 'How're things with you?'

'Good. Just going to put in for planning on a nice residential site.'

'Really, where?'

'Those disused light industrial units the Lamont's have had for years.'

'Who put you onto them?' Lunn asked, doing his best to hide his surprise.

'The grandson,' Bob replied. 'By way of your manager in the village.'

'Not my manager, mate. But good to hear he's putting you up for work,' he replied.

'Ah, the rumour's true then. You're not there anymore,' The developer said. 'He told me that they were going to knock down the old buildings and go for residential. It's a brownfield site, so they have a good chance of getting it.'

'The grandmother had always said she was going to keep the units as they were,' Lunn said. 'I told her husband years ago that they'd get planning if they wanted it. But they never did put in for it.'

'Well, the remaining family are all for it apparently and who am I to argue,' the developer said, picking up his rod. 'Mind you, I've had to give that manager a decent drink.'

Stacey saw the disapproval register on Lunn's face and changed the subject quickly. 'Any tips on fly choice, Jack?'

'I picked up a fish on a Pale Evening Dun,' Lunn replied, passing one across. 'Tied it myself.'

'Thanks.'

'How much did you have to pay him to get the land, Bob?'

'More than five hundred and less than a grand,' the developer replied somewhat shamefaced and tried to explain. 'It's more common than you think, Jack. You were always straight down the line, but that's the exception rather than the rule. So long as you got the best price for your client and the new houses came back to you to sell, you were happy.'

'Just make sure that you keep your wits about you with that one.'


Lunn packed his rod and reel away, stowing the rest of his gear in the boot of the Volvo. He thought about the near miss with the car and information he'd garnered over the last hour.

The old lady and her son were barely cold and the remaining family was running roughshod over the grandmother's decisions, whilst very quickly claiming ownership of the old lady's property. That near miss with the car could just be a coincidence, couldn't it?

Jack fumbled through his pockets to find his mobile, but Rhona Blacklock wasn't picking up. He left a message and called Mick Sparkes.

'I've just had a bit of news fall into my lap that might add to the Lamont case,' Lunn said.

'What case, Jack? It's closed.'

'Yes, I know the case is closed. But I think Rhona would be grateful of it anyway,' Lunn said. 'I've just bumped into an old acquaintance, who's a developer and the Lamont family have put some property up for sale that I know would have been directly against Elizabeth Lamont's wishes.'

'Jack, what they do with their inheritance is up to them.'

'The wills have barely been read and probate hasn't been granted, but the vultures are already circling, Mick. Make the Detective Chief Superintendent aware, please.'

'Okay,' Sparkes replied. 'Rhona's taken Geoff Cooke to the cleaners over hauling the poacher in.'

'Geoff will be blaming me for that, so keep your head down, Mick.'

'Will do. Oh, I've got a DC to call Mr Wiseman and they're going to meet with him at some point.'

'Look, why don't you and I go and see the old neighbours soon, as Rhona suggested?'

'I'm pretty tied up and Geoff isn't going to want you and me swanning around the place, stirring things up.'

'Rhona said that she wanted this watertight and so you'll just be tying up loose ends,' Jack retorted. 'I thought that at least some the names on that list would have been spoken too by now.'

'Let me see what I can do.'

'Thanks and keep in touch.'


Chapter 32

Jack's return home raised eyebrows.

'No dead bodies this time?' Eden asked, as she walked down the stairs to join her older sister. 'You look like you've been dragged through a hedge backward.'

'It's a new style I'm trying out,' he replied. 'I did bump into the rather live and objectionable Seb Lamont.'

'Really? Did he speak to you?' Gem asked.

'More like shouted and was generally bolshie. Calling me a poacher and trespasser, whilst trying to throw me off the river.'

'I hope you told him to bugger off,' Gem replied.

'Not in so many words and he asked to be remembered to you,' Lunn replied with a wink

'I'll bet he did,' Gem said. 'Last time he saw me I put him on the deck for being a dick.'

'It's nice to know that those judo lessons paid off and he's taken to referring to Mrs Lamont's house as his and carrying a shotgun like he's the lord of the manor.'

'I hope he didn't threaten you?' Eden asked. 'Was it loaded?'

'No, it was all for show. You guys were right about him being a bully,' Jack said. 'I'll get my stuff in.'

'What happened to you?' Sarah said, appearing from the direction of the kitchen and looking him up and down. 'You're all scratched up and limping.'

'I just took a tumble, love,' Lunn replied. 'Didn't see a rabbit hole.'

'Jack's been confronted by a shotgun-wielding madman, Mum. He should have a drink to steady his nerves,' Gem said.

'Let's not gild the lily too much.' Lunn interrupted. 'I just bumped into Seb Lamont, who was less than inviting when it came to me being on the river.'

'Go and take a bath and some painkillers for your knee,' Sarah said. 'Dinner won't be long.'

Rhona Blackwell called, as Jack was walking upstairs.

'You left a message, Jack?'

'I think there's some additional information you might find adds a little more background to the deaths of Elizabeth and Max Lamont,' he told the senior officer.

'Go on.'

'I was trying to have a few casts this evening and bumped into Sebastian Lamont by his grandmothers house,' Lunn replied.

'Not unusual, surely?'

'Toting a shotgun and being quite aggressive.'

'Not a cosy bankside chat then?'

'Hardly,' Lunn clarified. 'But it was more that I found his whole attitude disturbing.'

'In what way?'

'His grandmother and father aren't even in their graves and he's playing the Lord of the Manor.'

'The foolishness of youth, Jack?'

'Maybe. But then I was talking to one of the local developers and he's given to believe that some brownfield site that Elizabeth Lamont would never have sold is now coming to the market and that Seb Lamont is behind the sale.'

'That is a bit pushy, particularly when the wills haven't yet been even gone through probate yet.'

Jack decided to keep the near miss with the car under his hat for the time being.

'Just so long as you remember that you're no longer DI Jack Lunn. Whilst you're a highly valued member of the I.A.G, you leave policing to us. Is that fair enough?' the DCS said. 'Let's meet at The Blue Lamp at about half-past twelve tomorrow and you're buying.'

'It'll be my pleasure; I'll have a drink waiting for you.'

'Good enough. See you then.'

Jack put his phone away and turned to Gem, who had joined him. 'You say nothing about this to your Mother, understand and by the way, I didn't take a fall from stumbling into a rabbit hole.'

'What happened?'

'I was walking along the road back to the car park and some idiot ran me off the road.'

'What? It got a bit close to you?'

'No, I mean that if I hadn't jumped into the ditch I wouldn't be here,' Lunn replied. 'The car clipped my tackle bag. When I get a hunch about something, I'm seldom wrong. Why would someone try to run me over if the case is closed?'

'Who do you think it was?' Gem asked. 'Liam Galletly?'

'I didn't get even a glimpse at who was driving.'

'Are you sure it was deliberate.'

'I just have a feeling,' Lunn said.

*'By the pricking of my thumbs, something wicked this way comes,'* Gem replied.

'You can always rely on Mr Shakespeare.'

Chapter 33

Lunn nudged the sleeping body and Gem pulled the duvet down from her face.

'You look like something from The Walking Dead. Late night was it?' Lunn asked.

'I think it was about two-ish,' She replied, getting out of bed and shambled a few steps. 'Let me have a run and shower and I'll be with you.'

'Good. We have some work to do.'


Jack opened the shed and was soon joined by Gem, who made a start on the task in hand.

They worked quietly and quickly to produce the patterns.

Sarah appeared at just before eleven.

'How's it going?'

'Nearly done, love,' Lunn replied, easing himself out of his chair to take the opportunity of stretching his legs during the interruption.

'You look tired, Gem,' her mother said.

'Late night. No biggie.'


An hour later, Lunn was showered, shaved and dressed as Eden arrived with Grace, closely followed by Abi.

'I see you girls made your own arrangements for getting picked up,' Lunn remarked.

'I had some stuff to do this morning,' Emily replied. 'Eden volunteered to pick little sis up.'

He went back to the kitchen and took the pork joint out of the fridge, leaving it on the side in the kitchen, out of reach of the dogs. After retrieving his keys from the table. Jack shooed the kids and Sarah out of the front door. Jack and Sarah trailed the kids, as they talked animatedly and headed towards the pub.

'Mum's not very happy with you,' Grace announced, once they caught the group of youngsters up.

'So, no change there then,' Lunn replied.

'You've been embarrassing Geoffrey, Dad,' Abi weighed in.

'Geoff doesn't need any help from me.'

'He's not as bad as you make out,' said Grace.

'And he's not as good as he could be,' Lunn retorted.

'To be fair to your Dad, he did stop the police charging an innocent man,' Gem intervened.

'And as Martin Luther King said, *injustice anywhere is a threat to justice everywhere*,' said Lunn.

'Oh God, Dad!' Abi said. 'Next you'll be saying that *'with great power comes great responsibility'*.'

'And so it does,' Lunn said smiling. 'Let's move on to another and more pleasant subject.'

When they got to the Waterloo Arms, Gem and Jack made their way over to the bar, whilst the others looked for a suitable table. There was a small, but rowdy gaggle of young men, with what appeared to be the ringleader was holding forth, his back to Jack and Gem.

So where have you been, Liam?' one of them asked.

'A bit of business out of the area, that's all.' Galletly said, drawing a wad of cash out of his pocket and ordering more drinks.

'Must be nice to have a few bob, especially when you've only been out of jail a couple of weeks,' Jack whispered to Gem.

'He could have got the money from selling the old lady's rings,' Gem replied.

A couple of well-muscled men filled the bar space between the two parties. Jack recognised them as Neville Hayes' sons, Nick and Tim.

'Put your cash away, you're not impressing anyone,' Tim said.

'What's it to you?' Galletly replied, half turning to see who made the remark.

'Didn't you get a year for trying to rob old Mrs Lamont?' Nick remarked.

Liam Galletly slid off his stool and faced the pair, a waft of stale sweat and beer coming from him. 'Who the fuck are you two?'

'They're my sons, Liam,' Nevile Hayes said, as he arrived at the bar. 'Why don't you answer Nick's question?'

'So, what if I did?' Galletly spat back angrily. 'I've served my time.'

'I'm sure the Police will want to have a friendly chat with you about the murder of Elizabeth Lamont,' Neville replied. 'You're probably best off just turning yourself in, nipper.'

Jack saw fear in Galletly's eyes, as he recognised who was doing the talking.

Neville continued. 'When I say chat, I mean interview.'

The other local lads all made an effort to create some distance between themselves and Liam.

'You should listen to Mr Hayes, Liam,' Jack said. 'That's good advice he's giving you.'

'You lot don't scare me,' Galletly said loudly. 'I've got a perfect right to be here.'

'No, you haven't,' the Landlord said. 'You and your mates here are all barred, starting now.'

'It's time for you to leave,' Nick Hayes said. 'Or we can discuss it outside if you like?'

'I'd go quickly if I was you,' Jack said.

As Galletly made his way from the bar, he brushed past Jack.

'Yours,' he muttered, nodding to where Jack's daughters and Eden were seated.

'Not that it's any of your business.' Jack replied.

'They're filling out nicely.'

Lunn saw anger flash in Gem's dark eyes and as she moved forwards, Jack threw an arm out to bar her way.

'What are you going to do, girly?' Galletly spat out.

'I've put bigger and better men than you on their backs.' Gem replied.

'I'll bet you have,' Galletly said with a leer. 'You might be a bit on the skinny side, but I'd do you a favour too.'

'I'd rather go to bed with Ebola. The trouble with drunken oiks like you is that their mouth is always bigger than their dicks.' Gem parried.

'One more word out of you and I'll have the Police here,' Jack intervened.

Galletly leant in towards Jack. 'You'll regret this.'

They watched him retreat out of the pub.

'Nasty piece of work,' Neville said, then turned to Jack. 'You should get back to your family, Mr Lunn. I'll get some drinks sent over for you.'

'That's very kind of you,' Jack replied.

'We don't want his sort in the pub, spoiling our lunchtime, do we?'

'His sort?' Lunn asked.

'Ex-jailbirds,' Neville said with a wink. 'Lowers the tone.'

'What was that all about, Jack?' Sarah asked as they brought the drinks over. 'And wasn't that Liam Galletly?'

'It was and it was nothing, he'd just had too much to drink.'

'He was a spiteful thug at school. A bully and more than happy to prey on the weak. You stay away from him, Jack. And why did I hear mention of Elizabeth Lamont?' she asked. 'He must have been a suspect, having tried to burgle her house?'

'He lives with his mother, but the Police say he hasn't been there for the last few days.' Lunn clarified. 'He's on a list they're supposed to be following up.'

'But as Geoff is convinced the son did it, I'm guessing they're not in that much of a hurry to work through that list,' Grace chimed in.

'Can we talk about something else?' Eden requested.

'Good idea,' Jack replied, raising his glass. 'Cheers everyone, it's nice to have you all together for a while.'


An hour later and the family made its way back home. The girls taking over the family room, as Gem went to the shed to get on with some work. Jack busied himself with the pork joint, scoring the skin and rubbing in salt to get a good crisp crackling.

Cooking your family a roast dinner was one of life's true pleasures, he mused. It wasn't something the Lamont's would be enjoying anytime soon, but then it wasn't probably something they probably ever really enjoyed Jack thought, as he put the pork on a trivet in the roasting tin.

On the occasions when he'd come across them socially, it always struck him that they were on their best behaviour. The wife always made sure she spoke to and knew the right people. There was something else that he recalled, there are usually tell-tale signs and unconscious manifestations between a couple of their affection for one another. If they existed in the Lamont's marriage, they kept them very well hidden

Max had got an attractive, some would say borderline beautiful wife and Imogen Lamont had taken a big leap up the social ladder by hitching her wagon to the son of the local landowners. The children had followed the usual path of schools, which was where they'd crossed paths with Sarah's kids. Jack and Sarah had become accustomed to seeing them at the usual round of school plays, carol concerts and Summer Balls before the children had grown up and left for university. Now they occasionally bumped into them in the village, but it occurred to Jack how he didn't see them together that often. Social occasions yes, but every day was a rarity. But then the same could have been said of his own marriage.

The Lamont kids got the new cars, the right holidays, but then they took what could only be thought of as easy option courses at university and got jobs which had a career path that seemed to have a mainly social aspect, rather than anything else. Then Jack realised that on the odd occasions when he and Sarah had been guests in the Max Lamont's house, the only photographs of the family had been formal portraits. There were none of the informal pictures that littered their own home. It was a bit 'all fur coat and no knickers' as his own mother would have said.

He poured himself a beer and took a stroll out through the French windows and on to the patio.

If Max Lamont was a murderer, why had he waited so long to kill his mother and what was his motivation? He was going to inherit anyway, and he'd seemed to be the dutiful son to the outside observer. With the change to the old lady's will and the children and wife giving each other an alibi for the timeframe of the murder, Max was always going to be top of the list when he couldn't or wouldn't account for his whereabouts. But Jack couldn't shake off the impression he'd got from bumping into Max on the High Street Who else could it have been?

Sarah emerged from the shed and walked down the garden.

'Can I ask you a question?' he asked as she came back into the kitchen.

'Fire away.'

'Did the Lamont's strike you as a happy family?'

'What a strange thing to ask,' she replied. 'It's difficult for any outsider to really know, but I would say that it wasn't necessarily a love match and she always struck me as a bit of a cold fish.'

They walked back into the kitchen. Jack put duck fat into a roasting pan and slipped it in the oven.

'I just wanted to get your take on their relationship. You've known them longer than me and I wondered if you got the same vibe about them,' Lunn said, turning the water off under the potatoes and parsnips. 'What were the kids like when they were younger?'

'Bratty, very aware of being part of a well-known family in the area and feeling they had some sort of droit de signeur over other children,' said Sarah. 'And there were always some of the kids who were happy to reinforce that point of view, just to be accepted into their circle.'

'I suspect Gem and Eden didn't succumb?' Jack asked, draining the potatoes.

'Gem has never been impressed by position or wealth and Eden had her own circle of friends. They met at parties when they were at school, but had nothing more in common other than geography really,' she replied. 'What's bugging you? The police have closed the case, they seem convinced that Max killed his mother, then died in a drunken fall and yet you seem to want to keep picking over it?'

'I'll be honest. Max doesn't appear to stack up as a killer to me. He wasn't anywhere near the forceful characters that his father and mother were and although he doesn't have an alibi, when I saw the man in the High Street, he was beside himself.' Jack sprinkled ground semolina over the potatoes and parsnips, then gave them a good shake before putting them in the hot fat and transferring them into the oven. 'Why go to the trouble of bumping off your ancient mum, if you're relatively well-off anyway and you're going to get the old dear's dosh in the end? It just doesn't add up to me.'

'Jack, you're always like this when something has got under your skin. Like one of the dogs with a bone,' Sarah said.

'I don't know why I keep coming back to it. The case is closed, but there's just this nagging feeling that we don't know the whole story. When I spoke to Max after his mother was killed, he just looked stricken and I can't dismiss that.'

'Let sleeping dogs lie,' his partner said.

'You're right, though you've overdone the canine metaphors. Now would you do me a favour and set the table?' Lunn asked, shooing her out of the kitchen.

About an hour later he dished the meal up and Sarah took the serving dishes through, as the girls came to the table and a shout up to the shed brought Gem jogging down the garden.

With wine on the table and the food circulating the chat returned to the murder. Jack wanted to know what the kids had been like, as Eden and Gem had gone to the same schools.

'You've seen the film *Mean Girls*,' said Eden. 'Georgina was Queen Bee. She had all the boys chasing after her and a lot of the girls fighting to get into her inner circle. We saw her when Grace and I dropped in on Abi yesterday, she was buying underwear for her boyfriend.'

'What? She was buying boxer shorts?' Lunn asked.

'No, Dad,' said Emily. 'She was buying lingerie.'

'How do you know she was buying it for a boyfriend?'

'There are rules on underwear, Dad. If it's practical or pretty, women buy it for themselves. If it's sexy, then it's being bought for a lover or a hot date,' Grace explained.

'That was more information than I needed, but thanks for the explanation ladies. For your information when men buy underwear for themselves, we only ever buy practical?'

'What was the son like, Gem?' Lunn asked.

'A player,' Emily said before Gem had a chance to reply.

'And you know this how?' Jack asked.

'I've seen him in town. One of my friends fell for his patter and he slept with her,' Emily said. 'Then didn't call her. He's tried it on with me too. Good looking, loves himself just a little too much and he likes it rough apparently.'

'Seb Lamont was a nasty piece of work at school. He was a typical rich kid. Bit of a bully, who knew the cost of everything and the value of nothing and not that bright. Can you pass the potatoes?' Gem added.

'Gem had a run in with him,' Eden said.

'He liked to pick on the younger or smaller kids. He made the mistake of picking on one of my friends,' his partner's eldest daughter said, helping herself to a couple of roast potatoes. 'Those judo lessons paid off when he tried to bully me.'

'And you got suspended for it,' said Sarah.

'We don't have real money, Mum, and he does. That counts at some fee-paying schools and so I got a little lesson in economics,' Gem replied. 'But, he didn't ever trouble any of my friends again.'

The subject of the Lamont's was dropped, and the conversation swirled around the table as the meal was finished. Jack cleared the plates away into the dishwasher, brought out a cheese board. He smiled as the family talked, teasing each other, gossiping, passing plates and knives around. Sarah looked over and winked at him.


Jack volunteered to take Grace back home.

Pulling up outside the house he'd formerly called home, Jack walked his youngest daughter to the door. As they exchanged hugs the door was opened by his ex-wife.

'Come on in, Grace,' she said and as Lunn made to follow. 'Not you, Jack.'

'Always a pleasure to see you, Marianne and what's the reason for tonight's hostility?' he replied.

'I don't want you in the house. Geoffrey is in the conservatory having a drink. In fact, he's had several. You're the main cause and not for the first time.'

'I would imagine he's celebrating. Considering that the police believe the case is now closed,' Lunn said, trying to lighten the mood.

'Not before you embarrassed him though,' she said angrily.

'He embarrassed himself,' Lunn said. 'He nicked the poacher with only circumstantial evidence. If he'd completed the investigation, rather than going off half-cocked, he wouldn't be drowning his sorrows.'

'He's got the Chief Superintendent giving him a hard time about the poacher and for not getting a confession from Max Lamont before he died.'

'And that's my fault how?' Lunn asked incredulously.

'Geoffrey always seems to be following in your footsteps. He gets judged by your standards, Jack.'

'I have pretty low standards, Marianne and it's not like I've ever seen it as a contest.'

'But others do. Rhona Blacklock for one, Mick Sparkes for another and your own kids, Jack.'

'I can't speak for Rhona and Mick, but Geoff married you and the kids came as part of the package. Being a stepfather isn't all beer and skittles.'

'He's tried to be a father to them, Jack.'

'That's why Abi moved out, Marianne. She has a father and doesn't need another,' he snapped back. 'She certainly didn't need to be lectured by Geoff in the home she's lived in all her life. What he should be doing is supporting you.'

'And I suppose that's what you and Sarah do?' his ex-wife said angrily. 'Just keep out of his way, Jack.'

'Sarah and I try our best and of course, we don't get it right all the time. Look, the case is closed, so I've no reason to bump into him. But tell him Liam Galletly is back in the area.'

'I'll tell him,' his ex-wife said. 'And you keep your nose out of Geoff's case.

'Always happy to oblige,' Lunn replied and with that, the door was shut in his face.

Chapter 34

'Was that Grace?' Cooke asked as Marianne came back in the conservatory.

'Jack just dropped her back.'

'Did you say anything to him?'

'He's her father, Geoff. We have to talk.'

'I'll bet he couldn't wait to tell you about my situation,' Cooke responded glumly.

'I brought it up, actually,' she replied. 'And the situation was of your own making.'

'Oh, that's right, side with your ex.'

'I'm not siding with him, Geoffrey. But you have screwed up here and that's not Jack's fault,'

Marianne retorted. 'If you're honest with yourself, he just pointed out that you had the wrong man.'

'And didn't he enjoy every minute of it.'

'Well, don't give him another opportunity and stop feeling sorry for yourself. You know what

Jack's like and he feels involved in this case. Your case, Geoffrey.'

'He's not a bloody copper anymore,' Cooke snapped back. He took another swig of whisky. 'It was

bad enough when he was, always butting into my investigations and having Rhona's ear.'

'Then get him onside,' she replied. 'There aren't many people he doesn't know in the Forest, so in

the future use him. God knows, he's single-minded when he gets something to focus on. He told me

to tell you that Liam Galletly is back in the area, by the way.'

'He keeps bleating on about these other suspects. Galletly is one of them and I've got a couple of

DC's looking into it, but I'll kick them up the arse to get it dealt with,' Cooke said.

'No loose ends,' she reminded him. 'Look, Jack doesn't mean to, but he can get pretty oblivious to

what is going on around him if he's concentrating on something.'

'I know that's part of what caused you to break up, but why do you feel you have to be nice to

him?

'It wasn't his fault. I knew who I was marrying, and I knew how a case could consume him,'

Marianne replied, picking up her glass of wine she sat down next to her husband. 'When he got injured, I watched as he went through those operations and the rehab with such determination that he was going to get back to be an operational copper. Then his brother dying and leaving him the business. Realising that he wasn't ever going to be a policeman again and throwing himself into making a success of his new career.'

Geoff reached across and took his wife's hand.

'He thought he was doing the right thing for the kids and me, but I wanted more,' she continued. 'I wanted to be the centre of his attention and he really only had time for his work and the kids. It wasn't right what I did and I'm not proud of it.'

'Well, you won't find me making the same mistakes he did.'

'You need to focus on consolidating your new promotion, now this case is closed,' Marianne said, squeezing his hand. 'I know you don't like him, but if you're clever you'll work with him in the future.'

'Like you do?' Cooke asked.

Marianne smiled. 'Exactly, not that it's always easy.'

'I don't know why, but just the sight of him winds me up.'

'And don't you think he knows that?' she asked. 'Don't bite, love. That's my advice.'

Chapter 35

Sarah took one look at Lunn when he came back to the house.

'Bumped into the ex, did we?'

'Is it that obvious?' he said.

'She still knows how to press your buttons, Jack. What was it this time?'

'Poor Geoff is getting heat from above and that's apparently my fault.'

'Silly woman. He'll get over it.'

Lunn smiled. 'His problem is he doesn't know what his role in that house is.'

'Luckily that is not a problem for you, kitchen bitch. Now go and poke your head in on Gem. She's been working on the orders you had, and another came in today.'

'As you command.'

Gem was hunched over and adding the final touches to a Pale Evening Dun, her dark hair hiding her face and all her attention focused on the work in hand.

Jack watched and then she must have sensed him.

'Nearly finished, Jack,' she said, without looking round.

'Good,' Lunn said, producing two glasses with a flourish. 'Emerson said that 'The reward of a thing well done is to have done it'. I prefer a more practical appreciation.'

'Are you worried about the scene in the pub with Liam Galletly?' Gem asked.

'I know you're more than capable of looking after yourself. His sort is usually all piss and wind, bullying weaker kids and hitting women. But that wouldn't rule him out of killing an old lady who'd got him locked up. As a local, he'd possibly know about her morning and evening walks. As you pointed out, that wad of money he had could easily have come from selling Mrs Lamont's rings.'

'And Max?

'It could be just a fall and his confession wasn't really a confession at all,' Jack replied. 'Just an unfinished letter or message. I get that the Police have so few resources and are under pressure to get results, but there are still questions I'd want answers to first.'

They returned to the house just as Abi was getting ready to go, pulling on her coat and looking for her keys

'Thanks for lunch, Dad. I'm sorry I can't stay.'

'My pleasure, kiddo,' Lunn replied, giving his daughter a hug. 'Next time, maybe?'

Chapter 36

Sarah nudged him, as he sat on the bed the next morning.

'What?'

'Stay away from the river for the time being,' she ordered.

'Why?'

'Just do as I ask.'

'I have a right to fish there, Sarah. And some over-privileged upstart with an ill-deserved superiority complex isn't going to stop me.'

'You're a stubborn man at times, Jack Lunn.'

'I like to think more along the lines of determined and single-minded, thank you,' he replied, trying to lighten the mood.

'You can think what you like, but you can be stubborn. Which is not necessarily a strength by the way,' she said. 'I don't want anything happening that affects this family, Jack.'

'I know, I know. I'll stay away for a week or so until things settle down a bit. Has anyone ever told you, you can be a bit of a nag?'

'No one that lived for very long. Why?' she asked.

'Just that I was going to tell you that you're wise beyond your years and your advice is always welcome.'

'Good choice. What are you up to today?'

'Gem and I have the last few flies to tie for the group coming tonight. Plus, we have a couple of orders to complete and Rhona Blacklock has asked to meet up for lunch today.'

'Left the best till last, Jack. What does your old boss want with you?' Sarah asked.

'I don't know until I see her. She said a few days ago she'd call, and we'd have a catch-up.'

'Are you going to tell her about your meeting with the Lamont boy and that Galletly is back in town?'

'I think I should, don't you?' He replied, knowing that Rhona was already in the picture.

'Another good choice. Two in one day, Jack, that must be a record,' Sarah said, raising an eyebrow. 'Hand whatever information you have over to Rhona and step away.'

'Only record-equalling, my love. There's the day I made the decision to go to that Ball and then to ask you for a dance.'

'Ever the silver-tongued charmer,' she said, snuggling up to him.

They let Eden sleep in.


Jack met Gem in the hall, as she was coming in from her morning run.

'Just a heads up that your Mum knows I'm seeing Rhona today. But I've told her she's asked to see me,' Lunn informed his stepson.

*'Oh, what a tangled web we weave.'*

'Just trying to keep her from worrying,' Lunn said. 'Have you done any of your shrimp and crab fly designs for later yet?'

'I've got a couple more to do. Give me enough time to have breakfast and a shower and I'm all yours.'

Sarah came back in through the French doors and announced that the chickens were all well, fed and watered.

'Are you two ready for your, damn, what's the collective noun for a group of fishermen?' she asked.

'A tackle? An exaggeration?' The two men offered.

'Don't forget that there is housework to do whilst I'm out,' she reminded them. 'What's the point of having a dog and barking yourself?'

'Wait a minute. I have flies to tie, a meeting at lunchtime and then a group of potential buyers coming this evening,' Lunn protested.

'That gives you this afternoon to put your pinny on and get the hoover out,' Sarah explained. 'And have you forgotten your place here?'

Jack tugged his forelock and affected a West Country accent. 'No Ma'am, thank'ee for allowing me up from below stairs.'

'This is what happens when you're too kind to the hired help, Gem. Let it be a lesson to you.'

'Best keep him on though, mamma. He's a capital cook,' her daughter replied, in her best posh voice.

'Well, if it's okay with you landed gentry, I'm going to jump in the shower,' Jack said. 'Get some breakfast and then we need to get a move on, young lady.'


Jack was already working when Gem arrived at the shed.

'What are you going to tell your old boss?' she asked. 'Are you going to tell her about your near miss?'

'I'll leave that out for the moment. I'm not completely convinced there's a connection.'

'You don't think the Lamont deaths are as cut and dried as the Police, do you?'

'It just doesn't feel right. Plus, meeting young Master Lamont the other day and nearly getting run over has only reinforced that feeling,' he replied. 'What am I supposed to do, keep my mouth shut?'

'Not in your nature, Jack. I know you have to tell Rhona. Just so long as you're going to stay in her good books.'

'All I've tried to do point them in the right direction, letting them do the work and take the credit.'

At about twelve, they'd finished getting ready and Gem said she was going to take a lunch break and then maybe meet Mark to talk about some tweaks to the website.

'No problem. I'd better walk down to the pub and meet Rhona.'

'Starting to regret opening that can of worms, are we? Gem asked.

'Not at all. I'm happy that she values my opinion.'

Chapter 37

As he left the house, Jack stood on the porch for a moment. He set his shoulders and started off towards The Blue Lamp, wishing his leg wasn't playing up quite so much and at the same time knowing that the brace had prevented a worse injury from the near miss with the car.

DCS Blacklock was pulling into the car park as Lunn neared the pub. Going inside, she found them a quiet corner, whilst Lunn went to the bar and bought the pair of them a soft drink.

'Let's get on with it then,' she said.

'My step kids went to school with the two grandchildren and they're not nice, from what I can gather,' Lunn continued. 'Then, as you know, I had the run-in with the grandson yesterday. Also, Liam Galletly is back in the area, so has he been spoken to yet? He was waving a large bundle of cash about in here and we know that someone stole the old lady's rings.'

'I'll remind Geoff to get him interviewed.'

'He's a drunken thug, Rhona and he got barred from here, for which he blamed and told me that I'd regret it.'

'Not the first time you'll have been threatened by a drunk, Jack.'

'You're right about that,' Lunn replied with a wry smile. 'However, after my frank discussion with young Lamont, I was walking back to my car when someone tried to run me over. I ended having to dive into a ditch.'

Rhona looked shocked. 'Now you're pulling my leg.'

'No, I'm pretty certain that the car was aiming for me,' Lunn replied. 'So why, if Max is the killer, did someone else try to kill me?'

'Come on, it could be just bad driving?' Blacklock speculated. 'You were in your usual fishing stuff, so not exactly standing out from the surroundings.'

'If I hadn't jumped in the ditch, it would have hit me, Rhona and my gut tells me it wasn't just dodgy bit of driving.'

'Let's put that to one side.'

'You weren't the one picking yourself out of a ditch and whilst I might not have been wearing a high-viz jacket, it was no near miss in my opinion. I told you about the developer and the industrial units he'd been told are going to be up for planning and this is all coming from the remaining family members.'

'I know it seems a bit presumptive of them, with the probate still ongoing. But they are almost certainly going to be the beneficiaries.'

It just feels like too many coincidences.' Lunn replied. *'Once is happenstance. Two is coincidence. Three times is enemy action.'*

'I knew there was a reason why I put you at the top of the list when we set up the Independent Advisory Group for the New Forest,' Blacklock said.

'And there was me thinking it was my dashing good looks and connections.'

'Well, the connections went a long way, but it was you having been a copper that was the most important thing,' she replied. 'It's fine having local landowners, Verderers, businessmen, Uncle Tom Cobbley and all. But they don't think like we do, Jack and it's a real help having someone on board who sees things from coppers perspective.'

'So, not the good looks then?'

'I appreciate what you've done over the years. Crime rates in the Forest are at an all-time low, even with the cutbacks. In no small measure is that down to some of the initiatives, like the Safer New Forest Partnership and the efforts to reduce animal R.T.A.'s that you and the I.A.G. have helped introduced.'

'I appreciate the pat on the back, Rhona,' Lunn replied. 'Just sense that there's a 'but' coming.'

'The problem is that it's all just a bit circumstantial and the grandson has an alibi for the night his grandmother was killed.'

'Being alibied by your mother is flimsy at best and it doesn't stop me thinking that we're not seeing the whole picture. And there are at least three other parties who had a reason to take some sort of revenge on the Lamont family.'

'It's Geoff's case and he's closed it. The son killed the mother and was in the process of typing out a confession, then, pissed as a fart, he takes a header from the top of the stairs and breaks his neck,' she concluded. 'I'll mark Geoffrey's card about the other three though. Get him to dot all the I's and cross all the t's. I don't suppose that you got the registration or a look at the driver of the car that clipped you?'

'Sorry, no. I was too busy picking myself up out of the brambles. It was dark blue or black, that's all I got,' Jack replied. 'Back in the day, If I'd come to you with what I'd just told you, what would you have said?'

'Apart from, the case is sodding closed?' Rhona replied, shaking her head. 'You and your bloody hunches. You know what I would have said. Keep digging.'

'So, will you take this up?' He asked.

'I've already said that I'll get Geoff on to it,' she replied. 'But remember, Jack. You're not a copper anymore. Whilst we thank you, as a concerned member of the Independent Advisory Group, Geoff is in charge of the case and he considers it closed. So, that's the end of it.'

'Why, because it'll screw up the figures?'

'Don't push me. You know how this works, this was Geoff's case and how would it look if I re-open it without something concrete to go on? We don't have the resources with all of these cutbacks, so we can't go off on a wild goose chase. But I took this meeting because you have good instincts and you were right about the poacher.'

'I got enough grief about that from Marianne, thank you very much,' Jack replied.

'Geoffrey a bit miffed is he?'

'I got an earful from her about it, so he's not leaving it at the office.'

'I had to bollock him for cocking up on the poacher's arrest,' the DCS confided.

'I'm sure I'll get the blame if he ends up being moved to supervising pencils at Headquarters.'

'It's not as if we've had an advance in forensics on an old case to be able to go back over the evidence Your information offers nothing new to go on. We don't have anything new to go on and unless something else new comes to light, that's the end of it.'

'Are you saying that, if some new evidence came to light you'd be happy to re-open the case?'

'We'd have to. But that doesn't give you carte blanche to swan around poking your nose into every little corner,' the DCS said.

'I promise all I'm doing is talking and listening to people.'

She laughed. 'On the first day I met you, still wet behind the ears, I told you that this job was mainly listening and asking questions.'

'Best advice I ever got about being a good copper and actually, it's served me pretty well elsewhere too.'

'My official advice is to leave well alone,' Blacklock said, finishing her drink. 'Right about now is when I wish it was twenty-five years ago and I'd be ordering my second glass of wine.'

'Well, I'm trying to stay off the booze during the week. A moment on the lips and a lifetime on the hips, so I'm led to believe.'

'Helps with the knee, does it?'

'The less weight I'm carrying, the easier it is on the knee.'

'One of the worst days on the job when I heard you'd been hurt.'

'Wasn't great for me either and it got worse,' Lunn said. 'All those months of rehab and all they could offer me was a desk job.'

'I know it was rough at the time, but the rest of your life hasn't been so bad.'

'The divorce wasn't great, but I've got Sarah now. Even the redundancy has probably come at the right time,' he replied. 'I'd had enough of property and I loving working with Gem on the fly-tying. She's having her first casting lessons tomorrow.'

'I've got to get back to the office, as I'm drowning in paperwork these days and the thin blue line is ever thinner,' Blacklock said, pushing her chair back. 'If you do find anything out, call me. But do me a favour and make sure it's solid.'

'I need answers to a couple of questions,' he asked.

'Fire away.'

'Was there a search on the mobile masts and was anyone in the area of Mrs Lamont's house at the time she was believed to be killed?

'We did and Max Lamont's phone went dead shortly after he left the office, though he was heading in the general direction of his mother's house. What's the second question?'

'Didn't it seem funny to you that Max's confession, if that's what it was, consisted of just two words on a laptop? A laptop which could have been accessed by anyone.'

'The post-mortem didn't come up with anything suspicious. Forensics have come up with nothing, so we have to take it on face value,' Blacklock replied. 'If you've got any other questions, ask Mick.'

'Thanks for listening.'

They walked back to her car.

'Don't do anything silly,' Blacklock said. 'I don't want to end up with you getting nicked for stalking. I'll remind Geoffrey to work your list.'

They shook hands and as they separated, the police officer turned back to Jack and smiled. 'We've had enough death around here for a while, don't you think?'

'You'll get no argument from me on that.'

Chapter 38

Walking home, Jack mulled the conversation over. It was plain that the constraints on manpower in the Police meant that they'd be unlikely to act on the information he'd supplied with any sense of urgency. Geoff Cooke had this case off the books and a nice, neat clear up on it. But Rhona had confirmed she'd always trusted Jack's instincts in the past and that, so long as he stuck to talking to people and kept within the law, she'd consider at any new evidence he turned up. That gave him a little latitude.

He turned back down the road where he lived.

'Hello again, Jack,' a female voice called out.

He recognised it and turned to find Adele Porter with a slight smile on her face.

'You're like the proverbial bad penny,' he said.

'Another meeting with DCS Blacklock?'

'We're old friends and how did you know.'

'They've got another dead body on their hands and she's in charge of Major Crimes, so it's worthwhile tailing her. Then she went into your local pub, I took an educated guess about who she was meeting. Turns out I was on the money.'

'Both the cases are closed.'

'Really?' she replied, 'You don't think the son killed his mother any more than I do. Everything I've been able to find out about him screams 'I'm not a killer' and you're still poking around, aren't you?'

'Why should I trust you?'

'We both think there is still a killer out there and we want justice for the old woman.'

'It's not enough, particularly with your track record,'

'Point taken.'

'Listen,' Lunn replied. 'You will never get a quote from me and should we discuss anything, it's off the record. Understood?'

'You have my word.'

'Then keep doing what you're doing and I'll do my thing. Maybe, at some point, we can talk and compare notes.'

'Deal.'

'Look at the various disputes Mrs Lamont had over the years, including a court case over a boundary dispute. Then there was a builder who lost everything, killed his wife and himself, leaving a young son behind. Lastly, a local yobbo caught trying to steal from her house,' Lunn advised.

'I read about her holding Liam Galletly at gunpoint. I've got to give it to the old girl, she had balls,' she said. 'There's no sign of Liam at his mother's place.'

'You didn't doorstep her?'

The journalist shrugged her shoulders, 'I was doing what any reporter would do.'

'I'll bet you got short shrift.'

'Language that would make a sailor blush.'

'He's back in the Lyndhurst area somewhere,' Jack replied. 'Adele, if you try and screw me over, I will make sure that working in this area is no longer an option for you.'

'I'm not going to mess this up, Jack.'

'Make sure you don't,' Lunn replied. 'You know how to find me, or at least so far you have.'


The house was locked when he got home and the dogs corralled in the kitchen. Jack had a few hours to spare so called Steve Ingram.

'Hi Steve, just thought I'd touch base and see if we're still on for Avington?'

'Jack, good to hear from you, but I'm going to have to put Avington off for a few days.' Ingram replied. 'Nothing for you to worry about, just some last-minute business I need to take care of. Can I call you in a day or so?'

'No problem. I've got some people over looking at our saltwater flies this evening and if they order, we will need a couple of days to get that done.'

Good luck with that and I'll catch up with you soon.'

Chapter 39

Gem was sat in one of Lyndhurst's many café's with Henry when she saw Imogen Lamont walk past.

'Come with me,' she said.

'Why?'

'It's time to steal a phone.'

'No problem. Whose phone are we nicking?'

'Imogen Lamont's,' Gem replied.

'Why?'

'Because I want to hack it.'

'Good enough.'

'You take it and I'll do the rest.'

'What if she recognises me?' Mark asked.

'Doubtful,' came the reply, as they made their way out of the coffee shop. 'It's years since she's seen you.'

They followed Imogen Lamont down the High Street. She went into the butchers.

'Odds on she'll be coming back up towards the car park,' Gem said. 'All you need to do is just going to knock into her and get her to drop her bag. That should give you a chance to get her phone.'

'Oh, like I'm the Artful Dodger?'

'I'm confident you have skills. Now go and look interested in a shop window and do as I've said.'

As predicted, Imogen came out of the butchers a few minutes later. Henry barged into her, knocking her bag to the ground, with the contents spilling out.

'Sorry, love,' he said in a dodgy London accent, as he bent down to pick up the shoulder bag.

'You should look where you're going, you idiot!' she retorted, grabbing the bag from him and checking that her purse was still there. 'Now get out of my way.'

Smiling at her now retreating back, Henry fished in his pocket for the object he'd taken, giving Gem the thumbs up.

'Are you sure that you can hack this?' he asked, after crossing the road back to his friend

'It's a doddle, mate. We did this all the time in Afghanistan,' Gem replied. 'I just get access to the C7 network interchange service and all we need is her mobile number. I'll just call my phone from hers and that will give us the number. Erase the call from her records and then catch up with her to return her phone. Tell her she dropped it. Once I've done the hack, we can see her every movement, read her texts and even record her calls.'

'Has she got a passcode on the phone?' Henry asked.

'No. Her generation seldom does. This isn't a contract phone though, it looks like a Pay As You Go.'

Gem swiftly called her own mobile and then wiped the call from Imogen Lamont's phone and handed Imogen's phone back to Henry.

'I'll see you at your place,' he said and then hurried back up the High Street after the phones owner.

He caught up with her just as she turned left into the High Street car park.

'You dropped your phone, love.'

'What? My phone?' She rummaged quickly in her bag and then took the phone.

'You dropped it,' he said, noticing there was another mobile in the woman's handbag.

'I didn't drop it,' she replied. 'You nearly knocked me over and it must have fallen out of my bag.'

'Well, no harm done,' he replied and then turned back towards the High Street and Gem's house.

Chapter 40

Out on the patio in the sunshine, Jack was thinking about the killings. The first important step was that he thought of them as killings. The police just had one as a murder, but he wasn't anywhere near so certain. However, there was no clear evidence that Max Lamont's death was anything other than a fall, so he was back to square one. He sat, turning facts and assumptions over in his mind and trying to find an angle, reason or motive for what had happened.

His train of thought was broken by the sound of the front door being opened, which sparked the dogs to life as they sprinted back into the house. Dom and Mark emerged from the house and on to the patio.

'Spill the beans then, Mr L. How did it go?' Mark asked.

'Surprisingly okay. Rhona's basically told me the case is closed, but that if I find anything that looks like new evidence they'll take a look at it,' Lunn said and watched a conspiratorial glance shared between the two young men

'She didn't think the argument you'd had with Seb, the car near miss and the news about the redevelopment was relevant?' Gem asked.

'She understood why I think they aren't seeing the full picture, but they have to go with what scant evidence they have and that appears to point at Max killing his mother, then taking a fall whilst under the influence.'

'Are they following up on the other people you put in the frame?'

'I'm not holding my breath, Gem,' he replied. 'Geoff seems happy that they have their man and will get around to it when they have time, maybe.'

'What did she say about the car?' Mark asked.

'She didn't put any weight behind it.'

Gem looked sceptical. 'So, is that the end?'

'Well, that was the interesting part. She's basically telling me that they don't have anything solid to work on. Look, she trusts my instincts and encourages me to carry on talking to people,' Lunn continued. 'Warned me not to cross any lines. No stalking or invading people's privacy.'

'Sounds like your old boss wants you to keep snooping, Jack,' Gem advised.

'Yes, but I'll need a hand if you feel up to it?'

'I'm game, what did you have in mind?' his partner's daughter asked.

'I'm still mulling that over. Oh, we're going to have to put Avington off for a few days.'

'I think we may have something that will help us keep tabs on Imogen Lamont.' Gem said.

'What have you done Put a tracking device under her car, slipped a bug into her handbag?' Jack replied with a smile.

'All a bit James Bond, don't you think?' Gem retorted. 'Something much simpler.'


'You did what?' Jack asked, reacting to what Gem and Henry revealed to him.

'It was dead easy, Mr L,' Mark replied. 'Gem had it hacked in half a minute.'

'I'm not interested in how easy it was. It's illegal, you pair of dimwits!' He snapped back. 'Journalists have been locked up for this. How did you get hold of her number?'

'She hadn't pass coded her phone,' Mark said. 'It only took a few seconds to transmit her number to Gem's phone and then erase the call.'

Lunn turned to Gem. 'So, we've got theft and phone hacking have we?'

'Well, technically it wasn't theft, Jack. I had no intent to permanently deprive.'

'Oh, and I'm sure the Judge is going to entertain your discourse on semantics. Right up until they lock you up and that would sit so well with your mother,' he replied. 'Didn't it occur to you that what you were doing could have compromised any future investigation?'

'We just borrowed it for a couple of minutes and then gave it back to her,' Gem explained. 'And the truth is that there is no real ongoing investigation.'

'And you didn't think that there was a possibility that she'd recognise you?' Jack asked Henry angrily.

'She wouldn't know me from Adam,' Henry replied.

'We got some interesting stuff off her phone, Jack,' Gem chipped in. 'There are a number of calls to a particular number for about a week and then no more to that number. Then another number starts being called. Every week or so the same pattern and I'm sure the phone we got hold of is a Pay As You Go.'

'She had another phone in her handbag.' Henry explained. 'I just nabbed the one I could.'

'That does sound like calls to burner phones,' Lunn replied. 'And Pay As You Go phones are untraceable. Very interesting indeed, except that none of this would be admissible. You're a pair of idiots, albeit with your hearts in the right place. It is interesting, but she has at least some form of an alibi for the night her mother-in-law was killed.'

About an hour later Gem rather sheepishly came and found Jack in the shed.

'Don't give me another speech about just wanting to help,' Lunn said.

'I thought it seemed like a good idea at the time.'

'And now you've had a chance to contemplate a little?'

'Not one of my best moments of blue sky thinking, but we picked up burner phones all the time in Afghanistan. We soon learned to use the Dark Web to crack and clone them.'

'This isn't Afghanistan, Gem and you've broken the law.'

'I get that and I'm sorry. Sometimes I forget that civilians have rules.'

'Now I get why you don't talk about your time out there.'

'In the military it's a different set of rules. It's just about getting the job done and protecting your people.'

'Well, like it or not, us civilians have rights.'

Gem nodded. 'Mea Culpa.'


Jack and Gem spent the following hour going through their materials and ordering stock online.

Having sent an order off, they had a final tidy up of the workbenches.

'I've been having a think about what to do about the calls on Imogen Lamont's phone and young Master Lamont,' Lunn said.

'Go on.'

'Do you fancy keeping tabs on him?'

'What, follow him?'

'I'd like to know what he's doing, who he's meeting. Maybe it was him that had the untraceable phone his mother was ringing,' Lunn replied. 'I'm also going to see if I can get a look at the two files on the deaths from Mick. I'm pretty sure I can twist his arm to let me take a peek at them.'

'What do you hope to find out?'

'No idea, but most criminals are creatures of habit and that's how they get caught. Maybe a fresh pair of eyes will find something.'

'Looking for a pattern?'

'The organized ones are more difficult and this killer, or killers, seems to be very organized. Let's assume that one, maybe two persons killed both of them. There was no frenzied attack on either

Mrs Lamont or her son, so the killer or killers took real trouble to avoid leaving forensics behind. Like putting the old woman's body in the river, where any clues were washed away,' He explained. 'Also, she was hit just once and there were no signs of a violent struggle with Max. He did enough to do the job and no more. Didn't leave a weapon on site and took the trouble to mislead the Police with the fishing net. Other than the tracks in the grass the police couldn't get anything else. No imprints of footwear, nothing.'

'And statistically it's more likely to be a man, of course,' Gem replied. 'But what makes you so sure that it wasn't some random act?'

'No. This was planned. It was someone who knew the old lady's movements and I'd bet a pound to a penny they have to be a local,' Jack said.

'The family have an alibi.'

'It's pretty weak as alibi's go. Where was Liam Galletly? Where is the builder's son and what were the old neighbours up to? If I was in charge of the investigation we'd keep looking.'

The dogs barked in the house.

'Sounds like your Mum and Eden are back; we'd better go and help unload the car. Have a think about what we've talked about, Gem. But don't ever go off piste like that again, understand?'

'I promise,' Gem replied. 'And I'd love to have a snoop around, and I'll have a chat with a few people and see what I can come up with.'

'The basics of good policing and intelligence. Talk to people and be a good listener.

His partner and her daughter appeared to have emptied the contents of the supermarket into the back of Sarah's old Volvo and it took a few trips to bring all the bags into the kitchen.

'How was your meeting, Jack?' Sarah asked.

'Just a catch up with an old colleague,' he replied. 'You should come and inspect the shed. It's never looked so spic and span.'

'Let's go and look at the fly factory then,' Sarah said.

Sarah and Eden were impressed at how clean and professional looking the inside of the workshop now looked.

'I think you two will do fine this evening,' Sarah said.

'It looks amazing and the flies look great,' Eden followed on.

Jack and Sarah retired to the patio.

'When are these guys coming?' She asked.

'About six, love,' Lunn replied. 'We can eat afterward.'

A little after six the group entered the shed and shook hands with Gem, as Lunn introduced her.

'Gentlemen,' Lunn began. 'How many of you will be going on their first trip to Florida?'

Jack and Gem sat back in their chairs after their guests had left, nursing half a glass of beer.

'Have you looked at the orders?' she asked.

'We did okay, didn't we?' Jack said with a smile.

'Of course,' Gem replied. 'We'd better get back inside and have some food.'

'Good idea,' Lunn said, standing and flexing his knee. 'Time for some pasta, bring the glasses would you.'

'Jack?'

'Yes.'

'What are we going to do about Seb Lamont?'

'I've had some ideas, so let's talk tomorrow morning.'

Chapter 41

Lunn was already in the shed the next morning when Gem ambled in, wearing her running kit.

'I saw the light on. You're up early,' the young woman said.

'Looking to get ahead on this order and we have some work to do if we're thinking that there's still a killer out there.'

'You said you had some ideas?'

'First, I just want to absolutely rule out the rest of the family and let's start with the gun-toting son. Does he know what you look like now?'

'My hair's longer and he's not seen me for five or six years. I doubt he'd recognise me and if I keep changing my appearance, he shouldn't catch on.'

'As you know, the first thing is not to be spotted, to begin with,' Lunn said, finishing off the fly he had been working on. 'He's not expecting to be followed and working together will make it easier to keep him in the dark. As he's met me recently, you'll have to be the main tail.'

'If he gets too close, I'll swap with you and change how I look to take over again,' Gem said.

'That takes care of us on foot. When we're in the car, that's my call.'

'What'll I need to take with me?'

'A reversible jacket, a couple of different hats, sunglasses, that should give you enough looks.'

'Do you have headphones for your mobile?'

'Sure, good idea,' said Lunn, taking a drink of his coffee. 'Go and get your run in and I'll do some work first?'

'We can do a drive-by of the house and check he's still there, then lay up and wait to see where he goes. Surveillance work is mostly sitting around with nothing happening and we may get nothing for days if anything at all.'

'Now you understand why my old boss isn't willing to commit any resources to something like this,'

'It must just eat up man hours.'

'As far as they're concerned, they have a closed case. Why would they even bother sticking a tail on someone they don't even consider a suspect? Now, let's get some work done.'


Jack put various hats and coats in the back, along with a couple of bottles of water.

'Now I know why you picked out a 4x4,' Gem said.

Lunn smiled. 'Go on.'

'No one notices a 4x4 in the Forest,' she replied. 'Have you thought about where to park up?'

'There's a side road close to the house and before you get out on the main road. 'We'll park up there, keep a Mark One Eyeball on the target and wait until he moves. I'll call Mick Sparkes on the way, I need some more information from him and try to get a peek at those case files if possible.'

The DI didn't pick up Jack's call, so he left a voicemail.


'You know what to do?' Lunn asked Gem. 'You remember all your training?'

'Never look directly at the target. Use windows and reflective surfaces when you can, glance if you have to. Use peripheral vision and partial barriers and don't follow too closely. If we're on foot, you stay behind of him and on the opposite side of the road. I'll tail him, as he's less likely to be looking back and if he gets ahead of you or stops and goes into a shop or bar, you cross back over. Then do a walk past where he's gone in, check he's in there and then let me take over at the front. That's when change your appearance, pop the sunglasses on, hat, reverse the jacket, take the jacket off.'

'Nothing much like the cop shows then.' Lunn said, with a smile. 'Now, there are binoculars in the glove compartment. Assuming young Sebastian is in, your job is to keep watch and let me know when it looks like he's going to leave.'

'What are you going to do?'

'Have a nap. I was up earlier than you and I'm pulling rank.'

'Hang on Jack, how can you pull rank when you're an ex-DI?'

'And what was your rank in the job?'

'I was a Captain in Military Intelligence.'

'Ah, but this isn't Military Intelligence and it's my stag, so it's my rules,' he replied, with a wink.

'I'll give you that,' she replied.


Sebastian Lamont's BMW M3 convertible was parked on the gravel driveway outside the family home, so they turned into the side road about 50 yards away from the property. He turned the car around so they would see if anyone left the house.

'Shouldn't we have coffee and doughnuts?' Gem asked.

'I'm sure you had a ready supply of them when you were on covert operations. Put some music on and keep the binoculars handy.'

Two fruitless hours later they called it a day. Gem had spotted the target a couple of times when he came out to collect something from the back of the car.

'I really hoped he'd do something,' she said, disappointedly.

'Come on, you've done tons of surveillance. The bonus is that we haven't got a ton of paperwork to do waiting for us and we didn't have to submit a risk assessment before we went out.'

'Seriously, is this what Police obs are really like?'

'Nothing like yours, by a country mile. It's a lot of sitting around and a ton of paperwork. Nothing like the Sweeney. No tearing around the streets, tooled up and having punch ups with villains, then spinning someone's drum and shouting, 'You're nicked, you slag''.

'Did you ever tear around the streets, tooled up, fighting blaggers, Jack?'

Jack chuckled. 'Softly, softly, catchee monkey was more my approach. I did the driving and firearms courses. But what I was good at was getting a feeling about a case, digging clues out, making connections and getting people to talk to me. Seeing the bigger picture. *'Festina lente'*, as my old Latin master would have said.'

'Hasten slowly. Not much option with your dodgy knee though, is there?'

'Cheeky beggar. Let's get back and tie some flies and we can give Seb another go tomorrow. We just keep at it and stay patient. *All men commend patience, although few are willing to practice it.'*

Jack's phone rang.

'It's Mick,' he said to Gem and then answered the call. 'Mick, thanks for calling back. I've got an address for Mrs Lamont's old neighbours.'

'I'm not even going to ask how you got that,' Sparkes replied.

'Nothing underhand, I promise.'

'As you sold them the house, would you do the introductions and get me in to have a word with them?'

'I might not be flavour of the week, after what happened.'

'It'll just be a chat, background and that sort of thing. You know. I can play the 'good cop' at your expense,' Sparked replied. 'I'll be with you in twenty minutes

Chapter 42

'Their house is just along here on the left,' Lunn pointed, slowing the car down and then having to sharply stamp on the brakes, as a dark blue hatchback shot out of the driveway.

'Someone's in a hurry,' Sparkes said.

'Well, let's find out who then.'

The door was opened by a tallish grey-haired woman in her mid-fifties.

Jack recognised her straightaway.

'Mrs Brownlow, I don't know if you remember me? Jack Lunn?'

'I remember you. Who's this?' nodding towards Mick Sparkes. 'And what do you want?'

'This is DI Sparkes and he's looking into the death of Elizabeth Lamont. We were hoping that you could spare us a few minutes. It's just a formality. The Police are trying to speak to as many people who knew her.'

'So why are you here?' she asked Lunn.

'As you know Jack, I thought it might be a good idea for him to tag along. A friendly face,' Sparkes Interjected, showing his ID. 'It's just a chat, nothing formal.'

'I suppose you'd better come in then,' Mrs Brownlow replied grudgingly and opened the door fully.

They followed her from the hallway, through the kitchen and into a large conservatory, where a man sat in a wheelchair.

'I suppose you'll want tea?' she asked.

The man in the wheelchair took both the men in, said nothing and returned his attention to the TV in the corner of the room. Mick and Jack sat down at a small dining table.

'Please don't excite my husband. He's been in that wheelchair since the stroke. We have carers in to help me, now that our son's got his own place,' she nodded towards her husband. 'But he's pretty much a fulltime job.'

'Was that your son we saw as we pulled up?' Lunn asked.

She nodded. 'He comes and sees us almost every day unless he's away working.'

'He looked like he was in a hurry when he left?' said Sparkes.

'A work meeting, I expect,' she replied and then asked the two men how they took their tea.

'This shouldn't take too long,' Jack reassured the woman. 'But I wonder if you can tell DI Sparkes a little about Mrs Lamont and why you stopped being neighbours.'

'I won't mince my words, as she was the reason we moved. That damn boundary dispute is the reason he's in a wheelchair.'

'What happened?' Sparkes asked.

'It was a lovely house, as you'll remember.' she replied, looking at Jack for confirmation.

'I remember you viewing the place and the plans you had for it,' he said.

She nodded. 'We were building some additional garaging. Nick, our son, was getting to an age where he was going to take his driving test and get a car. We both had cars, plus visitors, that kind of thing.'

'Go on,' Sparkes urged.

'Tim wanted to put up a new boundary fence and some hedging at the same time, only the builders took the old fencing down and took nearly a metre or so of extra land, which smoothed out a slight kink in the existing fence line. Of course, Mrs Lamont noticed straightaway and was on to us to restore the boundary.'

'Why didn't you?' Lunn asked.

'If it had been up to me, we would have. But, my husband offered her money to leave things as they were. Well, it was like a red rag to a bull and the next thing is we have a civil action started against us.'

'That would have been a good time to wave the white flag, surely?' Sparkes remarked.

'You don't know what my husband was like, Inspector. He's usually a very reasonable man, but he had a stubborn streak in him.'

'But he was in the wrong here,' Lunn said. 'It was never going to end well for you.'

'I don't need you to tell me that. Tim wouldn't speak to a solicitor about it. He just banged on about the line on the Land Registry plan being the equivalent of at least a metre and it wasn't like they didn't have plenty of land to start with.'

'How did you get on with the Lamont's before that?' Sparkes enquired.

'Cordial, but hardly more than acquaintances. I'd sometimes join her for a walk along the river and we'd talk about the children. Nick was at the same school as her grandchildren.'

'How did your son take it when your husband was taken ill?'

'He was devastated, Inspector. He and his father were, are very close, and it didn't help that Nick found him. There was no need for any of this to have happened. I know that Tim was bloody-minded about it, but she needn't have been so vindictive. It could all have been dealt with civilly.'

'So, you felt it was Mrs Lamont who decided to escalate things?' Jack asked.

'You know the reputation she had.'

'What happened then?' Lunn asked.

'I sorted that damn fence out and at some cost. Then my husband had a stroke. Stress, the doctors Said. No doubt brought on by the court action. He was Nick's idol and reduced to a wheelchair, which Nick blamed the old woman for. That left us with really no option but to move.'

There was a moment's silence.

'Can you tell me what you were doing last Friday in the evening?' Sparkes asked.

'I have a husband to look after,' she replied testily.

'And it was just the two of you?' Lunn enquired, exchanging a glance with Mick Sparkes.

'I have a nurse come in the early evening to help me get Tim ready for bed, then it's just the two of us.'

'What about your son?'

'What about him?'

'Do you know where he was?'

'He has his own place, Inspector and no, he wasn't here. Probably working, or with his girlfriend.'

'Do you mind asking him to give me a call?' Sparkes asked, handing a card over. 'What does he do, your son?'

'Event management. He travels all over.'

They all sat in silence for a few seconds.

'I think we've taken up enough of your time,' Lunn said. 'Thank you for the tea and I'm sorry about what happened to Tim.'

'Some might say that he got what was coming to him,' she replied, looking over at the figure in the wheelchair. 'And some will say the same about Elizabeth Lamont.'

'Just a couple more things. You said that Nick went to school with the Lamont children?' Sparkes enquired.

'Yes?'

'Were they friends?'

'He and Seb were in the same year and were close.'

'Are they still friends?' Lunn asked.

'Nick took what happened to his father very hard but didn't blame Seb for it. He knew who caused his father's stroke.'

'And how did you feel about old Mrs Lamont?'

She looked over at her husband in his wheelchair. 'That's a stupid question. How do you think I felt. That woman put my husband under so much stress that he's now an invalid for the rest of his life.'

'Who put the floodlights up, Mrs Brownlow?' Lunn asked.

'That's enough questions. I need to look after my husband.'

'And the fly-tipping?'

'I'll ask you to leave now, please,' she said politely but firmly.

'We may need to talk to you again,' Sparkes said. 'You have my card, please ask your son to call me soon.'

They were ushered out of the house.


Once they were back in the car, Jack turned to Mick.

'Well, what do you make of that?'

'I can understand her harbouring a grudge against the old woman, but she is caring for her husband pretty much full time so probably wouldn't have had the opportunity. What was that about floodlights and fly-tipping?'

'At the height of the dispute, the Brownlow's put up floodlights pointing at the Mrs Lamont's house and someone fly-tipped a couple of loads of rubbish on the driveway.'

'So, it all got a bit out of hand. No wonder she wanted us out of the house sharpish.'

Jack nodded. 'As soon we started pushing her, she gave us the bum's rush.'

'We? It was you doing all the pushing. I thought it was going to be a nice cozy chat, but I suppose I should know you better.'

'All I'm saying is their son was tight with Seb Lamont and both mother and son blamed Elizabeth Lamont for the husband being in a wheelchair. It could have been her, it could have been her son or even the pair of them?'

'Why would they blame Mrs Lamont though? It was the husband who moved the boundary and then dug his heels in, so causing all of this.'

'I'm not so certain. My recollection of them was that she was the decision maker. When they bought that house, she was the one saying what they were going to do to it.' Jack replied. 'Maybe she was the one who was behind all of this and deflected her guilt at what happened to her husband on to the old lady?'

'That's a stretch, even for you.

'As a great detective once said, *'When you have eliminated the impossible, whatever remains, however improbable, must be the truth.'*

Sparkes chuckled. 'Even I know that one. Good old Sherlock.'

'You'll sort out the son?'

'All part of eliminating the impossible.'

Chapter 43

Having dropped Mick back at his car, Jack drove home and joined Gem in the shed, telling her about the conversation with the Brownlow's.

'I remember Nick,' Gem said. 'Never really understood why he was part of the crowd around Seb, as he seemed a decent enough bloke.'

'Sometimes it's all about being in with the 'In' crowd?'

They worked without interruption until Eden came up, telling them that food was nearly ready and they should come in.

'How's it going?' Sarah asked as they sat down to eat.

'We've nearly finished the first order for the Florida trip and Mr Wiseman's sent an order in for the tackle shop, so we're going to be busy,' Lunn replied.

'Where did you disappear to for a couple of hours?'

'There were a few things we needed for the orders, so we needed to get them pronto.'

'Are you going back to the shed after dinner?'

'We'll be an hour or so at the most.'

'Okay but call it a day then and come and watch some TV.'

As they walked back up to the shed after the meal, Lunn turned to his partner's daughter. 'I hate to lie to your mum, but it's best she doesn't know what we're doing.'

'I get that. What's the plan for tomorrow?'

'We need Mr Wiseman's order filled by lunchtime tomorrow, which gives us a reason to deliver it and do a bit of surveillance on Sebastian Lamont. I've still got to drop off the company car at some point and that might give us an opportunity to do a bit of evening snooping. I'm sure there's something the Police have missed.'

'The devil is in the detail.'

Jack called Mick Sparkes.

'I need a favour.'

'What?'

'I'd like a look at both the case files if that's possible?'

'You know those aren't supposed to leave the office.'

'See what you can do for a member of the I.A.G., please,' Lunn asked. 'Are you around tomorrow?'

'Do you want to meet up?' replied Sparkes.

'I'll call you and we'll sort out a time.'

'Okay. I'll see you then.'

Jack looked over at Gem.

'Let's get some of this done tonight. Tomorrow is going to be a busy day.'

'You do an hour or so and then go and spend some time with mum,' she advised.

An hour past as they worked and other than the occasional request to be passed something, silence reigned.


Lunn poked his head around the family room door where Sarah was busy marking.

'You up for a glass of wine, love?' he asked.

'Please. Have you finished?'

'Yeah, Gem will be about another half an hour or so. Anything worth watching on TV?'

'Have a look and choose something,' she replied. 'I'll be finished soon and Eden's not going to be back until late.'

'Everything under control with your orders?' she asked.

'We'll be a bit busy for the next few days, but Gem's a great help,' Jack said.

'What are you up to tomorrow?'

'We've got to deliver the order to Mr Wiseman and drop the first order off for the guys going to Florida,' Lunn replied. 'Oh, and I might drop the company car off tomorrow evening. But, Gem can do that with me. What about you?'

'Eden and I are meeting Grace for lunch in Hythe. There's a nice restaurant on the marina there and then we might go shopping in Lymington.'

'Sounds like you have a busy day planned too,' Jack said, as he flicked through the channels until he came across something acceptable. 'Have you managed to wheedle anything out of Eden about the new boyfriend?'

'Not a peep,' Sarah admitted. 'It's not like she's being cagey about him, she just plain refusing to discuss him.'

'She hasn't said anything to my girls. Gem hasn't seen anything on her social media that would give us a clue and let's face it, she's far more likely to turn up something than you or me,' Lunn confirmed. 'Is it something to worry about?'

'I don't know,' she replied. 'I just want her to be happy, but this is out of character for her.'

Jack sat in bed, later that night, ostensibly reading his book, whilst pondering what to do about keeping tabs on Seb Lamont. Due to the amount of work coming in, they had the same manpower issues as the police.

He tried to read a few pages, but couldn't focus as his tired brain tried to re-order the murder puzzle, knowing that he had pieces missing.

He recalled a Victor Hugo quote, *'Per angusta ad augusta'*, Through difficulties to great success.

Chapter 44


Standing in the kitchen the next morning just after five o'clock and he'd not slept well at all. Jack wrapped the dressing gown more tightly around himself and struck out across the lawn for the shed.

'You were up early?' Sarah said, when he returned a couple of hours later with a cup of tea for her.

'Couldn't sleep,' he replied. 'So, I've been working.'

'Are the chickens okay?'

'They're fine and I've got a got chunk of the next order done,' Lunn said, as he put his knee brace on, then slipped on his jeans.

'Are you going to give Gem a shout?'

'No need, she'll be up for her run in a minute.'


An hour or so later, with Gem beside him and their order in the back, they drove to Minstead and parked in a side road close to the Lamont home. Lunn sent a text to Mick Sparkes and shortly after their arrival he pulled in behind them. Gem moved to the back seat, so that the DI could sit next to Lunn in the front.

'What the bloody hell is this, Jack?' Sparkes asked. 'Vigilante surveillance.'

'We're just parked up having a little rest. Nothing sinister. Rhona gave me chapter and verse about what boundaries I shouldn't cross.'

'So, you're just pushing them as far as you can?'

'That's one interpretation; I prefer to think that I'm exercising my full rights as a citizen,' he replied with a smile.

'You're pushing it.'

'Did you bring the case files?'

'You know this could create real problems for me?'

'And you didn't bring them without Rhona giving you the okay, Mick. Your arse is covered and my lips are sealed.'

Sparkes handed over the files.

'How well do you know the case notes?' Lunn asked.

'I was in on two out of the four interviews, the mother and father.'

'Who did the son and daughter?'

'One of the DS's, but Geoff Cooke sat in on the interview. There are no inconsistencies, Jack,' Sparkes said. 'The mum and kids have the same story for the night the old lady was killed as their alibi.'

'So, Max Lamont refused to say where he was, only that he was driving around in the Forest. That tallies with what he told me and is where, conveniently, we have little or no CCTV. He goes to the trouble of turning his phone off shortly after he leaves his office in Romsey and doesn't turn it back on until he's home in Minstead.'

'I reckon that about covers it.' Sparkes replied.

Jack read through the statements and then passed them to Gem.

Sparkes started to protest.

'Mick. I've handled stuff marked Top Secret. In fact, I wrote some of the Top Secret stuff,' Gem said. 'I've signed the Official Secrets Act, so my lips are sealed.'

Sparkes didn't look to happy but nodded his assent.

'Okay, the first thing that stands out to me is that the statements are remarkably similar,' Gem mused.

'I know what you're getting at,' the DI replied. 'They seem almost rehearsed. But the fact is, they were tucking into a takeaway from the curry house at the time given for the old lady's killing. As they were all together and doing the same thing, there's not much surprise that their statements read the same.'

'I get that, but that they are so similar makes them feel a bit iffy, that's all,' she replied.

'Are you just reading too much into it?' Sparkes asked. 'What about Max Lamont?'

'I'd have bet a month's wages that he wasn't the type,' Lunn replied. 'What was he up to when he dropped off the map for a few hours that night?'

'Killing his old mum according to Geoff Cooke, simple as?' Sparkes replied.

'The kids were asked if they were in relationships and they answered no. Not surprising in young Seb's case, as I understand he's more a one-night stand merchant.'

'Yeah, I heard he's a bit of a lady's man,' Sparkes replied.

'The daughter has a boyfriend, according to my information,' he revealed, explaining about Georgina Lamont's lingerie buying.

'So, you're going with your girls' interpretation of women's underwear buying habits,' Sparkes said. 'Pretty tenuous at best.'

'You underestimate female intuition at your peril, Mick. But my first focus would be Sebastian Lamont. Applying to get that planning underway so quickly certainly shows a cold-heartedness and lack of empathy.'

'So, he's got some character flaws. But does that make him a killer?' Sparkes asked.

'No, I'm just saying he shows some interesting behaviours,' Lunn continued. 'This wasn't some spur of the moment killing, Mick. This was organized, pre-planned, cold-blooded, not something that happened in the heat of the moment.'

'What's still ringing your bells?' Gem asked.

'First, out of the box, the killer must have known her habit of walking the riverbank in the evening and early morning,' he replied.

'I'll give you that it does narrow the field,' Sparkes agreed. 'What next?'

'The killer planned his actions, came equipped to commit the crime and then dumped the poachers net to throw you off the scent. This was premeditated and so there had to be a motive, Mick. The victim was quite wealthy and her rings were missing. Good old financial gain would seem to top the list and next up, revenge.'

'So, you're back to the family again. If it's down to money the main beneficiary was her son Max. Surely you can see why he was put in the frame for this?' the DI replied. 'However, it's obvious that revenge puts a few others in the frame.

'And let's not forget a recently changed will.'

'Agreed.'

'There was a rumour around the village of a recent family falling out. We need to know what caused that?

'The will was changed,' Gem interrupted. 'Family's argue from time to time, but what makes it so strange?'

'A grandparent doesn't cut her grandchild out of her will unless they are doing it to make a point and old Mrs Lamont was fond of making a point,' Jack replied. 'We need to know more about what made her cut out Max's kids.'

'And your evidence for this is what?' Sparkes asked.

'It's about what's not there, not what is. The poacher wasn't the killer because there was no trace of his dog at the crime scene, this is no different,' he continued. 'What was the son really gaining? She hadn't cut him from the will, so he was going to get everything when she died. But the rest of the family?'

'No opportunity because of the alibi,' said Gem.

'Seb was seen picking up a takeaway and after that, they're alibiing each other. I'll grudgingly rule them out for the time being,' Jack replied. 'As there are other parties to be considered.'

'There was hardly any forensics recovered from Mrs Lamont's body,' the DI said, 'Not much of a surprise there, considering how long the body had been in the water.

'What about Max Lamont?' Gem asked.

'Again nothing. Wood floors and it hadn't been raining, so no strange footprints outside or inside the property.'

'Any sign of a struggle in the house?' Lunn asked.

'Nope, he was drunk and fell,' Mick replied.

'Or was pushed?' Gem threw in.

'What makes you say that?' Sparkes asked.

'It could have been someone who knew he was at his mother's house. There was no sign of a struggle and the killer would have had to know the layout of the house,' Gem replied.

'Or he was just pissed off his head and fell,' the DI insisted. 'Forensics have come up with nothing that's inconsistent with that.'

'Mick, I don't like that he went AWOL for those few hours when his mother was killed. But I still feel he wasn't the type and had no real motivation. The likelihood of him just falling down drunk, after typing out that he was sorry, too many coincidences for me. If he didn't do it, what was he apologising for?'

'The family say that they told him to move out, as they thought he'd killed the old dear. It's in their statements, Jack,' Sparkes responded.

'Their statements all read the same. And if you want to kill someone, then isolating them is a good start. What do your instincts tell you?' Gem asked.

'Okay, I'll give you that I'm not completely comfortable with the situation. But I'm buggered if I know where to take this,' the policeman replied. 'Rhona might have cut you some slack, but I'd be committing career suicide if I took this to my DCI or Geoff Cooke.'

'Best leave it with me then,' Lunn said. 'Let's get the Lamont's out of the picture and see where that takes us. You know what still bugs me?'

'I know you're going to tell me,' Sparkes replied.

'The old woman's missing rings. Where are they?'

'We've circulated the usual second-hand jewellers and the cash for goods places and come up with nothing so far.'

'The stones could have been taken out of their settings by now and the gold recycled,' Gem interjected. 'That would explain Liam Galletly waving a wad of cash around.'

'Jack, why are you so determined to get to the bottom of this case when it's closed?' Sparkes asked.

'It might be closed to you, but not to me,' Lunn replied. 'It wouldn't be right if whoever killed her went free and Max Lamont's name became a watchword for matricide, now would it?'

Gem put the binoculars down.

'Looks like Seb might be on the move,' she said.

'You'd better make yourself scarce, Mick.'

'Only too happy to do a vanishing act and I hope that if you're right you can prove it.'

'So do I,' muttered Lunn.

## Chapter 45

They waited for the BMW to pass before starting the engine and following, keeping a reasonable distance between it and them.

'Let's hope he's not expecting a tail,' Gem said.

'Why would he. The police have closed the case as far as he's concerned, and young Sebastian has just the right amount of arrogance to think he's bulletproof.'

'Looks like he's heading back towards Lyndhurst.'

'He might be going on into Southampton, Brockenhurst, or even Lymington,' Lunn mused.

They followed the car to the Romsey Road as it turned right and headed towards Lyndhurst. They were fortunate enough to get a couple of cars between themselves and the target as they pulled out, but knew that they would be close behind by the time they got to Lyndhurst High Street, where it became a one-way system.

The BMW turned off the High Street into the large car park by the Community Centre.

'If he is parking up, wait until he's got his ticket and stuck it in the car before you get out,' Lunn said.

'Okay. I'll stick a hat and a pair of sunglasses on and keep my distance. You go up to the top of the High Street and we should have him covered that way.'

Jack watched as Sebastian Lamont locked his car and turned away to walk into the village.

'Time to go, Gem.'

Lunn sorted a parking ticket out, then walked up to the car park entrance and called his Gem on his.

'You'll never guess where he's gone, Jack?'

'Where?'

'Your old office.'

'Really? He must be having a chat with Corporate Boy about the planning on those industrial units. I'll head back towards the car and I'll pick you up at the exit from the car park. Don't follow him back to his car.'

'Understood.'

Gem called him about ten minutes later.

'Looks like he's heading straight back to the car.'

'Fine, I'll pick you up in a minute. Try and make sure he doesn't see you.'

Jack watched as Lamont returned to his car, reversed it out of the bay and headed for the exit.

He followed the BMW out on to the High Street, picking up Gem when Lunn pulled up to the junction, then following Seb as he turned right into the one-way system.

'I'd have loved to be a fly on the wall in your old offices, Jack.'

'Well, we know he's got matey boy on board regarding the planning. So, I don't think we'd have heard anything too exciting. But it might be worthwhile having a chat with my old secretary.' Lunn replied as they followed Sebastian Lamont out of Lyndhurst and towards Brockenhurst.

'My bet is still Lymington,' Gem announced.

They drove through Brockenhurst, negotiating their way over the level crossing and on towards Lymington, passing a couple of pubs on the left-hand side. The BMW ignored them as it drove on towards the coast. Entering the outskirts of the Lymington, Lunn turned to his partner's daughter.

'Be prepared to jump out sharpish, as I'm really not sure where he's off to. It's probably a pub or restaurant, as it's lunchtime.'

'I'm bloody hungry myself,' Gem said.

'You'll have to wait until we get home, sorry.'

They followed the car to one of the several marinas and then hung back for a minute before driving in themselves, giving their target a chance to park up.

Seb Lamont was walking towards a bistro and so they turned into a parking spot to get a clearer view.

'How are we going to find out who he's meeting this time?'

'That's easy,' Lunn replied, grinning at companion. 'That bistro he's gone into?'

'Yes.'

'It's owned by an old school friend. I'll call him and find out,' he said, fishing his mobile phone out of his pocket.

'Is there anywhere around which The Old Boy network doesn't have its tentacles?' Gem asked.

'I confess; it's been pretty useful over the years.'

'Who's the owner?'

'Robin Millward, I've got his number somewhere in here,' Jack said, as he scrolled through his contacts. 'Here we go.'

The phone at the other end went to voicemail, so he left a message.

'Maybe he's not at the bar?' Gem said.

Someone called Jack's mobile.

'It's him. Hi, Robin, it's Jack.'

'Jack, how are you?'

'Good thanks, you?'

'Fine fettle. Busy, but what can I do for you?' the voice at the end of the line asked.

'A favour.'

'I'll see what I can do. What do you need?' Millward asked.

'You had a young man walk into your bar a few minutes ago, about six-foot-tall might have a table booked in the name Lamont.'

'Yes, Sebastian's here.'

'What's he doing and is he with anyone.'

'Well, he's seldom without company, Jack,' the bar owner continued 'Little sod's shagged half my waitresses over the last few years. But this time he's lunching with his mother and sister by the looks of it. What are you up to, Jack?'

'Can't tell you at the moment, but I'll book a table soon and come and tell you about it.'

'I'll try and earwig a bit of what they're saying as well,' the bar owner said. 'Say hi to Sarah for me and don't be a stranger.'

Good as his word the photo from Robin came through a few minutes later.

'Looks like Seb is being the dutiful son and brother, having lunch with mummy and little sister.'

'Now that would be a conversation worth listening to,' Gem said.

'We'll call it a day on this, get back to the house and get some work done. I'm just glad we didn't bump into your mum and the girls whilst we were over here.'

'Well, it was more interesting than yesterday. But what did we learn?'

'He's the one checking on things, whilst his mother and sister are shopping and lunching.'

'Bit like you and me then. We're working and where are Mum and Eden?' Gem chuckled.

'You're not far wrong there and we've got some work to catch up on.'


As they drove back home Lunn's phone rang again. It was the magazine editor, Steve Ingram.

'Hi, Steve. How are you?'

'Avington, Jack,' Ingram said. 'I was so sorry to have to delay our trip and wanted to know how you're fixed over the next few days?'

'Well, Gem is with me now,' Lunn answered.

'I'll let you know when I've booked it and if you guys would like to tie a few flies for me to use on the day, I'd consider it a fair exchange,' Ingram replied. 'Catch up with you soon and looking forward to meeting you, Gem.'

'Bye, Steve,' Lunn and Gem chorused.

'I need to drop the company car off this evening, if you'll give me a hand?' Lunn asked.

Gem nodded, 'Sure.'

Chapter 46

Later that evening, Jack tossed the company car keys to Gem.

'You can have the last drive.'

'Really? What if I ding it?'

'Then you get to pay for the damage,' Lunn replied. 'If you get it there in one piece, I'll buy you a beer on the way home.'

'Unscratched it will be then and a beer on the way home, I'll settle for that.'

It was about seven o'clock and Jack was reckoning that Corporate Boy would probably be at home cooking dinner, as they drove in convoy the short distance to the estate agent's cottage. He had instructed Gem to drive down the track and park the car in front of the manager's home. He parked at the top of the track that led down to the isolated cottage, swapped keys over with Gem and knocked on the front door. A few moments later the door was opened. Corporate Boy looked Jack up and down.

'Oh, it's you,' he said.

'I've brought the car around.'

'Didn't think to call, did you? Bloody inconsiderate.'

'Why, do you have company again?' Jack inquired.

'None of your damn business,' Corporate Boy snarled. 'I suppose you'd better come in, I'm in the middle of cooking.'

'Don't let me hold you up.'

Lunn followed into the sitting room and was once again struck by the feeling of everything being in its proper place and order. His attention was particularly drawn to the ego wall, with its souvenirs, photographs, etc.

'Where are the keys and paperwork?' he asked Jack.

'Here are the keys and the paperwork is in the car. Do you have the form for me to sign?'

'I need to check it over.'

'Be my guest.'

Corporate Boy ignored Gem and went over the Audi with a fine toothcomb, taking note of everything that even looked like a scratch or blemish.

'Heard you put Seb Lamont and Mark Stacey together on redeveloping that light industrial site of Mrs Lamont's,' Lunn said, seeing the surprise register in the younger man's eyes.

'What of it?'

'Just thinking that there it'll be a nice chunk of commission for you.'

'Again, I repeat. What of it?'

'Must be why you were looking at cars at the garage the other week.'

'You think you know everything that goes on in the village. Failed copper, redundant estate agent and now some sad fishing tackle business, I hear,' he said. 'It's none of your business anymore. You're now just a miserable, unemployed old man poking his nose in where it's not needed or wanted. You've dropped the car off, now don't bother coming into the office again and you're certainly not welcome here. Goodbye and good riddance.'

'When you do get found out, look over your shoulder,' Lunn said. 'I'll be there watching.'

'Why don't you just fuck off?'

'Hardly Oscar Wilde, are you?' Gem interjected, receiving an angry glance from the estate agent.

Corporate Boy turned his attention back to Jack. 'You come back here again, I'll call the Police and have you arrested for trespassing.'

'You really have been spending too much time with Seb Lamont,' Jack threw back at him.

He walked with Gem back up to the Volvo.

'You really do seem to enjoy his company, Jack,' Gem said.

'He's an arrogant wanker.'

'Anyone with him this time?'

'No.'

'Come on, let's have that pint. You must have a thirst on after that arguing?' Gem said.

'Good call.'

The two of them were nursing their pints when Jack's phone rang.

'Hi Jack, can you get to Avington for the day after tomorrow?'

'Sure, Steve.'

'Breakfast at seven thirty.'

'See you then.'

'Steve, the magazine editor?' Gem asked.

Jack nodded. 'Avington in a couple of days.'

His phone rang again; it was Mick Sparkes.

'Hi Mick, what can I do for you?' he said, handing Gem a tenner for another round.

'Just wondering how things are going, Jack?'

'Young Lamont went to lunch with his mother and sister,' Lunn replied. 'Maybe Geoff's right and it's as simple as, Max did it. We'll be following up a few more ideas tomorrow.'

'I'll bring Rhona up to date. You know she's going to ask you to step away soon,' Sparkes said.

'I know,' Jack said. He terminated the call and reached for the pint that Gem had brought over.

'Starting to feel the pressure?' she asked.

'Not really. I'm sure Rhona thinks that I'll toe the line,' Lunn replied. 'The problem for my old boss is that she can't really do anything if I choose to ignore her. Though the longer I can keep her onside the better.'

'How long will she give you?'

'A few days, maybe a week. She'll feel that she's given me enough rope by then and look to shut me down.'

'So, we're going to keep an eye on the Lamont's again tomorrow?' Gem asked.

'Yes,' Jack said. 'I've got to go and meet with Will Dowsett from the Florida trip at his shop, see if I can get him to take some of our stock.'

'That sounds like a readymade opportunity to keep tabs on them.'

Lunn's phone rang again. It was Robin Millward, the bar owner from the day before.

'Robin, sorry I couldn't come in to chat the other day.'

'No problem, I'd meant to call you back anyway and then forgot.'

'Old age creeping up on you, mate. It comes to us all,' Lunn replied. 'What can I do for you?'

'More what I can do for you. I did manage to catch the odd bit of the conversation the Lamont's were having. Sebastian was getting a hard time from the two women,' Robin said. 'There was mention of wills. We were busy and I only got snatches, but hope that's helpful?'

'Very. I appreciate the call and I'll see you soon.'

They pulled up on to the driveway at home.

'Gem,' Lunn said, 'I think we might have been following the wrong person.'

'You should have let me keep the hack on Imogen's phone.'

'Don't even dare go there.'

'We can't cover all three of them. What are we going to do?' asked Gem.

'I've got an idea about how to deal with that.'

Chapter 47

The next morning, Jack was in the kitchen taking the rabbit that Seth Walker had given him out of the freezer, when Gem appeared.

'What are you going to do with that?' she asked.

'There's a Nigel Slater recipe I thought I'd do for rabbit cooked in wheat beer, with rosemary and thyme and finished off with a little cream and tarragon.'

'That sounds good. Are you going up to the shed?'

'I'll be up in a few minutes. We can get the flies ready for delivery and get a few more tied.'

Music played as the two of them worked, and within three hours they'd completed the last of the orders for the Florida group, packed them into boxes and into the car.

Sarah was busy marking and surrounded by books.

As they drove away from the house Lunn turned to his partner's daughter.

'We've got somewhere else to go first.'

'Right.'

'I have an idea on who might help us out,' Lunn confided.

'Okay?'

'They said if I needed any help, I should ask. So that's what I'm going to do,' Lunn replied.

'And we're visiting them at home?' Gem asked.

'They still live at the same house that's been in the family for a good few generations,' Lunn said.

He headed off towards Cadnam, then turned off towards Bartley village before pulling off the tarmac road and on to a gravel track leading up to a small cottage. A lurcher dog was laid down by front gate.

'Stay in the car for the moment, Gem,' Jack said.

Lunn stepped out of the car and received a growl from the dog for his efforts.

'Here, Dan. Leave it,' said a voice from the cottage. 'What can I do for you, Mr Lunn?'

'Wondered if you could help me with something, Seth?'

'Is that Gemma with you? Get her out of the car and come in,' the poacher said.

Jack beckoned for Gem to join him and they went up to the front door of the cottage.

Seth Walker called them through from the kitchen.

'Come through and sit down, Mr Lunn,' the poacher said. 'You too, young Gemma. Or should I call you Ma'am?'

'Only if I have to call you Staff,' she replied with a smile. 'How are you, Seth?'

'All the better for Jack here helping me out,' the poacher replied. 'I heard you were finished with the Green Slime.'

'You can't keep a secret for long in the Forest. Yeah, I've been working abroad for the last year. Thanks for the chats we've had over the years.'

'Just two soldiers chewing things over. It was always a pleasure.'

The two visitors sat down at the kitchen table with their host and the lurcher curled up by the back door. The cottage had some land attached to it and Seth kept a few animals. A couple of pigs and some chickens, enough for his needs, particularly when he supplemented it with rabbit, pheasant, partridge and the odd salmon.

'Been a while since you've been here, Mr Lunn.'

Jack smiled. 'You know exactly when the last time was, Seth.'

'You got lucky and caught me with a couple of salmon in the back of my Land Rover if I recall,' Walker replied.

'The only time I caught you and not for the want of trying.'

'You and a few others came close a few times,' said the poacher.

'I'm still looking into the deaths of Elizabeth Lamont and her son.'

'Thought the police had that all tied up?' the poacher interjected. 'It said in the paper that the son was thought to have killed the old woman.'

'What do you think?' said Jack queried.

'She was a tough old bird and it certainly didn't sit well that someone tried to put the Police on to me. If it wasn't her son, then I'd like to know who that was.'

'We're singing from the same hymn sheet,' Jack said. 'Did you see anything in the day or two before the killing, or after your release, that might be of interest?'

'I know you found the body and you're ex- Old Bill, but why are you doing this?'

'The Police feel that Max killed her and Jack's not convinced he was the murdering sort, Gem said. 'He wants a bit of justice for Mrs Lamont and if Max didn't do it, then he shouldn't have that hung around his neck.'

Seth turned to Gem. 'What do you think?'

'I trust Jack's instincts. If he believes that there's a good chance Max didn't do it, then chances are he's right,' Gem replied. 'He's getting a bit of encouragement from his old boss and help from an old colleague.'

The poacher looked surprised. 'This true?'

'They've a closed case, so why waste man hours on it?' Lunn replied. 'I've seen the case files, the autopsy reports and forensics. There are definitely a few people that crossed her over the years and came out the worse for it. I'm just trying to wrap up a few loose ends.'

'So, they're letting you do their job?'

'I wouldn't quite put it that way, but they're under pressure to close cases with limited man power. Look, I know you had your run-ins with the old girl, Seth, but I got on okay with her and her husband.'

'I know you had a rod on their beat and I've seen you a few times. You're not a bad caster.'

Jack laughed. 'I didn't see you.'

'Didn't want you to,' Walker replied. 'Who do you think it was, Mr Lunn?'

'Though the Police have ruled the family out, I'm just taking my own look at them and a few others that might have had a grudge. I just want to be sure in my own mind, before we begin widening the net,' he explained. 'We've been tailing Max's son, Sebastian, but that hasn't got us anywhere and it appears that his Mother and sister seem to be running the show.'

'That pup? Flash bugger, I've seen him up at the old lady's place. Just the other day I saw him shouting at a fisherman, gun in hand like the lord of the manor.'

Jack grinned. 'You saw my argument with him?'

'Watched you catch that brownie just before too, Mr Lunn.'

'It really has annoyed you that someone tried to fit you up. Is there anything else that you've seen?' Gem asked.

'I've just been keeping an eye out, that's all,' the poacher replied.

'So, you'll help out?' she asked.

'I can spare a bit of time, so what do you need?'

'If you could keep tabs on the daughter that would be great,' Lunn said. 'We'll try and keep an eye on the mother and young Sebastian.'

'I'll do that for you. I appreciate what you did for me, so it's only fair I help you out,' the poacher said. 'I know where they live, so it won't be a problem following her. She'll not see me and no one notices an old Land Rover round here, do they? If I get anything, I'll drop a note to you.'

'Fair enough and thanks for offering to help out.'

'Good to see you, Seth,' Gem said as she shook hands with the poacher.

'And you,' Seth replied. 'Keep listening to the old man here. He's not too bad for an ex-copper.'

'He has been known to talk some sense occasionally.'

'Oh, one more thing, Seth,' Jack said. 'My brother's old cottage needs a re-decorate and I wondered if you'd like to earn a few quid and do it up for me?'

'I'm always up for a bit extra in the kitty.'

'I'll get you the keys,' Lunn replied, taking his wallet out and handing the poacher forty pounds. 'For diesel.'

'More than enough,' the poacher said, taking the cash.

They returned to the car, accompanied by Walker. Jack rummaged in the glove compartment, then passed a bunch of keys over to the older man.

'Go and take a look in the next few days and let me have an estimate.'

'Will do.'

Jack and Gem got back into the car.

'Old Seth's an interesting character and I didn't know you knew him well?' Jack asked.

'He's ex-Special Forces and served in the Falklands,' Gem explained. 'When I was thinking of joining the Army, I found out where he lived and had a chat with him. I wanted to know what it was like from a squaddie who'd served. I'd heard loads of stuff from officers and just needed a different perspective. If you're going to talk to someone, then you might as well speak to someone who served with an elite regiment.'

'Fair point,' Lunn replied. When he got out of the Army, he just couldn't settle and came home to his family here in the New Forest. He must be in his sixties if he's a day, but still pretty spry and sharp as a pin.'

'I knew he was a poacher, but I never really asked him how else he makes a living?'

'He does work on some of the farms in the area. He's got chickens, a couple of pigs and a good veg Patch. Plus, he sells some of what he poaches to local pubs and restaurants.'

They made the delivery to Will Dowsett's tackle shop and headed towards Imogen Lamont's home in Minstead.

Chapter 48

Parking up in the side road again, they clocked the two Mercedes SLK's on the driveway of the Lamont home, making it look like both the two ladies were in.

'Let's hope that if they're going out, they go in the same car,' Gem said.

'I doubt we'll have that sort of luck.'

Sure enough, they didn't.

The daughter came out first and drove away in a spray of gravel, as her mother watched with an exasperated look on her face. A few minutes later she also left, and they followed her at a discreet distance.

Isobel Lamont drove into Southampton, passing the Mayflower Theatre, turning left at the junction and following the road round to the right before turning left and parking in a multi-storey car park. Jack dropped Gem off outside, so she could tail her, then parked the car on the same level and called his partner's eldest.

'I'm heading towards London Road, Jack.'

'Stay on her. I want to know where she goes. I'm on my way,' Lunn replied.

He crossed Bedford Place as quickly as fast his knee would allow, cutting through to London Road.

Gem called him again.

'I'm outside Tesco's.'

'Did you see where she went?' he asked when they met up.

Gem gave him the name of a firm of solicitors.

'She's chivvying them up about the will, I expect,' Lunn said.

'What do we do now?'

'We? I'm off back to the car and you're going to follow her when she comes out of there.'

'I'll give you a call if it looks like she's heading straight back to her car.'

'Great. I think she'll come straight back, but let me know if she tales a detour.'

Gem called about twenty minutes later. 'She gone into a coffee shop.'

'Is she by herself?'

'Looks like it…no wait, she joined some bloke. I'll try to get a photo of him.'

'Just don't let them see you,' Lunn urged.

Half an hour later he got another call to say that she was on her way back towards the car park.

'I'll meet you at the front, and we'll see where she goes next.'


There was a rap on his car window, and he turned to see Adele Parker standing there. He wound the window down. 'Ms Parker, what an unexpected … no, pleasure isn't the right word. What can I do for you?'

'I'm just doing what you're doing, Jack.'

'Really?'

'Can I get in and talk to you for a minute or two, please.'

'I suppose so,' Lunn replied. 'Let it not be said that chivalry is dead.'

'Thank you,' she said and clambered into the front passenger seat.

'Well?' he asked.

'We talked about helping each other,' she replied. 'That Max Lamont didn't have anything to do with his mother's death. I know that you've been watching his family and that's why you're here now, following Imogen. I'll be frank, if Max didn't kill her then there was no motive for him to be writing a suicide note was there?'

'The police don't seem to follow your line of thinking and his missing hours during the murder time frame makes him favourite.'

'Look, I know you still think I'm some bottom-feeding journalist who'll do anything for a story,' Adele said. 'I know I made mistakes in the past, crossed lines and didn't act with very much integrity. But, when it boils down to it, I couldn't give a crap what the Police think. I do care what you think. You were right about the poacher and something about these deaths is bugging you. You knew her and apart from her own son, you were probably one of the closest to her.'

'Okay, everyone deserves a second chance. Frustratingly, I have nothing concrete to offer the Police and so they've closed the case.'

'You and I feel that there's a murderer out there, possibly a double murderer,' she said. 'If that's true, we want that person caught and justice to be served. I'm not so altruistic as to say that I'm not bothered about getting a good story out of it. But I'm not going to do a hatchet job on anyone, hack anyone or anything like that.'

'Just say I believe you for a minute. What are you bringing to the table?' Lunn asked.

'Another pair of eyes. We can share any information,' she replied. 'I need this. I need to be taken seriously as a journalist again, to show that I've learned my lesson and have some integrity.'

'Okay,' he said. 'Here's the deal. You get to follow the Imogen. We'll meet up in a couple of days and see what we've got. You do not publish anything without my agreement, you do not quote me and I'm not a source.'

'I can live with that. Who are you going to cover?' she asked.

'The son,' Lunn replied. 'I think he's the weak link and there's the matter of a changed will. I'm also looking for a Liam Galletly.'

The journalist's eyebrows rose.

'So, who's watching the daughter?'

'You don't need worry about her.'

'You've got the bases covered?'

'This is your second and last chance, Adele.'

'Thank you, Jack. Can I start tomorrow?'

'Fine,' Lunn said. 'We've got her covered today.'

They exchanged mobile numbers and the journalist left.


Gem returned, followed a few minutes later by their target. Imogen Lamont drove off out of the city and they followed at a discreet distance.

'We've got someone else who's going to help with the surveillance,' Jack said. 'That journalist, she has a nose for a story and is going to give us a hand.'

'Hasn't she got a bit of a dodgy history?'

'You're going to cast aspersions on her for phone hacking?' Lunn replied with a raised eyebrow.

Gem gave him a hangdog look. 'I should probably have left that particular can of worms with the lid firmly on.'


Imogen Lamont's next stop was unexpected, an undertaker in Romsey. Jack presumed that this was for the burial of her husband and mother-in-law.

'That service will be well worth attending,' Gem said. 'Some will want to make sure that the old dear is actually dead and the rest will want to see her suspected murderer buried. A proper double feature.'

'I suspect that the surviving family will be conspicuous in their absence from Max's service.'

The next stop was Elizabeth Lamont's house. Her daughter-in-law turned in to the drive and Jack drove a little further on, turning around and parking in a lay by on the opposite side of the road.

'We can see the entrance to the driveway from here.'

'I'll get the binoculars out,' Gem said.

Lunn noticed a car coming towards them. It turned down towards the house.

'Don't think you'll need them, as I think I've spotted why she's here.'

'And there was me thinking she was just measuring for curtains. What's she up to?'

'Getting the house valued. That's Corporate Boy who just drove up and turned in.'

'So, she's going to sell it then?

'She'll need to for the inheritance tax. I expect that our friend has been meeting her and getting the other properties valued, whilst we've been following the son,' Lunn answered. 'No wonder he was looking at cars. I think she's going to sell some of the properties, and he's got the development on the industrial site to come too and a nice fat commission to boot. She'll want the valuations as low as possible, to keep the tax liability to a minimum and he's just the one to call if you want a dishonest valuation. I wouldn't trust him to sit the right way on a lavatory.'

'Are we going to wait until they come out?

'No, I reckon she'll be going home next and we'll be missed by your mother if we take any longer,' Lunn said. 'Did you get a shot of who Imogen was meeting for coffee?'

'I did,' she replied, handing Jack her phone. 'No idea who he is.'

'I bloody do,' Jack blurted out. 'It's Steve Ingram, the magazine editor. Why the hell would he be meeting with Imogen Lamont?'

'We can find out when we're at Avington,' Gem replied.

'That we can.'


A couple of hours later Lunn was back in the kitchen and taking the meat out of the pan when Sarah walked in.

'Smells good, Jack,' she said.

'First time I've tried this.'

'I'll pop up to the shed and tell Gem that food's ready.'

Lunn gave the sauce a stir, set the table quickly and walked to the bottom of the stairs.

'Eden, food.'

'Coming.'

There was no sign of Gem and Sarah when he got back to the kitchen, but as he opened the French windows they emerged from the shed.'

'Grub up,' he called.


After dinner, Jack and Gem packed their fishing gear in the back of the Volvo, anticipating an early start.

'I'll give you a shout at about six tomorrow morning and we're leaving about half an hour after that,' Jack reminded him.

'When are we going to see Seth?'

'The day after tomorrow,' Lunn replied. 'And don't forget that your sister flies back in a few days, so play nicely until she does.'

'I'll try.'

*'Do or do not. There is no try.'*

Chapter 49

'There had better be a good reason why you're calling me at this ungodly hour, Mick.' Lunn said, answering his phone and seeing it was a little after 5.00 a.m.

'I'm at Bolton's Bench,' Sparkes replied. 'Get yourself up here sharpish.'

'Can't this wait?'

'I wouldn't have called you if it could.'

Sarah stirred. 'What's going on?'

'I'll pull some clothes on and be with you in ten minutes,' he said to Mick

'Who's calling you in the middle of the night?' Sarah asked.

'It's Mick. I'll go and find out,' he replied to his partner.


Lunn pulled on his jeans and a sweatshirt, made his way downstairs and slipped his shoes on. Grabbing a coat and car keys, closing the door as quietly as he could.

It was only a few minutes' drive to Bolton's Bench, which lay on the Southampton side of the village. The hill, which overlooked the village cricket pitch, was topped by a large old yew tree and Jack had sat on the bench many times over the years and watched a game. He was waved through a roadblock and drove over to the gathering of police cars, parked up with lights oscillating.

Sparkes walked over.

'Why the urgency, Mick?'

'Another death.'

'Not the same family, surely?'

'No,' Sparkes replied. 'That reporter.'

'Adele Porter?'

'Hung herself.'

'From the yew tree?' Lunn asked incredulously.

'Looks like she came up here, tied the rope around a branch, put the noose around her neck and stepped off the bench.'

'Show me,' he asked.

Sparkes started up the hill and Lunn limped after him. There was a flock of rooks on the slopes of the hill, barking out their caws as the two men worked their way towards the old tree at the summit. The black feathered birds brought to Jacks' mind a gathering of undertakers.

'Mick, this isn't right at all. I only spoke to her yesterday and she seemed in a good frame of mind. Another death, you have to agree it's no coincidence'

'I do, but I'll leave that to the pathologist.'

They reached the summit and tree. Jack took in the scene, as a little breeze gave movement to the barefoot body hanging by the noose.

'Where are her shoes?' Lunn asked.

'I haven't seen any. Oh shit, she was brought here. I'll bet her car's not anywhere nearby either,' the detective thought out loud.

'Where was she living?' Lunn demanded agitatedly.

'Totton. I've got a car on its way to her house.'

'Well, that rules out her having walked here. You've a murder on your hands, I reckon,' Lunn concluded. 'Where's Geoffrey?'

'On his way.'

'Rhona?'

'Also on her way.'

The police tape surrounding the summit of the hill flapped gently in the light breeze and causing the body to swing a little.

'Jesus, can't we get her down?' Lunn asked, the scene making him sick to his stomach.

'You know we can't. Scarlet's on her way and I'd be right in the shit if the crime scene is corrupted.' Sparkes replied. 'I've got some screens coming and I've blocked one of the roads off.

'Who found her?'

'Early morning dog walker.'

'Why is it always dog walkers? Name?'

'An old bloke called Ben Youngs. He's down in one of the cars,' Sparkes replied.

'I know Ben,' Lunn said. 'Let me talk to him.'

'You'll get me strung up, Jack.'

'It'll be at least ten minutes before Geoff and Rhona are on site. Just give me five with him?'

'If they turn up and see you with him, I'm denying all knowledge,' Sparkes said.

Lunn limped off down the hill as fast as his knee would allow, making a beeline for the car with the internal light on.

He knew the constable by the car and raised a hand as he approached.

'Hi, Sam. Mick said I could have a few words with Mr Youngs, if he's up to it.'

'Not sure what to tell you,' the old man replied. 'But I could do with the chat, just to try and..., I don't know.'

The constable excused himself, explaining that he had to help seal the road to Beaulieu off from civilian traffic.

'Let me ask you a few questions and just answer honestly. If you don't know, just say I don't know,' Lunn said.

The old man's Jack Russell lay on his lap with his head on his master's hand and Jack slipped into the back seat alongside them.

'Why were you out so early?'

'Since the wife passed away, I don't sleep so well. Sophie and I come out for a walk early quite regularly.'

'Did you see anyone or anything out of the ordinary, other than the victim?'

'Not a soul.'

'How long were you out before finding her?'

'Ten minutes, I guess,' the old man replied. 'You know where I live.'

Jack knew that it would take about that time to get to the hill from his house.

'Vehicles coming and going?' he asked.

'Not a thing.'

'Did you touch the body?'

'No. It was obvious she was dead.'

'Look, the police will want to talk to you, take a statement and fingerprint you. That kind of thing,' Lunn said. 'Don't worry about any of that, it's just procedure. No need to tell anyone else that we've spoken and just tell the police what you've told me. They'll offer you counselling, and my advice is to take it.'

The old man nodded. 'Thanks.'

Jack got out of the car as the constable returned.

'If you're asked, no one's spoken to him,' Lunn advised.

'I wondered if you had permission,' the policeman said tersely.

'DI Sparkes was fine with me having a chat with Ben,' Lunn replied. 'But you'll drop him in it if Superintendent Cooke finds out and you wouldn't want to do that, would you?'

'Never mind what that bad-tempered bugger Cooke would do to me,' the policeman said, 'I'd be directing traffic for the rest of my natural born.'

'Glad you understand,' Lunn said and made off back up the hill.

He just about made it to the top as four cars arrived in convoy. Two figures made their way up the hill, as the third donned overalls and organised two figures from the fourth car.

'Mick got you out of bed then?' DCS Blacklock asked.

'I was due up early anyway. Just not this early and not for this.' Lunn replied.

'Suicide,' Geoff Cooke said. 'Out of favour with the gutter press. Down on her luck and decided to end it.'

'I don't know why the rest of us are here, Geoff. Might as well tell Scarlet and the rest of the Forensic Team to pack and go home. The Superintendent has spent all of twenty seconds at the scene and has solved the case,' Lunn replied.

'Oh, you'll have a different theory of course,' Cooke snapped back.

'Where's her car and where are her shoes?' Jack asked.

'No sign of either,' Sparkes said.

'She lived in Totton, for Christ's sake. It's five or six miles to her home, Geoff.'

DCS Blacklock held her hands up. 'Let the C.S.I.'s do their job and can everyone stop jumping to conclusions.'

'You should try doing some investigating, Geoff,' An incensed Lunn said. 'You know, examine the Evidence and talk to witnesses, that sort of thing. I gave you a list of suspects and I'll bet you haven't spoken to any of them. Now we have another body and your theory about Mrs Lamont and Max has more holes in it than a colander.'

'I don't need a civilian telling me how to do my job and you least of all, thank you,' Cooke replied indignantly.

'Enough, the pair of you,' Blacklock intervened. 'Like a pair of squabbling kids. Geoff, I told you that the people on Jack's list had to be spoken to and I'm your superior. See to the forensic team and get them up here asap. I don't want that body hanging there any longer than it has to. I'll be the lead from here on.'

Cooke looked suitably crestfallen and ambled off, heading down towards the assembled cars.

'Mick, I need more manpower here soonest. Get some uniforms out here and a cordon organised. I don't want any rubberneckers and I especially don't want any photographers, if we can help it.'

Blacklock turned to Lunn.

'You'd better tell me what you know.'

'She was trying to help, Rhona,' he said. 'I honestly believe that she'd had a 'road to Damascus' moment and was trying to do something worthwhile.'

'What did she tell you?'

'That she doubted that the son did it and felt that there might still be a killer out there.'

'She was probably just flattering you, hoping to get some inside information.'

'I honestly don't think so and you know I have decent instincts about people.'

'So?' Blacklock asked.

'She was brought here, there's no sign of her car and she's no shoes with her,' Lunn expanded.

'That means she was probably either drugged, unconscious or already dead. Either way, to get her up that hill and then hang her took a couple of people, I reckon.'

'Who found her?'

'The old gent in the patrol car, Ben Youngs. He lives about ten minutes away and was out walking his dog.'

'Isn't it a bit early to be out and about?' Blacklock probed.

'Not when you recently lost your wife and you've only got a Jack Russell for company. He's genuinely shocked and doesn't have a motive, never mind that he's seventy-five, if he's a day.'

'Fair enough. I'll get one of the uniforms to run him home and take a statement. Next time you leave it to us to speak to witnesses first.'

'I just thought that someone he knew might get a bit more out of him, that's all.'

The forensic team was now huddled around the murder scene, cameras flashing, lighting up the area and casting odd shadows. Three more police cars had arrived and a cordon of blue and white tape was being strung out along the roadside. A figure detached itself from the cluster and made its way over to where Rhona and Jack were standing.

'I know it's early doors,' Scarlet Ribbans, the senior C.S.I. said. 'But my initial findings are as follows. She was dead when someone hung her.'

'You're sure?' Blacklock asked.

'It's an initial finding, but I'd bet this month's pay on it,' she replied. 'There's a second ligature mark under where the rope marked her. She was strangled and then brought here.'

'These killings are all connected, Rhona,' Lunn said.

'Why? Because Ms Porter was nosing around these two deaths. There's nothing to directly connect her to the Lamont's and let's face it, she'd made a good few enemies over the years,' Blacklock replied.

'I'm going to get back to the body,' Scarlet said, as she turned away from the pair. 'I'll know more once we get the body down and back to the pathologist.'

'Look, Jack, let's see what Scarlet comes up with and I promise I'll keep an open mind,' Blacklock said. 'You know that if these are linked, then we could be looking at a serial killer?'

'I can count,' Jack replied. 'Look, I know it's circumstantial, but she was convinced that the deaths of old Mrs Lamont and her son were linked. I know Geoff doesn't want two unsolved murders on the books, but he jumped to a conclusion with the old lady death and the son's looks less accidental by the minute.'

'You've made that bloody obvious and you're sure that you've not let personal enmity creep into your thinking, Jack?'

'I just want justice for the two of them and Adele too.'

'I know what you get like, Jack. Look up tunnel vision in the dictionary and there's a picture of you.'

'I'm not being blinkered about this,' Lunn insisted. 'And I agree that there's every reason to have some concerns. When you look at the methods used to kill the victims, they're all different. Not the usual pattern for a serial killer at all. But Adele Porter was deliberately hung in that tree and whoever killed her must have known she'd be found quickly. The killer, or killers, are sticking two fingers up to the Police and telling the world how clever they are.'

'Same rules, Jack. No stalking anyone and keep away from Geoffrey.'

'Easy to do the last.'

'You get on now and I'll keep you posted on any other findings,' Blacklock said. 'Let me know if anything else come up.'

'It's a deal.'

Chapter 50


Lunn shook Gem.

'You awake?'

'I am now,' she replied.

'We're off in thirty minutes.'

'In that case, I'll see you downstairs in about thirty minutes.'

'Make it twenty.'

'Okay.'

Good as her word, Gem was putting her shoes on a little over twenty minutes later.

'I got a call from Mick Sparkes this morning,' Jack told her.

'Really, what did he want this early?'

'You know that reporter that's been nosing round?'

'The one who was going to help us out?'

He nodded. 'She was found dead this morning.'

'What? Gem replied incredulously. 'This is getting out of hand and a little too close for comfort. Where was she found?'

'Bolton's Bench, hanging from the yew tree.' Lunn explained.

Gem shook her head, like she was trying to get her mind around what she'd just been told. 'Hanging from a yew tree? That's bizarre, like Odin from Norse mythology. Her killer is trying to make a point.'

'And Scarlet, the senior C.S.I., says she was dead before she was hung.'

'That's someone advertising their work and taunting the Police at the same time, surely?'

Jack nodded in agreement. 'If there is a connection, then our killer or killers have got very bold and if they've got cocky, they'll get careless. Let's just hope no one else has to die before they're caught.'

'I'll second that,' Gem replied.

'Let's go and find out a bit about Steve Ingram's connection to the Lamont's.

As they drove into the fishery, past the carrier stream, they saw Ingram sitting on the tailgate of a Land Rover Discovery and pulled up next to him.

Steve, Gem. Gem, Steve.' Lunn introduced them.

'I loved those flies you tied. Great work,' the editor said to his partner's daughter.

'Thank you. Coming from you, that's a real compliment.' Gem replied.

Ingram turned back to Jack. 'We'll get some footage for the online magazine too if that's okay with you?'

'Can I get copies for my website?' he asked.

'I'm sure we can sort out getting the video over to you and any photos you want too.'

'Great. Should we set up first or have breakfast and do some tying first.'

'Let's set up and then have some breakfast,' Steve replied. 'Avington's a morning and evening fishery, so we'll do the tying around lunchtime when the fish are less active.'

'Nice motor, Steve,' Lunn commented, nodding towards the Land Rover.

'Not mine, I'm afraid. Mine is being repaired, so I cadged a lift,' nodding towards the photographer.

'It wasn't a problem, as you were staying down this way,' the photographer said.

They walked down the steps of the Lodge, having made a good fist of clearing the food on offer.

'Where are you going, Jack?' Steve asked.

'Middle Lake, I'll see what I can find cruising around. What about you guys?'

'We'll start at Top Lake and see how we go; we've got the fishery to ourselves for the day.'

'I'll be on my mobile if you need to get hold of me. Otherwise, I'll see you around and tight lines,' Lunn said, then turned to Gem. 'Listen carefully to Steve, just do what he says, and you'll catch some fish.'

Jack turned and walked purposefully towards Middle Lake, slipping his sunglasses and baseball hat on as he went. Keeping back from the edge of the bank, rod in hand and fly in the other, ready to cast if he caught sight of a decent fish. There was a spot by the side of a chestnut tree, about a third of the way along, that had been productive for him in the past and he crouched down and quietly edged closer to the bankside. Spotting a Rainbow of about six pounds cruising about forty feet out, he stripped off some line and started false casting, watching as the fish slowly swam to his right and then made the cast in front and beyond it. The nymph landed with a small splash and the trout altered its course slightly towards the splash, increasing its speed as Lunn stripped the line back towards it in a series of irregular motions designed to mimic the underwater dance of the natural nymph. As the fish zeroed in on Lunn's fly and he increased the speed of the motion and retrieve, lifting into the trout as it took the fly.

About five minutes later he slipped his net underneath the fish, put his rod down and fumbled for his priest to kill the fish. Two sharp raps over the head and the fish was dead.

He stood up and looked at the piece of wood and metal in his hand. He'd felt it as he'd brought the priest down on the fish's head. In the same way that it was designed to kill trout quickly, whatever had been used to kill Elizabeth Lamont was designed to perform the same task on a human.

'I got some decent shots of you,' a voice said from behind him. 'Can I get a couple of the fish with the fly beside it?'

Jack looked over his shoulder to see Steve's photographer, camera in hand.

'Sure,' he said, stepping away from the now motionless body. He hadn't even noticed the photographer. 'I hope it wasn't too much of an issue having to pick Steve up this morning?'

'He was staying in the New Forest and I'm only at Romsey,' the photographer explained.

As the man busied himself with composing the shot, he was trying to comprehend how the pieces fitted together.

With the photographer done, Lunn picked up his rod and with the trout still in the net started walking back towards the fishery office when his mobile buzzed. It was Karen Pusey, the chair of the New Forest Independent Advisory Group.

'Karen, how are you?'

'I'm fine, Jack. Thanks for asking,' she continued. 'Sorry if I'm disturbing you, but I'm calling an extraordinary meeting of the I.A.G. for nine o'clock tomorrow morning. After that poor woman was found at Bolton's Bench, I was hoping that you could ask one of the senior investigating officers to attend and bring us up to date.'

'I'll see what I can do. Are people getting twitchy?'

'Of course they are,' she replied. 'Summer isn't that far away, and you know that traders, pubs and hotels rely on the tourists.'

'And those tourists aren't going to come if they think there is the possibility of a killer on the loose.'

'Precisely. See you at nine tomorrow.'

As he got closer to the Top Lake, he could see Steve standing with Gem who had a nice bend in her rod and a fish on. Lunn stood back a little way, so as not to distract them, as Steve talked her through the fight with the fish. Eventually, the trout capitulated, and Gem was able to net it.

Jack could see her face was flushed with success.

'Good job,' he called out.

The two of them turned towards him.

'Looks like you've done okay, Jack,' Steve said.

'On the damsel with the Krystal Flash. Your guy got some photos,' Lunn replied. 'We'll drop the fish off with Andy Fairford on the way home, Gem.'

'I love this. You were right, catching a fish on a fly you've tied yourself is something very special.'


Gem and Steve had moved on from Top Lake when Jack returned to the bankside, so he crossed over to the other side of Middle Lake from where he'd been fishing. He could see the other pair in roughly the same place he'd been earlier, so continued down towards Bottom Lake. He paused at the far end of Middle Lake where it was at its deepest, to have a cast at a double-figure trout. It studiously ignored his nymph, even when it was retrieved just a few inches past its nose. Jack continued down to Bottom Lake, looking in the margins for a fish to flip a fly to.

He wasn't really concentrating on his fishing now. There was that growing sense of anticipation he hadn't experienced for twenty odd years. A sense that he'd always felt when a breakthrough on a case was just around the corner.

There was no scintilla of doubt in his mind that the weapon used to kill Mrs Lamont wasn't just some random piece of varnished wood, but that it had been designed to kill. He fumbled for his mobile and called Mick Sparkes.

'Jack, how are things going?'

'I've had a nice rainbow on the bank. Look, someone was seen having coffee with Imogen Lamont, I'm with him today and I've some thoughts on what was used to kill Mrs Lamont.'

'Do you think he was involved?' Sparkes asked.

'He's been seen with one of the suspects, was in the Forest last night and says his car is being repaired.'

'Really?' Sparkes replied, with a note of surprise. 'Sounds like we'll need to speak to him.'

'Add him to the list.'

'What's your thinking about what killed Elizabeth Lamont?' Sparkes asked.

'Every fly-fisherman carries a what's called a priest. It usually made of wood, but with a lump of brass, or lead at one end.'

'A priest?'

'It delivers the 'last rites' to the fish.' Lunn replied. 'My point is, whatever was used to kill Mrs Lamont was designed to kill.'

'A club of some sort then.'

'That's my best guess. Has the pathologist had any ideas?'

'I haven't had sight of the report, but let me see what I can do,' Sparkes offered.

'A couple of other things,' he said. 'Is Rhona around?'

'In a meeting with the ACC. Why?'

'I need to talk through a couple of things with her. I'll text her. One other thing, do you know when they're burying Max Lamont?'

'Eleven in the morning tomorrow.' Sparkes said. 'Right after his mother.'

'Hopefully, I may have some more information for you in the next day or so. Can you and Rhona keep this under your hats until then?'

'We'll have enough to do tracking Liam Galletly and two missing sons down.'

Jack found Gem on Top Lake with the carrier stream at his back and another rainbow on the bank. The photographer was taking the last few shots.

Lunn waited until the man was out of earshot and then turned to her.

'I've had some thoughts about the case.'

'I thought you might,' she replied.

'It was a 'road to Damascus' moment earlier and whatever was used to kill Elizabeth Lamont was designed to kill, not something just picked up at the last moment. Whoever killed her knew her movements, planned to kill her and went equipped for that purpose.'

'And how does our friend Mr Ingram fit into the picture?' Gem asked.

'Have you seen him use a phone?'

'Just the one. But that fishing vest is like Mary Poppins carpet bag. It's full of stuff, so he could easily have another phone in there. Do you think he could be who Imogen's been calling?'

'It's a possibility. Max could have been killed to cover the killer's tracks?'

'That's a hell of a leap to make and what do we do next?'

'It's in hand,' Lunn replied. 'I've spoken to Mick, left a voicemail for Rhona to call me and we have a couple of funerals to attend on Monday.'

'The Lamonts?' Gem asked.

'Right first time.'

'To see who turns up?'

'And who doesn't,' Jack said. 'We're going to drop in on Seth when we go home, just to see if he's got any information for us.'

'What do we do now?' she asked.

'Act naturally, enjoy the fishing and keep our eyes peeled for a second phone.'


Jack was setting up the fly-tying vices when Rhona Blacklock called.

'Are you positive about the weapon being made for purpose, Jack?'

'I know it was designed to kill, but just not what it is exactly,' Lunn asked.

'Scarlet says the varnish is significant, but she'll need the actual weapon to be absolutely sure.'

'What I'm not sure about is how this all fits together. You have a bundle of suspects to sort through.'

'Geoff Cooke is less than happy with being taken off the case, so expect some grief from Marianne when you see her next. I've got Geoff's team trying to track down your tackle shop owner's grandson and the Brownlow kid.'

'It's not like I've ever been on his favourite people list. How are they doing trying to track down Mr Wiseman's grandson?

'Not great. Social Services are doing their best, but the lad seems to have just vanished,' Blacklock answered. 'Mick said something about a bloke you're fishing with?'

'He stayed in the Forest last night and knows Imogen Lamont.' Lunn replied. 'I'm going to the funeral services on Monday. I just think it might be interesting to see who turns up for Max's service. Also, I need a favour.'

'Go on.'

'An extraordinary meeting of the IAG has been called for tomorrow at nine and they want a senior officer to come and give them an update.'

'Natives getting restless, are they?'

'They have legitimate concerns.'

'Okay. Usual place is it?'

'I'll see you outside just before nine.'

'Let me know if we need to speak to your fisherman friend.'

'Will do and see you tomorrow,' Lunn replied. 'Maybe we can grab a drink in the evening?'

'Sure.'

A few minutes later Gem arrived with Steve, who had got the rainbow he'd been hunting.

'What did you get him on?' Jack asked.

'I used that Gold Head Viva pattern with the Krystal Flash.'

'That's one of Gem's designs.'

'What do you think weight wise?'

'It looks about thirteen pounds, maybe a shade more,' Lunn replied.

'Got some nice footage and photos too,' Steve said.

'I'm nearly ready in here if your guy wants to set up?' said Lunn.

'Yeah, let me sort this out. It's coming up on midday, so the fishing is going to get quieter.'

'Good time to have a break then.'

'I'll be back in a minute,' Steve said, leaving Lunn alone with his partner's son.'

Ingram re-joined them as a mobile phone went off and Jack watched as the magazine editor started hunting for it in his fishing vest. Lunn looked across at Gem, who held two fingers up to him.

'I can't really talk, Imogen,' Ingram said. 'I'll call you back later this afternoon.'

He listened for a moment and then terminated the call.

'You must know the rivers around here well, Steve?' Lunn asked.

'The Itchen and the Meon pretty well, but I adore fishing the Test,' Ingram replied.

'Where's your favourite spot?'

'The Stockbridge area is fantastic, but there is a stretch below Romsey, couple of miles or so on from the Broadlands Estates water and it's just a delight there.'

Jack knew he was talking about the beats belonging to the Lamont family.

'Do you get to fish there much?' Gem asked.

'Not as much as I'd have liked, but that's set to change,' Ingram said with a smile. 'There was an old woman who owned the water, but now she's dead and the relatives are looking to make some changes.'

'Oh, what sort of changes?' Gem pressed him.

'Make it more commercial or sell it off.'

'Did you know the old woman well?'

'Not really. I'd see her walking the bankside occasionally and exchange a few words, but I know the daughter in law.'

'Really.' Lunn responded. 'And you stayed in The Forest last night?'

Ingram nodded.

'Somewhere nice, I hope?'

'Terra Something or other.'

'I know it, Terra Vina. Decent restaurant and good cellar.'

'If you say so,' came back the non-committal reply.

Jack and Gem exchanged a meaningful look.


It was around four in the afternoon by the time they'd finished filming some of the fly-tying, whilst they chatted about Jack's business and other places they'd fished. The two older men knew that the fishery often came alive in the late afternoon and evening.

'Why don't I take Gem off and see if we can't find a bigger fish for him?' Ingram suggested.

'I'm going to try the carrier stream with a dry fly and try and winkle out a wild brownie,' Lunn replied.


A couple of hours later they adjourned to The Trout Inn, about half a mile from the fishery, for a pint and final chat. Ingram left shortly after that with the photographer to start back towards London.

'Do you think he suspected anything?' Gem asked.

'Hopefully not,' Lunn replied. 'We know for sure that he's connected to Imogen Lamont, so we'll check with the hotel first and before the Police get to him.'

They dropped the fish off at Andy Fairford's for smoking and then drove to Terra Vina, Jack told the receptionist that his friend, Steven Ingram, had possibly left a jacket in his room and would they mind checking. They were informed that neither Mr Ingram, nor his female companion had left anything behind.

'You're thinking that's Imogen Lamont, aren't you?' Gem asked.

'You've got to admit that it's hardly a leap in the dark,' he replied.

'CCTV at the hotel?'

'They're not going to hand it over to the likes of us. I'll let Mick and Rhona sort that.'

Chapter 51

'How'd you get on?' Sarah asked, when they arrived home. 'And where are my fish?'

'Getting smoked at Andy Fairford's,' Jack replied.

'And are you now a great hunter-gatherer, Gem?' her Mother asked.

'I had a wonderful day, mum. I caught some trout, tied some flies, plenty of fly-fishing bonding,' came the reply.

'Well, I thought we might treat ourselves to a curry tonight, as it's coming up on seven o'clock,' she announced.

Jack hunted for the restaurant menu and then called the number to book a table.

Twenty minutes later they assembled in the hall, locked the dogs in the kitchen and left and for the restaurant, which was a couple of hundred yards away.

As always, they were greeted like old friends by Mr Khan and his staff, Jack buttonholed the restaurant owner.

'Mr Khan, do you mind me asking again about the night that Mrs Lamont was killed again?'

'Not at all. You know the son was here and I've told the police this. The boy made a bit of a fuss about the bill, but that was about it. Why are you asking, I thought this was all finished with?'

'It's nothing really, just something I had in the back of my mind and wanted to clear up,' Jack said. 'Nobody came with him and did he make or get any phone calls whilst he was waiting?'

'I don't remember seeing him talking to anybody, on the phone. Dreadful thing with that journalist and not good for business,' the restauranteur continued. 'She came here asking questions, you know.'

'Really, what sort of questions?' Lunn asked.

'Trying to get some information on the night old Mrs Lamont died. Asking about you. I told her nothing, of course,' Khan said. 'No one knew this was going to happen though and no one deserves to die like that.'

'The police will find out who did it, you can rely on that,' Lunn responded.

'The rumour around the village is that the police now have three unsolved murders, Mr Lunn, and some locals are claiming they're all linked.'

'Opinions are like noses, everybody's got one.'

'Agreed,' the restaurateur replied with a smile. 'Let me get your drinks sorted.'


'What are you up to tomorrow, after your day out today?' Sarah asked as she lay in bed later that night.

'I've got an I.A.G. meeting first thing. Gem and I have some orders to fill and we thought we'd go to Max Lamont's funeral.'

He saw the look on his partner's face.

'I don't think he killed his mother and not many will be going. So, we thought we'd show our faces.'

'Are you going to his mother's service too?'

'She left me the rod on the beat, so it's only right I show my respects.'

Jack tried to read his book, but he kept returning to exactly what was the connection between Steve Ingram and Imogen Lamont and who was this mystery man with a dark coloured car that Eden was dating?

Chapter 52


Jack thought that Rhona looked a little uncomfortable as she stood with the local uniformed Inspector. But then it wasn't every day that she had was summoned on behalf of the chairperson of a worried I.A.G.

'Morning, Rhona and morning Matt,' Lunn said as he shook hands with them both.

'This feels like an ambush,' Rhona whispered to him.

'Just friends here,' he replied. 'They're just looking for some reassurance.'

'And there's the rub. You know I can't really tell them much, other than we have three dead bodies on our hands and we're pursuing a number of leads.'

'The fact that you're seen to be leading the inquiry is a good start.'

'You know that's bollocks though and Mick will be the real lead on it.'

'They don't know that and you've got the local uniform Inspector here. It all helps.'


Karen Pusey, the Chairperson and a local farmer, called the meeting to order.

'I don't like calling emergency meetings of the I.A.G.,' she said. 'But I think we can all agree that these recent deaths more than warrant it.'

There was a confirmatory murmur from the other parties.

'I'm sure we all appreciate Detective Chief Superintendent Blacklock taking the time to be here today, along with Inspector Matt Holroyd from Lyndhurst. DCS Blacklock heads up the Major Crimes Unit in Southampton and it's her team that's dealing with the murders. I'm going to ask her to talk us through what the Police are doing and intend to do, then open it up to any questions from the floor. DCS Blacklock?'

Rhona got to her feet. 'As you all now know, there have been three killings in the area in the last couple of weeks and three killings in a year would be a statistical anomaly. We can't say for certain, but there is probably a connection between the first two and possibly all three of them. We have a number of people who are of interest, investigations are ongoing and we're keeping an open mind.' She sat back down.

'Well, thank you,' The Chairperson said. 'Questions?'

'This has been a right cock-up by the Police, hasn't it?' Eric McKinley, a local hotelier stated. 'These murders are driving visitors away from the area. Every morning I have calls or emails cancelling bookings. I want to know what you're going to do about it and don't give us that load of old guff that you've just parroted out.'

'There were some mistakes made in the early part of the investigation, I'll grant you. But we now have some additional members of the public we need to speak to and we're re-examining the forensic evidence to see if there's a tangible connection between the crimes,' Rhona replied.

The hotelier looked to interrupt, but Rhona silenced him with a glance and wave of a finger.

She continued, 'I appreciate that this is putting pressure on local businesses, but the important thing is to catch the killer or killers. I've asked Inspector Holroyd to ensure that we have an increased visibility and we'll be having a press conference later today in which we'll outline some ways that residents and visitors can increase their safety and vigilance. My advice to you, Mr McKinley is to let us do our job.'

'That's just a sop,' McKinley spat out. 'If it wasn't for the man sat next to you, you'd have a decorated Falklands War veteran locked up and poor Max Lamont labelled as his mother's killer.'

'To be fair,' Lunn interjected. 'DCS Blacklock wasn't in charge of either of those investigations and I trust her to be thorough and open-minded. You want someone locked up quickly, Eric? As you've just pointed out, it's just as important to lock the right person, or persons up.'

'I can see the connection between Old Mrs Lamont and her son, but where does this newspaper reporter fit in?' asked Terry Knight, the Chief Verderer.

'We know she was investigating the killings and that her body was found in the Forest.' Blacklock responded. 'As I said, we haven't had all the forensics back yet, but that gives us some hope of getting some evidence.'

'So, who have you got to see?' McKinley asked.

'You know I'm not going to discuss any lines of inquiry in detail, never mind naming persons of interest,' the DCS replied. 'We all want the same thing here, a safe New Forest and the swift arrest of whoever has been committing these murders. The Police appreciate the support that this I.A.G. has given to us and that you've worked with us to significantly reduce crime in the area, but this is different. We go years without a murder in this area and we're now dealing with three. We have to be meticulous, exhaustive and absolutely sure when we make any arrests.'

'We do understand that and you have our backing,' Karen Pusey conceded and then asked if additional officers would be tasked to the Forest.

'There will be increased visibility,' Inspector Hayes said.

'That's not what I asked, Inspector,' the Chairperson replied.

Matt Holroyd looked to Rhona for support.

'There are budgetary considerations,' Blacklock answered. 'You all know that we have constraints on manpower and that there have been significant cuts to Police funding. That being said, we're looking at making sure that there's an increased and visible Police presence.'

'Can you be more specific?' the Chief Verderer asked.

'You'll see more cars and more foot patrols and that's as far as I'll go at this stage.' Blacklock said.

'Well, Chief Superintendent, I'm sure you have work to do, so let's not keep you any longer,' Karen Pusey said. 'That was the only matter on the agenda, so I'll call the meeting closed unless anyone has any other business pertinent to this? No? Then I declare this extraordinary meeting over. Jack, a word.'

Lunn told Rhona Blacklock that he'd see her outside and made his way over to Karen Pusey.

'How involved are you in this?' she asked.

'I'm not sure that I'm involved at all, other than being a member of the I.A.G. and finding the body.'

She raised an eyebrow. 'I know that you got the poacher off and that you were seen talking to the newspaperwoman, so don't go trying to pull the wool over my eyes.'

'With respect, I can't tell you anymore than DCS Blacklock told you and for the reasons she gave.'

'But you know who the persons of interest are, don't you.'

'Is that a statement or question.'

'The former.'

'I can tell you that it was no one that was in this meeting.'

'Well, I should be grateful for small mercies then.'

Look, the old woman wasn't exactly the most popular person in the area and so they have a number of people they need to speak to,' he said. 'This isn't like a TV drama, where it's all wrapped up in a couple of hours. They have to be interviewed, their movements and stories verified, any CCTV looked at, phone records, forensics, DNA. It all takes time.'

'I know, I know. Is she any good, your DCS Blacklock?'

'The best investigating officer I ever worked with and the DI on the case is my old DC, so we're in good hands.'

'And you're not involved? She looked at him quizzically, 'Do I like look like I just fell off the hay cart?'

'Anything but, Karen,' he replied with a wink.

Rhona Blacklock was waiting just outside, having a furtive cigarette.

'That wasn't so bad,' Jack said.

'Who was the rather rude bloke?'

'Eric McKinley, local hotelier and general pain in the rear.'

'Let me have a guess, he's always got a bee in his bonnet about something?'

'A one-man complaints department.'

'So, first up we're going to revisit the ex-neighbours and their son.'

'Has Mick heard from the son?'

'No, but we've been round to the business address, which is his home and it looks like he's been away a few days. You know, the usual, mail sat on the doormat, etc. He organises events for companies, so he could be on a job. Mick has emailed him through the company, so I'm pretty certain he knows we want to see him.'

'What about Galletly?'

'Still no sign of him, but we've circulated his picture. He'll turn up, his type always returns home,' she replied. 'What about this fisherman you were with yesterday?'

'You'll need to speak to him for sure. He knows the daughter-in-law, knew the old woman walked the banks and had fished the river several times. There's a possibility that he could profit from the deaths too,' he replied. 'There are so many loose ends, Rhona.'

'Well' I'd better make sure that a few of them tied up then,' she said. 'Drink this evening?'

'Of course,' he replied.

Chapter 53

Jack and Gem left the house later that morning and walked up towards the Church, which was a magnificent Gothic Victorian building with a fabulous fresco and famous for being the last resting place of Alice Hargreaves, the inspiration for Lewis Carroll's Alice, of Alice in Wonderland. It was now going to be the last resting place of Elizabeth Lamont and her son.

There was quite a crowd assembled for the old lady's service. Whilst she hadn't been the most popular figure, she'd served on quite a few local committees and no doubt quite a few of the people there were attending out of a sense of duty, rather than affection. Lunn noted that the daughter in law and grandchildren were present, suitably attired and accepting the condolences of other attendees. Jack joined the queue, to pay his respects.

Gem nudged him. 'Do we really want to do this?'

'Let's see what sort of reaction we get from the grieving family,' Lunn said, as they approached them.

'What the hell do you want here?' Seb Lamont said angrily when he noticed Jack.

Before Jack had a chance to reply, Imogen Lamont interrupted her son. 'I'm sure Mr Lunn has just come here to offer his condolences and pay his respects.'

'No shotgun today, Sebastian?' Lunn asked.

'I don't need a shotgun to deal with a cripple,' the son replied threateningly.

'You're not trying to intimidate anyone, are you Seb?' Gem said, as she joined Jack.

'Here's another bad penny, Gemma Bryce. What business is it of yours?' the son spat back.

'Jack's my mum's partner and like him, I'm paying my respects. If you want to discuss that, we can take it elsewhere? But, as it didn't end well for you last time, you might want to skip that.'

'You've got a big mouth.'

'Five years in the Army and two tours in Afghanistan will do that for you, Seb and I like to keep my combat skills up.'

Seb was left open-mouthed.

Imogen Lamont interrupted. 'I won't have any arguments today. This is a sad occasion and I won't have anyone behaving disrespectfully.'

'You're right of course,' Lunn replied. 'This is a celebration of Elizabeth's life and time for all of us to reflect on the lives we've led. Wouldn't you agree?'

'What do you mean?' she asked.

'Well, no one lives a guilt-free life, Imogen.'

'I'm sure you're right,' she replied. 'And now you're holding up other people.'

'Will I see you at Max's service later?' Lunn enquired.

'I think not.'

'He killed Granny,' the daughter added.

'What on earth makes you say that?' Gem asked.

The young woman hesitated for a moment before answering.

'It's what all the newspapers, TV and the Police say.'

'Good point. But the Police thought the poacher had killed your grandmother and they were wrong there, weren't they?' She let the words sink in for a few seconds before continuing. 'Of course, they couldn't possibly be wrong again, could they?'

Imogen Lamont turned away towards the other mourner waiting in the queue without answering.

Jack saw Neville Hayes near the entrance to the church and they walked over to him.

'Come to pay your respects?'

'Yes,' the big man said, then turned to Gem. 'I see you and the son don't exactly get on?'

'Let's just say he's not on my Christmas card list, Mr Hayes' she replied.

Big Nev looked the young woman up and down. 'Army Officer, weren't you?'

'Intelligence Corps,' Gem nodded. 'Did you serve, Mr Hayes?'

'Only at Her Majesty's pleasure. What are you going to do now?'

'I've only just got back from working abroad, so I'm helping Jack out. At least until I can figure out what I want to do next.

Hayes turned back to Jack. 'I heard about the journalist.'

'She was convinced there was a killer on the loose,' Lunn replied.

'She came knocking on my door. Wanted to see if I knew anything.'

'And?'

'Gave her short shrift as soon as she said she was from a newspaper and I recognised her as the one who got kicked off that Fleet Street rag.'

'I think she'd changed, and that she saw the killings in a similar way to me. They also offered her a chance to prove herself as an investigative journalist again, like some form of redemption.'

'Leopards don't change their spots.'

'You did, Neville.'

The big man smiled. 'Touché.'

'Are you staying on for Max's service?' Jack asked.

'I thought I would, but no. All this death is rather upsetting, Mr Lunn.'

'Is there's anything that the journalist said to you that you thought was odd?'

'Not really. But you're right, she did refer to them as murders and not deaths.'

'Thanks, Neville,' Jack replied, offering him his hand.

Taking it, the big man leant in towards Lunn. 'I know you're on the case. See what you and your old boss can do to get this sorted pronto. I came here for some peace and quiet, not to end up living somewhere with a killer on the loose.'

'I'm looking into it,' Jack replied.

'Well, look a bit closer and quicker then,' Hayes said and made his way into the church.

'That's quite a scary bloke,' Gem said, watching the retreating figure.

'He likes to make sure that the rumours about him appear true, but he's got his heart in the right place. He might have got up to some shenanigans in the past, but I think he's legit and has been for a good few years.'


It came as no surprise to Jack that Max Lamont's funeral was poorly attended. Imogen Lamont and her children were conspicuous by their absence. There was no eulogy and the short service had almost finished when Lunn heard heels on the stone floor of the church and turned to see a blonde woman in her early forties take a pew at the back. She kept her head bowed and left as soon as the service was over.

Jack emerged from the church and turned to Gem.

'Did you see the woman arrive and sit at the back?'

'I heard someone come in, but didn't look,' Gem replied. 'Did you know her?'

'I can't say I did. Blonde, early forties.'

Other than the minister, Gem and Jack were the only mourners at the graveside. As the minister said a few more words, Jack heard the sound of high heels again and turned to see the same blonde woman watching a short distance away.

He whispered to Gem. 'Stay here.'

He walked away from the grave as if he was leaving and then changed direction to approach the woman. She didn't notice him initially and only turned to walk away at the last moment, but Lunn caught up to her and decided to shoot for it all.

'You were close to him,' he said.

'Who are you and why are you asking me questions?'

'It wasn't a question,' he replied. 'It was a statement. Look my name is Jack Lunn. I'm an ex-copper and I found his mother's body. Tell me if I'm wrong, but my guess is he was with you when his mother was killed.'

'Why would I feel the need to talk to you?'

'I'm convinced that Max didn't do it. I saw and spoke to him the day after his mother had been killed and there was no way that he was involved in my opinion. I've told the Police as much.'

She remained tight-lipped.

'If you were with him and say nothing, then some people will always think of him as a murderer,' Jack reasoned.

'He said it would all blow over. That I shouldn't say anything. Then he had the fall and they called him a murderer.'

'But if you knew differently, why didn't you come forward?'

'I'm married.'

'Ah, awkward,' Jack said. 'Look, I'm convinced that Max's mother was killed and you've just confirmed that Max was unlikely to have been her murderer. If he really meant something to you, then make a statement and help clear his name.'

'I can't do that. What if my husband finds out?' the woman said.

'Can I buy you a coffee?' he asked.

She nodded and they made their way to a nearby café.

Jack brought the drinks over, sat opposite her and said, 'I'm hopeful that the case could be made without you. But, a statement from you would pretty much take Max out of the picture completely. When the Police catch whoever killed them both, it will stop the defence muddying the waters.'

'He was going to leave his wife,' she said.

'Were you going to leave your husband?'

She nodded.

'Then why are you still so concerned about him finding out,' said Lunn. 'If you're unhappy in your marriage, you should just be honest with your husband. And if it can't be fixed, then get out.'

'Are you speaking from experience, Mr Lunn?'

'I've been there and got the t-shirt.'

'I'm still trying to deal with what's happened.'

'Look, I'm not going to apply pressure on you to come forward, but you have to know that there's a killer still out there,' Jack said. 'You'd be doing the right thing speaking to the police, helping clear Max's name and getting them to focus on getting the real killer locked up.'

'Why are you so involved, Mr Lunn?'

'I'm just looking for some justice for Mrs Lamont, to get an innocent man's name cleared and whoever killed them behind bars.'

'Do the police know what you know?' the woman asked.

'Most of it and they're coming around to the idea that there's a connection between the deaths of Max and his mother and the reporter that was found yesterday morning. I've a meeting with the senior officer in charge this evening and it would really help if you were prepared to speak to her,' Jack said. 'Why don't I give you my mobile number and you can call me after you've had a chance to think about it. The senior officer is a good friend and will treat your information with total discretion, I promise.'

'Okay, give me your number. I'm not saying I'll call you, but I'll think about it.'

Lunn hunted through his pockets for a piece of paper and found one of his old business cards, he scribbled his mobile number on it and handed it over.

'Text or call me either way, withhold ID if you feel more comfortable,' Lunn said. 'Can I just ask you one other question, please?

'Depends what it is.'

'Was Max left-handed?'

'Yes,' she replied. 'Is that important?'

'It might help clear him completely I think and thanks for talking to me.'

He walked her back to her car, thanked her for talking to him and then noted the registration number.


'Well?' Gem asked, when he came back.

'She alibi's Max for the night his mother was murdered.'

'So, they were both killed?'

'Every possibility. She might well talk to the Police, but I noted her registration just in case.'

'A bit sneaky, Jack.'

'No point in getting older, if you don't get craftier. Come on, we'll get back home and get on with some of those orders.'


Jack got a phone call at about four thirty.

'Mr Lunn?' a female voice asked.

'Yes. How can I help you?'

'We met this morning at the church.'

'I'm glad you called me.'

'I'll only speak to your contact if you're present and I'm not going to appear in Court. Is that clear?' the woman said.

'Crystal,' Lunn replied. 'I'll need some details for my contact. Are you okay to let me have your name and a contact number?'

'My name is Naomi Cooper and you should have my mobile number on your phone.'

'I do thanks, Naomi. My contact is called Rhona Blacklock, she's a Detective Chief Superintendent and I'm meeting with her later this evening. Would it be possible for her to meet you tomorrow?'

'Late morning would be good.'

'I'll let her know and thank you again.'

With the call ended, Jack rubbed his hands together and looked over at Gem.

'That should put the lid on Max as the killer,' he said with a smile.

'Are you sure Rhona will be as happy?' she asked.

'Let's cross that bridge when we get to it.'


In the pub Jack bought pints.

'See if you can find a table in a quiet spot,' he said. 'I don't want anyone eavesdropping on us.'

'It looks like outside might be the best bet then. I'll see what I can do.'

'Take the beers, I'll be with you in a minute.'

Jack was just getting his change when Rhona Blacklock arrived with Mick Sparkes in tow.

'You in the chair then, Jack?' she asked.

'Looks like it. What'll you have?'

'I'll have a nice glass of Pinot Grigio and DI Sparkes will have a soft drink, as he's driving,' Blacklock replied. 'Get me some nuts too, I haven't eaten since breakfast.'

'Nuts don't count as one of your five a day,' Lunn remarked and ordered drinks and some nibbles. 'Gem is finding us a quiet table in the garden.'

'What the bloody hell is she doing here?' Blacklock asked as they made their way out into the beer garden.

'She's been with me on the surveillance.'

'She can't join us, you know?'

'She's ex-Military Intelligence, Rhona. She's signed the Official Secrets Act, is used to handling sensitive information and looks at things slightly differently from those of us with a copper's background.'

Rhona looked sceptical at best but nodded her consent and they walked out into the garden

'Nice to see you again,' Gem said, as she shook hands with the senior police officer.

'And you, Gem. It's been a while,' Blacklock replied. 'I was going to ask you to leave us to speak privately. But Jack has persuaded me otherwise and says you may be able to bring a different angle of thinking. You understand that everything we talk about is strictly confidential?'

'No problem.'

'It's appreciated,' Lunn replied. 'As you know, I'm pretty sure I know that what killed Mrs Lamont was designed to kill, not just something that came to hand. I just can't quite pin down what it might be.'

'Okay, what else?' Blacklock asked.

'We know that the family are alibiing each other, but is there any way you can get a look at their mobile activity?' Gem asked.

'It's not as easy as that, I'm afraid. You two having a hunch isn't enough for us to access any of their phone records,' Blacklock said. 'Neither is the kids saying they're single when one of them may be in a relationship. The mobile phone data we do have points to them all being at home together.'

'What if they have more than one phone?' Gem asked and getting a warning look from Jack.

'We've got no proof of that.' Sparkes interjected.

'I'm just not ruling anyone out. Maybe if they'd had a call it could have told them two things, that the old lady was dead and the takeaway from the curry house was an effective alibi,' Jack replied. 'As for the daughter saying she didn't have a boyfriend, my daughters saw her buying underwear.'

'What has that got to do with anything?' Blacklock asked.

'It wasn't the type of underwear a woman buys for herself apparently,' Lunn explained. 'Pretty and practical is what women buy for themselves. Sexy is because they have a man.'

'Well, it's good that you men learn something new every day. Any other reasons why you think the daughter-in-law and her children could be involved?' Blacklock said, putting her wine glass down. 'I'm still far from convinced.'

'I have a witness that says Max Lamont wasn't at his mother's house at the time she was killed,' Jack said. 'I have Imogen Lamont meeting with Steve Ingram and talking to him on a second phone, Ingram was in the Forest the night Adele Porter was killed. The report on old Mrs Lamont said she was killed by someone who held the weapon in their right hand.'

'And?'

'Max Lamont was left-handed, so you also need to check which hand typed the message on his laptop,'

'Okay, so that would rule him out as his mother's killer and there would be no need for a note saying he was sorry,' said the DCS, leaning forwards. 'We can check the fingerprints on the laptop. What about this witness?'

'Jack and I went to Max Lamont's funeral,' Gem explained. 'He spotted a woman at the service and got talking to her and she says she was with Max when Elizabeth Lamont was murdered.'

'How do you mean 'with'? As in having an affair?'

'So it seems.' Jack replied.

'Will she talk?' Mick Sparkes asked.

'She took a bit of convincing, but she'll talk,' Lunn replied. 'I've given her your name, Rhona. You can get in touch with her tomorrow. You'll need to send her a text, she'll be in Southampton and will meet with you in the late morning.'

'Her name and number?' asked Blacklock.

Lunn handed over a slip of paper.

'Her number plate is on there too. I'm pretty sure she must be from somewhere in the Forest, which is quite possibly why you have no footage of Max on CCTV,' said Lunn. 'She's asked that I'm present when you meet with her.'

'And she definitely his mistress?' Sparkes asked.

'In love and both going to leave their partners, according to her.'

'Why the bloody hell didn't she come forward before now?' asked the DCS.

'Max had told her to lay low when his mother was killed, as he thought it would all blow over,' Lunn said.

'Okay,' Blacklock said. 'If Max Lamont was elsewhere, then we have an unknown killer. We still have the rest of the family having a family meal on the evening of the murder. But, if Imogen Lamont knew about her husband's affair, then the family do have motive.'

'I have something to say about my near miss too,' Lunn said.

Rhona Blacklock raised an eyebrow. 'And?'

'Seb Lamont was on the phone when I walked away from the house and about twenty-five minutes later a car tries to run me down. It could just be a coincidence, of course.'

'I'm not saying that we don't believe you,' Sparkes said. 'You've given us a crowded field of suspects to look at and we need to whittle that down first.'

'What about Galletly?' Lunn asked.

'Not at his mother's house and the talk is he's holed up somewhere. Let's just say that the search for him is ongoing,' Sparkes replied. 'We're getting nowhere with the son of the builder. Social Services have given us what they have, but we seem to have run into a brick wall. We'll ask the Met to have a chat with your magazine editor. They'll have the background about his meeting and knowing Imogen Lamont. I've also told them to look into his car being off the road. Do you really think it could have been this Ingram bloke who that nearly ran you over?'

'Anything is possible,' Lunn said. 'Okay. You'll let me know when you're ready to speak to

Naomi Cooper and have a time for me to come into the nick?'

'I'll call you,' Blacklock said. 'But you understand that you're only there as a facilitator and can't be part of any interviews.'

'No problem. I just want her to be sure that she's comfortable with you and that she gets the discretion she wants.'

'Obviously, we'd like her as a friendly witness and so I'll be the genial auntie, Jack. We'll need to re-interview the Brownlow's too.'

'Have you heard from the son?' Gem asked.

'Nothing,' Sparkes replied. 'I've spoken to the neighbours and he's frequently away for a few days at a time.'

'Come on, we'll give you two a lift back,' Blacklock said, getting up from the table.


Lunn knew the manure had connected with the air conditioning when he saw Sarah in the front window.

'Better put your flak jacket and tin helmet on. I think there is incoming fire,' Gem said.

'Have you not kept your nearest and dearest in the loop?' Rhona Blacklock asked.

'That flapping you can hear, Detective Chief Superintendent. That's Jack's chickens coming home to roost.' Gem chipped in.

Lunn sighed. 'Better face the music, I suppose.'

'My best guess is it's the 1812 Overture, cannons and all,' Gem said with a smile.

'Not helping, Gem. Really not helping…,' said Lunn resignedly.

'I've got to get back to the office,' Blacklock muttered, taking in the situation.

'There's not a chance of that, Rhona,' Lunn said. 'You'll get your arse in the house and tell my other half how instrumental I've been to you in cracking this case and that Gem's been a great help too.'

'I'm more than happy to be left out of this,' his partner's daughter replied. 'After all, I was only following orders.'

'Didn't work at Nuremberg and I have a feeling that it's not going to work here, Gem,' Blacklock said.

Sarah was sitting in the front room with her sternest schoolteacher face on, as the four of them sidled in.

'Hello, love. Look who I bumped into at the pub,' Lunn said.

'Do you really think I'm that naïve?' she said. 'Hello, Rhona. Perhaps I can get some sense from you?'

'You're looking particularly lovely today, Sarah,' said the DCS. 'New hairstyle?'

'Cut the flattery. What have you got him involved in?' she asked.

'No, no, you've got it wrong there. It's Jack and young Gem that have been doing all the work,' Blacklock replied.

'Thanks, Rhona. Couldn't you have dropped me any further in it?' Lunn said, then turned back to his partner. 'I'm sorry I didn't say much to you. I just didn't want you worrying.'

'But you thought it was okay to involve my daughter in your activities?' she asked.

'I kind of involved myself, Mum,' Gem said.

'So, the only innocent party here is you, Rhona?'

'Well, let's just say I didn't discourage him,' the DCS replied.

'What in hell are you thinking, Jack?' his partner asked.

'I found the body, Sarah. I want justice for her,' Lunn explained. 'I knew Max hadn't done it and I was right. Now someone has killed the journalist, who was also convinced of the same.'

Sarah turned to Blacklock. 'Is he right?'

'Looks that way. We have a witness that puts Max Lamont somewhere else. Jack's made some connections to other suspects and we're looking into the car that nearly ran Jack down the other evening.'

'What bloody car, Jack?' Sarah asked. 'Was this when you told me you fell over?'

'Technically, I had to dive out of the way, It might have looked like a fall from a distance,' Lunn replied, giving Blacklock a look that could kill.

'Don't think for one minute that you're in my good books,' Sarah said. 'Are you taking over from here, Rhona?'

'I just need Jack to meet with a witness tomorrow and I'll need statements from both your men.'

'I bloody knew you were up to something, Jack,' Sarah said and then turned to her eldest daughter. 'As for you, Gemma, I don't know what to say.'

'I didn't mean to cause any upset, mum. But it wasn't right for Max Lamont to carry the can for his mother's murder,' Gem replied.

'Rhona, you and Mick can go. I'm surprised at you though, Mick,' Sarah said. 'Gemma, get me a whiskey and don't think for a minute that I'm finished with you yet.'

Blacklock took the hint and after telling Jack and Gem to be at Southampton nick after nine in the morning, she left hurriedly with Mick Sparkes in tow.

Gem brought a large whiskey through for Sarah, having poured one for herself and Jack as well.

'Thanks,' Sarah said, taking a sip of her drink and fixing her eyes on Jack. 'I think I know why you got so caught up in this.'

'Apart from having the body float down to me?' Lunn asked.

'No need to be sarcastic, Jack.' Sarah replied. 'I know she was about the same age as your mother and another difficult woman. That doesn't excuse you from lying to me.'

'Maybe subconsciously that had an effect,' Lunn replied. 'You know I've got regrets about the relationship that I had with my mum and this was a horrific attack against another defenceless old woman that I knew, I want whoever did this brought to book. I didn't lie to you though, just didn't tell you everything.'

'You're going to try semantics on with me, Jack Lunn? You're feeling brave. You barely told me anything. I know you have this inordinate need to see that justice is served, but that includes being honest with me.'

'I am sorry, and I should have told you what we were up to.'

'You know that I mean what I say.'

'I'll keep my nose clean in future and not let Jack lead me astray, I promise,' Gem chipped in from the doorway.

'I doubt there was much leading required, Gemma,' Sarah replied. 'I feel very let down by the two of you.'

'But, Sarah,' Lunn intreated.

'Don't even go there, Jack,' she interrupted.

Chapter 54

Jack could hear raised voices from the kitchen as he came out of the bedroom and onto the landing later that evening.

Gem was sat on the stairs.

'What on earth is going on?' Jack asked.

'Mum and Eden are having a full and frank discussion about boyfriends.'

'I'd better see what I can do to settle things down.'

'I can't work out if you're brave or foolish,' Gem replied.

'As Wilde said, *'Everything is dangerous, my dear fellow. If it wasn't so, life wouldn't be worth living.'*

As Lunn walked through the kitchen door, both women turned towards him.

'I'm just a worried mum and you haven't always made the wisest choices in the past,' Sarah said to Eden then turned to Lunn for support. 'Has she, Jack?'

'Your Mother makes a good point, Eden.'

'Oh, and I'm going to take relationship advice from the two of you with your divorce track records?' she scoffed.

'We're speaking from experience,' Sarah said in exasperation.

'I know you've had Gem trying to poke around my social media and Jack's been using the girls to try and find out about him. Frankly, how dare you.'

'You've been so secretive about who he is and that's why we've been worried,' her Mother replied.

'Look, we want to respect your privacy. But you have to meet us halfway,' Lunn reasoned.

'I don't have to do anything, and my privacy is a right.' Eden replied dismissively.

'Whilst you live under this roof, I'm not going to stick my head in the sand and surrender my responsibility for you,' Sarah argued back.

'Can we just calm down a little?' Jack pleaded.

'No problem,' Eden replied. 'I'm packing some things and going to stay with friends for a few days and you can't stop me.'

Sarah glanced at Lunn, 'Jack?'

'What? Should I wrestle her to the ground and chain her up in a tower,' he replied and turned to Eden. 'Are you staying with friends or him?'

'You don't need to know.'

'We want to know you're safe, that's all.'

'I'll call or text you,' she said and opened the kitchen door to find Gem lurking outside. 'Don't even think about trying to track me down. You all just have to stop treating me like a baby.'

Sarah sat down on a kitchen chair and Gem came in from the hallway.

'Didn't go so well?' Gem asked.

'You heard,' Lunn replied.

Gem put a comforting hand on her mother's shoulder. 'She'll be back before you know it.'

'That's not the point,' Sarah said. 'Why is she being so bloody-minded?'

'She knows you care, but maybe we were all just a little heavy-handed with her?' her eldest replied. 'It could have gone worse.'

'Really?' his mother replied with a sigh.

They heard the bedroom door slam and the tattoo of steps down the stairs.

Sarah looked at them both. 'I want her back under my wing a.s.a.p., do you both understand?'

Jack heard the front door slam and hurried to the front door to see Eden getting into a dark coloured car. He couldn't really see anything of the driver in the darkness, but as it drove away, he noted the registration and returned to the kitchen.

'Well, I think the new boyfriend just picked her up, so I'm guessing that she's staying with him,' he said, as he rummaged by the phone for a pen and some paper. 'I got the number plate and can ask Mick to run it whilst we're in Southampton tomorrow.'

'Make sure you do,' Sarah said emphatically.

Chapter 55

Gem was just getting up for her running shoes when Lunn knocked on her bedroom door the next morning.

'We leave in about forty-five minutes,' he reminded her.

'Okay, I'll have a quick run and shower and be with you.'

In the main bedroom, Sarah was already awake.

'How was the spare bedroom?' she asked.

'Not somewhere I want to revisit.'

'Is Gem getting up?'

'Run and a shower, she'll be ready in thirty minutes,' Lunn replied. 'She's nothing if not low maintenance.'

'When are you going?'

'In about three-quarters of an hour.'

'What have you got to do, other than making a statement?'

'Not much and we should be back later this morning.'

'And the boyfriend's car registration?' she asked.

'Yes, I'll get it sorted.'


As he left the house with Gem, Jack called ahead to Mick Sparkes.

'I'll meet you at Reception when you arrive, get you badged up and signed in,' The DI stated.


As good as his word, Mick ushered them through the building, into the lift and up to Major Crimes where DCS Blacklock was waiting.

'Morning, you two,' she said. 'This way.'

They followed her through the main office and Jack noticed DCI Richardson, Geoff Cooke's right hand man, scurrying off towards the Superintendent's office. No doubt to let Geoffrey know they were in the building, he thought ominously.

'Gem, I'll get DC Taylor to take your statement,' Blacklock said, beckoning the young detective over.

'Just stick to the facts. Nothing subjective, no speculation,' Lunn advised.

'Understood,' Gem replied, blushing slightly as Marcus Taylor joined them.

'Marcus, Gemma is just going to give you a background statement. Take her through the usual, please,' Blacklock ordered.

'Will do, boss,' he replied and turned to Gem. 'You're with me.'

'I can think of worse ways to spend a morning,' Gem said, as she followed him dutifully.

'You're with me and Mick,' Blacklock said to Lunn. 'My office and a coffee, I think.'

Another DC was called in to take Jack's statement and in about an hour he was done.

'Summing up, you think that the old woman, her son and the journalist could have all killed by the same person?' Sparkes asked once the DC had left Blacklock's office.

'There's a common link, so that seems the most likely,' Lunn replied. 'Two members of the same family and a journalist investigating the first two deaths. The incongruity is the three different ways they died. But we know whoever did this made sure there was little or no chance of any evidence from the lack of forensics at the first two crime scenes and they actively put you guys on the wrong trail.'

'They frame your poacher, then you were right about the few words on a laptop to implicate Max. The word 'sorry' was all typed with the right index finger.'

'Somebody got sloppy,' Lunn replied. 'As my old boss used to tell me, the Devil is in the detail.'

'Mick tells me that you haven't ruled out the family,' Blacklock said.

'I can't see how anyone can be ruled out. But you need to narrow the field, Rhona. Where are you with the other names, that I gave you?'

'We'll get to your list in a minute. Going back to the family, you say that the daughter lied to us about having a boyfriend,' Sparkes speculated. 'Any idea who he is?'

'I've got Seth Walker on the girl,' Lunn told them. 'But I've not heard from him for a couple of days. Do you know when the Met is having a chat with Steve Ingram.'

'They're going to update me later today,' Sparkes replied.

'Why's the poacher helping you out?' Blacklock asked.

'He feels he owes me. When he wants to be, he's practically invisible.'

'Call him and see how he's getting on,' Sparkes said.

'Seth doesn't even own a TV, never mind a mobile phone.'

'We've currently got no one who stands out,' the DI muttered.

'Let's see what the Met come back with,' Blacklock replied.

'And the others?' Lunn asked.

'Still drawing a blank on the builder's son,' Sparkes replied. 'We've widened the search parameters. But, if someone makes a determined effort to disappear, or even assume a new identity, they can do it. You could walk past him in the street and be none the wiser.'

'And it was much easier to do fifteen years ago.' Blacklock added. 'What's the latest on Galletly?'

'We have surveillance at his mother's and his description is circulated, but no sign currently.'

'The former neighbours have to stay in the frame too. He might be in a wheelchair, but his wife and son aren't, and she certainly isn't the forgiving type,' Lunn said.

There was a knock on the door.

'Come,' Blacklock called out and Marcus Taylor stuck his head around the door.

'I'm all finished,' he said.

'What have you done with Gem?' Jack asked.

'Sat at my desk, with orders not to touch anything,' Taylor replied.

'You don't know Gem, that's like an invitation to her.'

'I'd better get back then.'

'Hang on a minute, Marcus,' Blacklock said, then turned to Lunn. 'Look, I'll put what we have in front of the CPS, but I wouldn't bet too much on them saying we can get access to phone records for any of our front runners. We need something more tangible.'

'I understand that, but when you look at all the events, even me nearly getting run over, it keeps leading me back to the killings being connected,' Lunn answered. 'I know it's circumstantial, but I feel we've missed something and you need to start putting suspects under the microscope.'

'Get surveillance organised on the family, Mick,' Blacklock ordered. 'Get it started this evening and I want the old neighbours properly interviewed and find me Liam Galletly.'

'Marcus, ask one of the DS's to come I and see me when I'm finished in here, please,' Sparkes requested.

'What about the PM on Adele Parker?' Lunn asked.

'She was drugged, and a ligature was used to asphyxiate her,' Blacklock replied. 'You were right about her being brought to Bolton's Bench. Scarlett confirmed that she was hung in the tree after she was dead. They're going over her clothes with a fine toothcomb. Her Mother and brother are coming down from Reading to I.D. the body.'

'Any sign of her car and shoes?' Lunn asked.

'Car turned up abandoned in Sway with the keys still in it. Forensics are dealing with it. No sign of her shoes,' Sparkes said.

'When's Naomi Cooper due in?' he enquired.

'About twenty minutes,' the DI replied.

'Do you think she'll be put at ease by seeing you here, Jack?' Blacklock speculated.

'It's what she asked for, Rhona and I'm happy to help in any way I can,' he replied. 'And speaking of help, can I ask a favour?'

'Fire away,' Blacklock said.

He fished a piece of paper out of his back pocket and handed it over. 'Can you run a check on that number plate?'

'Is this a suspect?' she asked.

'I think it's Eden's boyfriend's car,' he explained. 'There was a bit of an argument last night and she went off.'

'And it will help get you back Sarah's good books.'

'It can't do any harm. If Eden's not contactable, Sarah will assume she's lying in a ditch somewhere.'

The DCS took the note from him. 'Give me a few minutes with Mick to get this surveillance organised and approved, then we'll meet your witness. Go and see what mischief Gem's getting up to.'

'No problem.'

Gem and Marcus Taylor were talking animatedly, so he wandered over to a nearby window, taking in the view of the traffic streaming in and out of Southampton. Sensing someone behind him, he turned to see Geoff Cooke and Jack held up both of his hands.

'I come in peace and at the behest of the DCS, Geoff.'

'Happy with your day's work, are you?' the Superintendent asked angrily.

'Happy that a dead son isn't thought of as a murderer, yes. But, I'm certainly not happy that there's a killer, or killers, still out there to be caught.'

'Well, I'm off the case. So, you and your mentor will have to figure that out.'

'Don't try and put this all on me, Geoff,' Lunn replied. 'And before you say anything, I didn't get involved to screw up your career.'

'Oh, you're just the cavalry arriving at the right moment, are you?'

'I found the old woman's body. I knew her. She'd been kind to me in the past and we got on. I just felt some sort of responsibility to make sure that her killer was found. I gave you a list of suspects to follow up on, but you made the decision not to do that and that's on you, Geoff .'

'Who the fuck do you think you are?'

'I'm sure you think I should have left it to you?' Lunn spat back. 'You tried to hang her murder on an innocent man and then put her son in the frame. You're a bloody detective, Geoff. You should have done a proper investigation and not have gone looking for a quick clear up.'

The rest of the office had gone quiet and the two men noticed a tall dark-haired and uniformed man, observing them form the end of the row of desks.

'So, you're Jack Lunn,' he said.

Lunn noticed the rank badges. 'Yes, sir.'

'No need for the 'sir', Mr Lunn. I think you and I had better step into Rhona's office,' the Assistant Chief Constable said. He then took in Geoff Cooke. 'I'm sure you have something important to deal with, Superintendent?'

'Yes, sir,' Cooke replied and scurried back towards his office.

'Your girl?' the ACC asked, nodding towards where Gem and DC Taylor now appeared to be in earnest discussion.

'My partner's eldest daughter,' Lunn replied.

'And you've got daughters, haven't you.'

Jack raised an eyebrow.

'I like to know who we're dealing with, Mr Lunn,' the ACC answered. 'But then you were one of us.'

'It was a while ago.'

'Well, it appears that time hasn't dulled your wits,' the senior officer replied, as the door to Rhona's office opened and Mick Sparkes emerged, closely followed by a DS. They both chorused 'Sir,' and Rhona looked up from her desk.

'I see you've met Jack, sir,' she said, as she stood up.

'He was having a full and frank exchange with Superintendent Cooke,' the ACC replied. 'Where are we?'

'We have a witness coming in who'll confirm that Max Lamont was with her at the time his mother was killed,' Blacklock informed the senior officer.

'So, it's now three murders and we are no closer to making an arrest. Suspects?' he asked.

'I have surveillance starting on the remaining Lamont family, but they have an alibi for the night the old lady was killed. We have a list of other persons of interest and we're in the process of tracking them down.'

'Your thoughts, Mr Lunn?'

'There's a missing link. Whoever killed Mrs Lamont went equipped with something specific to kill her with, so it was planned. The old lady had a habit of walking the riverbank every morning and evening and whilst not everyone knew the route she took, I'm pretty sure the killer must have known. Max is a different kettle of fish and I was convinced from the start that he had nothing to do with his mother's death. I talked to him after she'd been killed and he looked utterly bereft. I think whoever killed him, knew he was by himself and then set the scene up to cast suspicion on him.'

'What about the reporter?'

'She'd told Jack that she thought the murders were connected and supported the theory that Max hadn't killed old Mrs Lamont, sir,' Blacklock replied.

'I think she got too close to the truth and was murdered for it,' Lunn added. 'I do feel some responsibility for that, as I encouraged her.'

'That's bollocks, Jack and you know it,' the DCS interjected. 'She was doing her job. Whatever you had said to her, it wasn't going to put her off the scent of a good story.'

'When's your witness due in?' the ACC asked her.

'A few minutes, sir. I need to get downstairs with Jack and meet her.'

'Keep me updated,' the ACC said and then made to leave the office. 'Good to have met you, Mr Lunn.'


Naomi Cooper was on time and Lunn introduced her to DCS Blacklock.

'You understand that I don't want to appear in a court?' she asked.

'Your statement should be ample, Mrs Cooper,' Blacklock replied.

The woman took a deep breath. 'Let's get this done then.'

An hour later and Jack shook Mrs Cooper's hand. 'Thank you for clearing Max's name, Mrs Cooper. You've done the right thing.'

'I couldn't let him be thought of as a killer. I loved him.'

'I knew he couldn't have done it,' Lunn replied. 'Will you be okay?'

'I'll be fine,' she assured him. 'I just want his killer found.'

'Well, that's in the police's hands now.'

She smiled briefly. 'I suspect that we wouldn't be at this point without your intervention.'

'We certainly wouldn't be here without your help.'

He watched as she walked away and then turned back to Rhona Blacklock, who was waiting by the entrance.

She handed him a slip of paper. 'Here's the information on that car reg.'

Jack stuffed it into his pocket. 'I'll collect Gem and we'll get off home.'

'Let us know if you hear from your poacher,' Rhona reminded him.

'I'll keep in touch.'

Jack opened the car and Gem clambered in the other side.

'You seemed to be getting on with DC Taylor.'

'He gave me his mobile number. Just in case I may have forgotten something, you understand.'

'When's the first date?' he asked, with a smile.

'Jack, don't push it,' came the reply.

'We've got some work to do in what remains of the day.'

'I'll check the website when we get back,' Gem said. 'I see you couldn't resist having words with Geoff Cooke?'

'He started it. He's angry at being taken off the case and blames me.'

'The important thing is that the murders are now being properly investigated, surely?'

'Exactly,' Lunn replied. 'I don't know about you, but I'm starving.'

'I could eat the south end of a donkey heading north.'

Chapter 56

It took them about half an hour to get home and after parking, Jack pulled the slip of paper out of his pocket and quickly scanned it.

He handed it to Gem with a grimace. 'Your mother isn't going to like this.'

'Nick Brownlow! Eden's seeing Nick Brownlow?'

'So it would seem. At least we've got the address of his flat now,' Lunn said.


Sarah and the dogs greeted them as they came into the house and she asked how things had gone. Jack and Gem brought her up to date.

'I'm glad it's out of your hands now, Jack. Have either of you heard from Eden today?'

They both shook their heads.

'I've tried calling her and left a voicemail.' She continued.

'She almost certainly stayed at the boyfriends last night and I have an address for him now.'

'Who is he?' Sarah asked.

'Someone she knew from school.' Gem said. 'I remember him vaguely.'

'If we don't hear from her soon, I'll drive over there.' Lunn volunteered.

'I'm going up to the village and I'll try her mobile whilst I'm out,' Sarah replied.


Shortly after Sarah had left the house the doorbell rang, setting off the dogs and as Jack walked up the hall he saw a familiar outline.

'Seth, nice to see you,' he said, as he opened the door and then took in the bandaged head partly hidden by an old cap. 'What happened?'

'Got clobbered at the cottage.'

'Which cottage?'

'Your brother's cottage,' the poacher replied. 'I went there to spec the job and got hit from behind.'

'Have you been to the hospital?' he asked in an anxious voice. 'If you lost consciousness, you must get checked out.'

'Knocked me cold for a few moments, but I'll survive.'

'Come in, come in,' Lunn said. 'Let's get you a cup of tea or coffee?'

'I can spare a few minutes and a mug of tea wouldn't go amiss. Anyway, I have some news for you.'

Jack led him through to the kitchen, where Gem was making a sandwich.

'Get the kettle on and make a brew, Gem.' Lunn ordered. 'Seth got attacked at my brother's cottage.'

He saw the shock and worry cross her face.

'Who was it?' Gem asked in a concerned voice, as she busied herself with the kettle and mugs.

The poacher fished around in his jacket and tossed a wallet onto the kitchen work surface, 'Someone who was in a hurry to get away.'

Lunn opened the wallet to find Liam Galletly's face staring at him from the driving licence inside.

'How long did it look like he'd been there?' he asked.

'A few days, maybe. There was stuff in the fridge and one of the beds had been slept in.'

'So that's where he's been laying low.' Gem said. 'You'd better let Mick know.'

Jack nodded. 'I'll call him. You'll give the Police a statement, Seth?'

'If it helps lock that scumbag up.'

'Assault, A.B.H. and breaking into the cottage should take care of that.'

Gem handed the poacher a mug of tea. 'If he bashed you over the head, there's no reason why he couldn't have also bashed old Mrs Lamont too.'

'Lucky for me, I've a thick skull,' Seth replied.

'You should have a doctor check you out.' Lunn said.

'Wouldn't want to waste their time.'

'If you're sure you're okay.'

'Nothing a good mug of tea can't help,' the poacher said, taking a slurp. 'Have the Police spoken to anyone else?'

'They've made a start,' Lunn replied.

'Which reminds me, you asked me to keep an eye on young Miss Lamont.'

'And?'

'I've got an address and she stayed the night.'

'Boyfriend?' Dom asked.

'Looks like it.' He said, passing Lunn a scribbled note.

'The main thing is that you're not badly hurt, but you should get yourself checked out.'

'Can't be doing with doctors and hospitals,' the poacher replied.

'Then finish your tea and get off home and take it easy. I'll get the Police sorted out and you can make your statement tomorrow.'

Seth took a good swig from the mug and glanced towards Gem, 'Thanks for the tea, Ma'am.'

Gem smiled. 'Don't you Ma'am me, Seth. He obviously did more damage than you'll admit.'


As soon as Seth had left, Lunn passed the note to Gem, who couldn't hide a look of surprise.

'I'm going there now. Call Mick Sparkes and Rhona and give them the address. As you know it's not easy to find, so get them to pick you up to show them the way. And tell them, no blues and two's.'

'Don't you think it would be better just to hand this over and let them do their job?' Gem asked.

'If I tell them what we've found out, I'll be told to butt out and I want to be there when they make any arrests.'

'I don't know, Jack,' Gem replied. 'I think you're crossing a line this time. Let the Police do their thing and don't get into any more trouble with mum. We could just do a drive-by?'

He started rifling through his desk drawers. 'After the way Geoff has handled the last two killings, I'd rather just make sure that it's dealt with properly this time.'

'Please, Jack. Just let Mick and Rhona handle it.'

'It'll be fine, Gem. Just do what I've asked,' Jack replied, as he pulled some nitrile gloves from a drawer and stuffed them in his jeans pocket.

Chapter 57

It didn't take long to drive to the address on the scrap of paper. Jack parked a couple of hundred yards away from the house. After waiting a couple of minutes to check that no one was around, he set off as quietly as possible down the track and towards the house.

The cottage was set back from the road and well screened with trees and bushes via a dogleg. He stopped on the corner of the sharp bend in the track, sneaking a glance or two to the property for any signs of life. Jack let a few moments pass. All that could be heard, apart from birdsong, was the occasional car passing on the road some way behind him. With no lights showing, curtains twitching, or movement apparent, he walked quietly towards the house.

Peering through the front window of the cottage, Jack could clearly see the object that he was looking for. He looked at the adjacent garage and it was obvious from the ground in front of it that the doors had been opened. Wondering if it held anything else of interest, he pulled on the gloves from his pocket. As the garage had no windows, Lunn tried the doors. The hinges creaked and the old doors grated on the ground, but he managed to open one of them a couple of feet and eased his way in.

The air was musty and tainted with the smell of motor oil. Jack could see a car in the thin shaft of light coming through the open door. He looked around for a light switch and in the gloom took a few seconds to find it. The strip light sputtered into life, illuminating the interior in flickering white light, before settling down to a steady buzz and an unforgiving brightness. Jack stared for a few seconds at the rear of the dark coloured Audi A3, not recognising the vehicle at first. Then he caught sight of the passenger side wing mirror, its glass broken and wrapped in duct tape. He tried the car doors, but they were locked and there was no sign of a key.

This had to be the car that tried to run him down. Having seen enough, he switched off the garage light and sidled out of the door, lifting and edging it closed.

He didn't hear the blow coming, his right knee collapsed under the assault and he fell forward, his body slamming against the wood of the garage door.

It took him a moment to gather his wits, then he looked up at his assailant. Framed by the sunlight, the silhouette figure was swinging the baseball bat that had dumped Jack in a heap.

'You enjoyed that.' Lunn said through clenched teeth.

'Not as much as I'm going to enjoy bashing your head in.'

Jack held a hand up. 'You've certainly had the police running around in circles, but killing the journalist was a mistake.'

'I didn't think you'd put two and two together,' Corporate Boy said, wrapping a second hand around the bats handle. 'And why aren't you rolling about in pain?'

''You hit my knee brace, rather than the knee. I think I understand how you became involved and as the police know most of what I know, time's pretty much run out on you.'

A smile flickered across Corporate Boys face. 'Time enough to finish you off and vanish, so no trying to shout for help.'

'Why the old woman?' Lunn asked.

'You actually don't have a clue, do you? If the police have only got what you know, I'll be long gone before they work anything out.'

'I know you've been sleeping with her granddaughter,' Lunn said.

'Well, you've got half the story. The daughter and her mother both, though not together. That would be a little perverse, even for me. Imogen came up with the plan to kill her mother in law. She'd found out about her husband's affair and that the old woman had written the two children out of the will recently, so her future seemed less than rosy.'

Lunn adjusted his position, leaning back against the garage door. His leg throbbed from the shock of the blow, but the brace had taken most of the power of the bat's swing.

He looked up at Corporate Boy and then past him to the driveway leading back to the road. 'So, you've been leading everyone a merry dance.'

'And with you here, there's a certain symmetry. First, I take your job, then I take your life.'

'You killed old Mrs Lamont with the knobkerrie on your trophy wall and threw her in the river.

Was it your idea to take her rings and leave the net in the area?' Lunn asked.

'The rings were my idea and Seb came up with the net. He knew that it had been in the hut for months and thought it would wrong-foot the Police. Taking her rings just added a misleading motive,' Corporate Boy replied. 'Frankly, it was about the only decent idea Seb came up with.'

'Apart from trying to get you to run me over.'

'Well, that was just too good an opportunity to miss. All he did was call, let me know you'd been poking your nose where it wasn't wanted and that you were on your way back to your car. The decision was easy.'

'And where are the rings?'

Corporate Boy reached inside his shirt and revealing the rings on a leather thong around his neck. 'They make a nice trophy, don't you think?'

'And the reporter was killed because she was getting closer to the truth?'

'I was doing the world a favour,' Corporate Boy responded. 'She thought she was on to something. A way of clawing her way onto another gutter red top. Funnily enough, she was asking questions about you at first. I just invited her in, offered her some wine and slipped something into her drink.'

'It wasn't your place to decide if she should live or die.'

'She brought it on herself and should have kept her nose out,' Corporate Boy said. 'Bit like yourself really.'

'And that was excuse enough for you to strangle her? But you didn't hang her in the tree all by yourself?'

'Seb does have his uses. He helped me get her wrapped in plastic sheeting, into the car and up to Bolton's Bench, but nearly threw up twice. It seems he's a bit squeamish about handling the dead.'

'And I'm guessing you've got her shoes?'

'Just another keepsake.'

'And Mr Lamont?' Lunn enquired.

'As I said, Seb turned out to be squeamish,' Corporate Boy responded. 'He was supposed to bump his father off. All he had to do was get him to the top of the stairs and just give him a shove, nothing complicated.'

'But you had to give him a hand?'

'There was Mr Lamont, a few whiskeys under his belt standing on the stairs and Seb bottled it.'

'Whose idea was it for the message on the laptop?'

Corporate Boy gave a small bow.

'No fingerprints, no footprints?' Lunn asked.

'You can buy latex gloves just like you're wearing, coveralls and overshoes in any DIY store.'

'So how did you get Max's fingerprints on the laptop?'

'A dead man isn't going to complain about what his fingers do. I just pressed them on the keyboard.'

'And that's what helped clear him,' Lunn said.

'How?'

'You assumed that he was right-handed and he's a southpaw,' he replied. 'So, Imogen Lamont came up with the plan to get her hands on the property and money, putting her husband in the frame for the murder of his mother and the kids went along with it?' he then offered.

'Everyone knows that the first people investigated in a murder case are the family,' Corporate Boy said. 'But with a nice alibi from the Indian restaurant, the missing rings and the fishing net all leading the police in the wrong direction, until we could kill Max, it was pretty easy. The kids knew granny had left them nothing and it looked like their father would be leaving their mother, so they were on board. Trouble is, like most over-privileged kids, they just didn't want to get their hands dirty.'

'I still don't get why Imogen had got to the point of hating old Mrs Lamont so much.'

'The old bird has always thought her son had married beneath him, so there was always friction between them. When Imogen found out about Max's affair, all she wanted was the money, the property, her mother in law dead and freedom from her husband.'

'And I suppose you're the one who told her about Max's mistress?'

Corporate Boy smiled slightly, 'I wish I could claim that one too, but Max was not that careful about covering his tracks. Imogen sensed that he was up to something and when he'd told her that he was supposed to be working late one night, she followed him to a liaison with his mistress.'

'Did the daughter know about you and her mother?'

'About me sleeping with her? God, no.'

'But a chunk of cash wouldn't be enough to get you get involved?' Lunn asked.

'Well, the money will come in useful, but you still don't get it do you? That old woman and her husband ruined my father. Drove him to kill my mother and then himself, leaving me an orphan.'

Jack stared at his attacker with incredulity at first, as the truth dawned on him. 'You're George Wiseman's grandson?'

'Now the penny drops.' Corporate Boy replied. 'That old bitch deserved to die.'

'What killed your parents was your father's greed and stupidity. He bodged work he was doing for Mr and Mrs Lamont and got sued for it. He brought that on himself and your poor mother got caught up in his self-destruction.'

'Shut your lying mouth.'

'This was all about you getting revenge?'

'Well, life is about the paths we choose, isn't it?' Corporate Boy said. 'Look at you. Failed cop, failed husband, redundant cripple and about to die. Think of your choices and where it's got you. It'll almost be a mercy killing. You're just plankton caught by the current, going where it takes you. On the other hand, I go where I please and do what I want.'

'So, no voices commanding you, then?' Jack asked. 'No acts in the heat of the moment.'

Corporate Boy chuckled. 'Voices? Commands? What else? Was I abused as a child? Did I wet the bed? Was I a mummy's boy? I don't buy into any of that crap. The old woman and her husband killed my parents, Max was an adulterer and inconvenience and the journalist was just scum.'

'Three innocent people have died because of your warped desire for revenge?'

'You'll be number four and five is in the cottage. I'll just set fire to the old place when I'm finished. I'm sure the Landlord will have insurance.'

'Who's number five?' Lunn asked.

'All in good time,' Corporate Boy replied, as he hiked the baseball bat up a little.

'What gives you the right to be judge, jury, and executioner?' Lunn asked.

'You really are tedious. I don't have to justify myself to you.'

'Who's number five?'

'Your partner's youngest daughter.'

'You've got Eden here?' Lunn was stunned and angry, he tried to get to his feet but was pushed back down by the end of the baseball bat.

'To be fair, she put up a bit of a fight.'

'How the hell did you get her here?' a bewildered and frustrated Lunn asked.

'I was in the pub when she had an argument with her boyfriend. He walked out and I told her that you and I used to work together. I bought her a drink and offered her a lift home. Slipped something in her drink and she was already a bit out of it by the time I got her into my car.'

'But why?' he demanded angrily.

'I'd missed you with the car and it was an opportunity to fuck your life up.'

'You hate me that much?' Lunn asked.

'You think you're so superior, like some sort of moral crusader. The reality is, you're just a loser.'

'One more thing.'

Corporate Boy rolled his eyes, 'If you must.'

'I'm not alone.'

Corporate Boy laughed. 'What am I supposed to do, look over my shoulder to see the Old Bill rolling up with blue lights flashing.'

'They arrived a few minutes ago and heard you confess to all the killings and the family's involvement,' Lunn said. 'It really is worth a look over your shoulder.'

Chapter 58

'Christopher Farringdon, I'm arresting you for assault and threats to kill and on suspicion of the murder of Elizabeth Lamont, Max Lamont and Adele Parker,' DCS Rhona Blacklock said in a commanding voice. 'You do not have to say anything. But it may harm your defence if you do not mention when questioned, something that you later rely on in court. Anything you do say can be given in evidence. Now put the baseball bat down.'

Corporate Boy's shoulders slumped and he half turned away from Lunn to look at Rhona, as two uniformed officers appeared from the bushes on the corner, both with Tasers drawn.

'Why couldn't you have been a few minutes longer?' Farringdon asked. 'I wasn't finished yet.'

'You're finished, now put the bat down,' Blacklock ordered.

Farringdon's knuckles whitened as he gripped the bat more tightly. Jack shrank back against the garage door. The red dots from the Tasers played on Corporate Boy body, who had second thoughts about taking another swing at Jack and dropped the bat.

'Cuff him,' Sparkes ordered. 'Get him to the car and call for support and we need SOCO's here now.'

'Rhona, you heard what he said about having Eden in there. I have to get in that house and make sure she's okay.' He insisted.

'Not a chance, Jack. I'll go, make sure she knows she's safe and that it's over. Then we wait for the SOCO's. I can't have you traipsing through the house and corrupting the crime scene.'

Is Mick on his way?'

'He'll be here very shortly. I've got Marcus waiting with Gem at the top of the track and I guess you'll want to stay here?'

'Damn right I do,' Lunn said emphatically, as Rhona offered him a hand to get back to his feet.

They could hear the approaching sirens now.

'Right, I'm going to sort Eden out,' Blacklock said and instructed one of the uniformed officers to come with her and the other to stay with Jack and the prisoner.

Within a couple of minutes Mick Sparkes jogged down the driveway, a couple more uniforms in tow and Marcus Taylor and Gem in close formation.

'Are you alright, Jack?' Mick asked anxiously.

'I wish everyone would stop asking me that,' Lunn replied. 'I'm fine.'

'Right. Where's Rhona?'

'That creature's had Eden in there,' he said, pointing at Corporate Boy. 'Rhona's inside letting her know she's safe and I want to know she's okay before I leave here.'

'What on earth was she doing here?' Gem asked.

'He'd drugged and brought her here,' Lunn explained.

'I want to see my sister now,' Gem demanded.

Marcus Taylor took Gem's arm. 'They have to secure the house forensically and follow proper procedure,' he explained.

Gem turned angrily back to Jack. 'Mum told you to keep your nose out of this.'

'I didn't know this maniac would target the family and we've both helped to catch a killer.' He replied.

'At what cost though, Jack?'


Rhona Blacklock reappeared from the rear of the house.

'Tell me Eden's okay?' Lunn beseeched.

'We'll need to get her checked out, but she knows it's over and that we have to get Forensics in before we can get her out,' she replied and then turned to Mick Sparkes. 'Where are the C.S.I.'s?'

'Getting their kit together,' Sparkes said, pointing back up the driveway.

'If the back is open, the forensic team can enter there, ma'am,' Marcus Taylor said.

'I've got an officer at the rear door, he can do the Log,' Blacklock said.


The C.S.I.'s appeared and jogged down the track, led by Scarlet Ribbans.

'Are you okay, Jack,' she asked.

'He's fine,' said Blacklock and Taylor together.

'I'll get on with my job then,' Ribbans responded. 'Is there a Log Officer on site?'

'Set up by the back door,' Blacklock replied. 'Get up to the master bedroom, as there's a girl being held there. I've been up to reassure her that she is safe and that you'll be onsite shortly. Her name's Eden.'

'Will do,' Scarlet pulled her hood up and mask on and started towards the rear of the cottage.

'Scarlet, make sure the knobkerrie on the wall in the sitting room is bagged up soonest,' Lunn called after her. 'It's what he used to kill Mrs Lamont and I'm pretty sure he's got trophies from his other kills somewhere in the house. The car that nearly ran me over is in the garage. There should be some decent forensics in it. I'm betting that he used it to transport Adele Porter's body to Bolton's Bench.'

'How did you know it was him, Jack?' Blacklock asked.

'I didn't. Gem and I been following the family. Well, Seb and his mother to be exact,' Lunn said. 'I had Seth on the daughter and he followed her here.'

'That's not much of a link.'

'It led to the knobkerrie,' Lunn explained. 'It's designed to break skulls and the fragments of wood and varnish in Mrs Lamont's head wound will match up to it. I couldn't work out what had been used to kill her, but when Seth told me that the Lamont girl had been seen at Farringdon's cottage, it triggered a memory. I finally knew what the murder weapon was and where I'd seen it.'

'DCS Blacklock!'

All heads turned to the sound.

'You need to come into the house,' Scarlet Ribbans asked, then glanced over at Lunn. 'The girl's going to be fine. Her mouth, arms, and legs are all taped up and my guys are taking it off. But they need to preserve evidence and it'll take a few minutes.'

'The paramedics will be here very soon. Just let us and them do our jobs, Jack,' Blacklock said and then disappeared around the back of the cottage with the forensic scientist.

Geoff Cooke arrived a few minutes later, hurrying down the track.

'Where's DCS Blacklock?' he asked.

'Stay here, Jack,' Sparkes ordered and then turned towards Superintendent Cooke. 'DCS Blacklock requested for you to get and execute warrants for the rest of the Lamont's. She wants them at Lyndhurst nick within the hour.'

'Where the bloody hell is the ambulance?' Lunn asked.

'Five minutes away at most, Jack. Scarlett and Rhona are with her, so she's in good hands.'

'This is going to be my fault,' Lunn replied.

'How's that?' Sparkes asked.

'Sarah warned me not to let this investigation affect the family.'

'So long as Eden's okay, I'm sure Sarah will be okay,' Sparkes reassured him, but Gem looked less certain.

Rhona Blacklock returned from the rear of the house, as the increasing volume of a siren announced the arrival of the ambulance.

'She's going to be fine, Jack. No cuts or breaks, but a few bruises. We've found what may be Rohypnol in the house, it must have been what he used on Adele Porter. Let the paramedics give her the once over first,' Blacklock said. 'We're going to need to recover her clothes and she'll need to be examined. Then she can give her statement as soon as she's been given the all-clear.'

'Did touch her in that way?' Gem asked.

'She says no. But as he used a common date rape drug on her, the exam is necessary but only precautionary.' Ribbans replied.

Rhona beckoned to Jack.

'A word in private,' she said. 'Best leave Gem here to be with her sister when she comes out,' Blacklock said. 'Eden's not best pleased and it might be a good idea if you're out of sight when she comes down.'

'I understand,' Lunn replied. 'She needs some time and you need her head as clear for her statement.'

'I need your statement too, Jack. I'm going to get one of the DS's to run you and Mick back to the station.'

'I'll explain things to Gem,' Lunn said and they walked back to the front of the cottage.

'Everything okay, Jack?' an anxious-looking Gem asked when they re-appeared.

'Yes,' Lunn replied. 'I've got to go to the police station and give my statement. Mick is going there to formally charge Farringdon, so I need you to go with your sister when she comes down.'

'I told you not to come here,' Gem said.

Jack ignored the accusation.

'If the paramedics say she's going to be okay, then we're going to take her into Southampton. We have special facilities and officers there, so we'll get the Police Doctor to check her over and her injuries photographed,' Blacklock clarified. 'She'll be far enough away from that scumbag and the Lamont's that way. We can take your statement there too.'

'I'll call mum,' Gem said.

'No,' Lunn said firmly. 'I'll call her.

Chapter 59

It wasn't an easy call.

'How did it go?' Sparkes asked when Lunn came off the phone.

'As well as could be expected.'

'So, a stay of execution?'

'Not a chance,' Lunn replied. 'But that murdering scumbag had to be taken off the street.'

'Let's hope Sarah sees it that way,' the DI observed, as they pulled into the car park at Lyndhurst Police Station.


Jack was ushered into an interview room with a DS he didn't know, but he settled down to giving his statement in a quick and efficient manner that he knew the policeman would appreciate. He'd nearly finished when Rhona Blacklock poked her head.

'Are you nearly done?' she asked.

Jack looked over at the DS, who nodded.

'Get it transcribed asap,' Rhona ordered. 'Jack, come and join us in the conference room.'


'What's the latest?' he asked, as he entered the room with its familiar big oval table.

'We picked up both the kids at their home and interrupted the mother's shopping trip,' Blacklock replied.

'I'd have loved to have been a fly on that wall when Imogen got nicked,' he replied.

'I understand the language would have made a drill sergeant blush,' she replied. 'Serves her right, spending her ill-gotten gains before she'd gotten them.'

'What about Eden?' Lunn asked.

'As well as can be expected. They've got her at Southampton finishing her statement and I've got a DC interviewing the pub staff where she got slipped the Mickey Finn.'

'Are Gem and Sarah with her?'

'Gem's given her statement, Sarah's there too,' Blacklock replied. 'It appears the remaining Lamont's were up to their necks in it. Scarlett has the club, C.S.I.'s are all over the house and we have him bang to rights with what I witnessed, added to your statement.' Blacklock said. 'By the way, we'll speak to Eden's boyfriend to confirm their argument in the pub.'

'What about Steve Ingram?'

'The Met interviewed him earlier today. Apparently, he's known Imogen Lamont since they were children and she used to get him occasional days on the river. She'd contacted him about a week ago asking his advice about making the fishery more profitable. He says that they'd had a meeting in a coffee shop, which is what Gem witnessed.'

'And their overnight stay at the hotel?'

'He's a single man, Jack and she's an attractive widow.'

'I'm glad he's not involved. But what about Liam Galletly?' Lunn asked.

Blacklock grinned. 'I just had word he's been picked him up at his mother's house. It doesn't appear that he has a connection to this case. However, we've arrested him for the assault on your poacher, criminal damage for the break-in at your cottage and whatever else we can make stick.'

'Who's going to interview Corporate Boy?' he asked.

'Mick and I,' Blacklock replied. 'And Jack, going to the house on your own was a very bad idea.'

There was a knock at the door and Mick Sparkes poked his head in.

'We're just waiting for the CPS to give us the thumbs up,' he said.

The three of them left the room and walked down the corridor and into the main office, where the assembled officers and detectives were working.

There was a few that Lunn knew, who nodded and smiled at him and a chorus of 'Well done, guv' aimed at Rhona.'

'There's still a long way to go,' Blacklock said to them. 'Just do your jobs, as we don't want any of these bastards slipping through our fingers.'

They left and crossed the courtyard, to where the holding cells and the custody sergeants desk were located.

'Any issues with our guest?' Blacklock asked.

'Not a peep,' the sergeant replied.

'Right,' she said. 'Let's go and chivvy the CPS along, shall we?'

Lunn and Sparkes waited whilst Blacklock sat down with the CPS lawyer, which didn't take too long.

'They're happy that we can charge him,' she said. 'Jack, you remember the small room just by the duty sergeant's desk, get yourself in there and we'll bring him up.'

They made their way back across the courtyard and Lunn tucked himself in the anteroom.

'Fetch the prisoner up,' Blacklock said.

Lunn could hear the footsteps down to the cells and the keys jangling in the lock.

'Out,' the officer ordered and then steps came back towards the desk sergeant's area.

'I see an audience has gathered,' Farringdon said, in a slightly mocking tone.

'Shut up and listen,' Sparkes snapped.

A throat was cleared and then the desk sergeant read out the three charges of murder, one of abduction, one of possession of a Class C drug without a prescription and another of assault with the intent of committing grievous bodily harm.

'I'd like to have a lawyer now, please,' Farringdon requested.

'Is there one particular you want us to call, or do you want the Duty Solicitor?'

'I'm sure the Duty Solicitor will be adequate,' he replied.

''I'll make the call,' Sparkes said.


The footsteps retreated, the keys jangled again and the door to the cell slammed shut.

Mick Sparkes leaned into the anteroom.

'All clear,' he said, sotto voce.

Returning to the conference room, they found the ACC sat there.

'Thought I'd come and see how things are going, Rhona.'

'Just charged him, sir.'

'I hear he'd abducted someone, as well as assaulting Mr Lunn?'

'He kidnapped Jack's partner's youngest daughter, sir. Knocked her about too,' Blacklock replied.

'How is she?' The senior officer asked, turning to Jack.

'She should hopefully be on her way home now. The paramedics checked her out on site, but she will have had some further examinations,' Lunn replied. 'Thanks for asking.'

'And I understand you've been instrumental again, Mr Lunn?

'If it wasn't for DCS Blacklock's quick reactions, I'd have my head bashed in and he'd have killed Eden, torched his house and be long gone,' Lunn replied.

'Next time don't go turning up to a suspect's home,' the ACC said meaningfully.

'The point has already been well made by DCS Blacklock,' Lunn replied.

'As soon as the brief is here, we'll transport him back to Southampton nick and I've asked for the Lamont's to be taken there too,' Blacklock said.

'All the bad apples in one barrel,' the ACC added ruefully.

'Yes, sir,' she replied.

'Okay. As you have everything under control, I'll leave you to it, Rhona. But keep me up to speed.'

'Of course, sir,' Blacklock replied. 'I have a meeting arranged with the media relations people when I get back and then we can get down to interviewing Farringdon and the Lamont's.'

'Are the family lawyering up too?' the ACC asked.

'First thing they requested,' she replied.

'Should be interesting when they realise our friend in the cells has completely dropped them in it,' he said. 'Phones, computers, etc?'

'We already have their phones with Tech Branch. I've got uniform sealing off their house, we'll get it searched and any additional evidence collected asap, sir.'

'No stone unturned, Rhona. You know the old copper's saying, 'A confession is an admission of guilt, later retracted on the advice of a solicitor',' he looked over at Lunn. 'Haven't you got a home to go to?'

'If I'm not needed here anymore,' he replied.

'You should get home to Sarah and Eden,' Blacklock said.

'We can supply counselling,' the ACC added.

'Thank you again. I'll tell her mother.'

'Rather you than me, Jack,' Blacklock said.

'Can I get a lift back to my car, Rhona?' he asked.

'Mick can drop you off to get your car.'

'I'd better go and face the music then.'

Chapter 59

Pulling up outside the house, he saw the lights were on and Sarah's car was parked on the driveway. Eden's bedroom light was also on and he felt a wave of relief that she was home and safe.

Putting his key in the lock, he took a deep breath in anticipation of the full broadside he was about to receive from Sarah.

The key wouldn't turn.

He tried again.

It still wouldn't turn.

He rang the bell, setting the dogs off.

Sarah came down the stairs and opened the door.

'You forgot to put the latch on,' Lunn said.

'No, I didn't.'

'What?'

'There's an overnight bag in the sitting room for you,' she said calmly.

'You can't be serious? I know it's awful that Eden got hurt,' Lunn said. 'But she's okay and home. The police have offered counselling too.'

'Awful?' Sarah retorted angrily. 'Have you got any idea what Eden's been through and what you've put this family through?'

'I thought.'

'No, Jack. Thinking is the one thing you didn't do. There was no consideration for anyone's needs apart from your own,' she interrupted.

'Sarah, I understand you're upset,' he tried to interject.

'I'm so far beyond upset,' she shouted at him. 'I told you to leave this alone. I warned you, but you didn't listen. Now my child is upstairs battered and bruised, knowing that you're the cause of her abduction, drugging and assault. They took her to a Rape Suite, Jack. My girl in a Rape Suite and that's on you.'

'If I can just speak to her, Sarah,' Lunn said. 'I'll apologise, try and explain.'

'Are you kidding? She doesn't want you anywhere near her and even if she was okay with it, I wouldn't be,' she responded scornfully. 'You've totally fucked this relationship up and you have to go. I warned you there would be consequences, now take the overnight bag and go.'

'Is that it, Sarah?' he asked. 'What about us?'

'At this moment in time, Jack,' she said. 'There is no us.'

'But I did the right thing, Sarah,' Jack appealed. 'I got justice for Mrs Lamont, Max and the journalist. If I hadn't been nudging the investigation in the right direction, they'd have got away with it. Would it have been right for me to just stand by the wayside? To see Seth possibly wrongly convicted, or Max thought of as his mother's murderer?

'Don't be so bloody sanctimonious, Jack. That poor journalist is dead because you encouraged her to keep investigating. I told you to keep your nose out of it, but you just bloody ignored me, dragged Gem into it and I dread to think what could have happened to Eden,' she replied.

'That's completely unfair,' he replied. 'I can't be held responsible for what that man did.'

'But you'll happily take the credit for stopping him.'

'Somebody had to. Too many people just walk by.'

'Oh, now you're the Good Samaritan? There's nothing saintly about what you've done to my child or this relationship, so just get out of my sight. I'll call you tomorrow and tell you when you can pick the rest of your stuff up. Don't come back to this house, unless you've arranged something with me.'

With that, she ushered him out of the door and locked it.

He turned back down the path, noticing a couple of the neighbour's net curtains twitching, no doubt alerted by the raised voices.


His phone pinged with a text message. It was a text from Gem.

'Meet me at The Blue Lamp in twenty minutes?'

Jack text back, 'Okay.'

Chapter 60

He was sat at the bar nursing a pint when Gem arrived.

'Does your mother know you're here?' Lunn asked.

'Look, Jack, you're not expecting me to take sides, are you? She's my mum and whilst you've been a pretty good surrogate father over the years, I have a sister who could have died today. You need to see things from Mum's perspective,' Gem replied. 'Get me a pint and let's find a quieter spot.'

The pair of them settled at a corner table.

'You know she's kicked me out?' Lunn said.

'I imagine most of the street know,' Gem answered with a smile.

Lunn chuckled. 'Your mum didn't come with volume control, did she?'

'As she said, it's not like she didn't warn you.

'But doesn't your Mum understand that a killer has been stopped?' Lunn asked.

'She only cares that the same killer nearly added Eden to his victims,' Gem explained.

'Do you blame me too?'

'How can I, when I was part of what happened and understand what you were trying to do. But, I don't think you took account of the possible consequences and neither did I. Something neither of us will forget in a hurry.'

Lunn nodded in agreement. 'I'll try to make amends and I hope we can carry on tying some flies together?'

'I think we'd better keep that between us for the time being?'

'I want you to carry on being involved with our business, Gem,' Lunn said. 'And I do understand that your mum is naturally protective of you both. I just didn't imagine you guys would be dragged into this.'

'Well imagine this,' Gem replied. 'What if Farringdon had kidnapped one of your girls and it was because of something that your best friend had done and despite you warning them not to do it?'

'I do get it.'

'Where are you going to stay?' Gem asked.

'I'll find a hotel tonight and then crash at my brother's cottage, once the Police have finished gathering evidence against Galletly.'

'Give it some time, keep in touch with mum and take your medicine when she dishes it out.'

'I've got to get the rest of my belongings,' Lunn said.

'Leave that to me. I'll get some stuff packed and ready for you tomorrow and we can go and walk the dogs together,' Gem suggested.

'In hindsight, I should have expected something like this to happen,' Lunn said.

*'Expectation is the root of all heartache,'* Gem replied.

'Did your mum give you an ear bashing too?

'Let's just say that I'm not her flavour of the month. But she's more focused on making sure that Eden is okay. We're a good team Jack and I enjoy working with you on the fly-tying, but the investigation was what really brought us both to life.'

'Well, it's over now.'

'There's always something we can be looking at together and you now have very senior Police Officers who will listen to what you say and take it seriously.'

'What are you saying?'

'I'm in for the business, but I'm also in for anything your asked, or want to investigate. You know I'm good at this.'

'You have great instincts and I should have listened to you when you told me to leave it to Rhona and Mick.'

'We all have perfect vision in hindsight,' she replied. 'Do we have a deal?'

Jack nodded and stuck out his hand.

'I'm not going to shake on it, but I'll give you a hug,' Gem replied.

They broke apart.

'You'd better get home and I'd better get off. Tomorrow?' Jack asked.

'Tomorrow, Jack.'

The End

Printed in Dunstable, United Kingdom

66479883R00163